ALBA

Ron Culley

Grosvenor House
Publishing Limited

This book is published by
Grosvenor House Publishing Ltd
Link House
140 The Broadway, Tolworth, Surrey, Kt6 7Ht.
www.grosvenorhousepublishing.co.uk

Photograph of Willie McRae used with the kind permission of Aberdeen
Press and Journal. Photograph of the Saltire used on the front cover used by
kind permission of Hamish Irvine. Hamish's photographs can be viewed at
https://www.flickr.com/people/topaz-mcnumpty/

Edited by John McManus

ISBN 978-1-78148-995-6

Previous books by Ron Culley

The Kaibab Resolution. Kennedy & Boyd 2010.

I Belong To Glasgow [foreword by Sir Alex Ferguson]
The Grimsay Press, 2011

A Confusion of Mandarins. Grosvenor House. 2011.

Glasgow Belongs To Me. Grosvenor House
[electronic media only] 2012

The Patriot Game. Grosvenor House 2013

Shoeshine Man. A one-act play. SCDA. 2014.

One Year. Grosvenor House 2015

Web address
www.ronculley.com

CONTENTS

"Scotland Needs Its Troublemakers."
Ian Robertson Hamilton Q.C. *

*Ian Robertson Hamilton, QC is a lawyer and Scottish Nationalist. He is perhaps best known for his part in the removal of the Stone of Destiny from Westminster Abbey in 1950.

ACKNOWLEDGEMENTS

Many thanks to friends and family for encouraging me to write a book that I believe requires to be written, a book that may help shed some light on the controversial death of Willie McRae. I've told the tale, set out those areas where there remains disagreement on matters of fact and offered my own assessment of the circumstances surrounding his death at the conclusion of the book.

A huge thank you to my editor, John McManus. His ability to find flaws in plot, spelling and punctuation as well as helping me determine a general direction of travel has been essential and has made for a much improved end product.

Thanks also to the Justice for Willie McRae Campaign, and especially to the campaign's leading light, Mark MacNicol whose energy and determination has ensured that the intransigence of the authorities in refusing to release information on the circumstances of McRae's death will not be permitted to go unchallenged. Equally helpful has been the investigative work of retired police officers John Weir and John Walker who have unearthed information which has shed fresh light – without discovering proof positive – on the death of Willie McRae. However, the interpretation of facts and any errors surrounding the death of McRae are mine.

Finally, much respect and grateful thanks go to the countless numbers of concerned individuals in Scotland and further afield who continue to push for transparency and honest explanations of Willie McRae's sad demise.

DEDICATION

The book is dedicated to my current crop of grandchildren; Arran, Eilidh, Olive and Emily; Culleys all, in the hope that they grow up in a country which, unlike the United Kingdom of 1985, holds to morality and ethics as fundamental principles governing public and private behaviour.

FOREWORD

All governments lie. All governments dissemble. Not all governments assassinate their own people, even when they view them as a threat to the state. But the British Government stands accused of just that by a great many people.

Many words have been written about the life and death of Willie McRae. He was a controversial character, of that there is little doubt. He was a committed Scottish Nationalist and beyond peradventure was someone who worked diligently to advance the circumstances of those who felt betrayed and who sought to oppose the imposition of disadvantage upon the Scottish people.

He was an alcoholic, a homosexual, a heterosexual, an academic, the life and soul of the party, a gun-toting depressive, an optimist, a fantasist, a kind man, a firebrand, a shrewd politician, and a brilliant orator depending upon which newspaper you opened of a morning. Perhaps unsurprisingly, those within the British Establishment who found him inconvenient tended to uncongenial views which suited their political bent. To others he was a hero.

McRae came from humble stock; his father, an electrician. Born in the township of Carron, reputed then to host the largest ironworks in Europe, McRae read history at the University of Glasgow where he gained a first-class degree. During the Second World War he was a commissioned officer in the Seaforth Highlanders but transferred to the Royal Indian Navy where he became first a lieutenant-commander and subsequently *aide-de-camp* to Admiral Lord Louis Mountbatten during the period when he occupied the post of Supreme Allied Commander, South East Asia Command based in India. Perhaps unsurprisingly, McRae supported the Indian Independence Movement.

Following the ending of World War Two, he returned to the University of Glasgow and studied law. Later, he was responsible for sculpting the maritime law of Israel and was emeritus professor at the University of Haifa. Following his untimely and controversial death in 1985, a forest of 3,000 trees was planted in Israel in his memory.

He set up as a practicing solicitor in Scotland, establishing the law firm Levy & McRae which still exists today in Glasgow's St Vincent Street. His political life was dominated by his Scottish National Party activism and his opposition to the plans of the nuclear industry to bury waste beneath the soil of Scotland. In the 1979 General Election, McRae stood for Parliament as the SNP candidate for Ross and Cromarty, where he narrowly lost to Hamish Gray of the Conservative and Unionist Party. Scotland was a different place in those days. He was a contender for leadership of the SNP in 1979 but lost to Gordon Wilson and to Stephen Maxwell who came second.

This book, however, is a tale within a tale; a work of histori-cal fiction which deals substantially but *inter alia* with the death of Willie McRae. I have remained true to the facts such as are known and where I have deviated in the interests of narrative, I explain these at the conclusion of the book. I also show where the facts as presented are contested.

It is a tale based in Scotland in 1985 which centres upon notions of perfidious Albion and deals with some of the political circumstances of the day but it is not a dry, biographical, blow-by-blow account of McRae. Those who seek this will be disap-pointed. It is but a semi-fictive work that *en passant*, attempts to help make the death of Willie McRae aged only 61, understanda-ble in the context of the political objectives of the British Establishment. The story is told with strict observance of all dates – before and after the untimely death of McRae.

Chapter One

WEDNESDAY 6TH MARCH 1985

Glasgow, Scotland

The downpour had eased to a deluge.

Having lashed Glasgow all day sending uninterrupted almost solid rods of water to flood streets, the rain had now reduced slightly in intensity. Despite this minor blessing, a strong wind continued to threaten trees and a dark murk settled over the city as nightfall compounded the day's meteorological felony.

Hector McLeod pulled his grey tweed bunnet down tighter around his head leaving most of his long locks unprotected, turned up the collar of his tweed overcoat and inspected the storm raging outside the front door of the Auld Smiddy from its entrance. *Christ Almighty! See rainy days in Glasgow?* he mused to himself. A cigarette cupped in his right hand as much for warmth as inhalation, glowed red in the gloom before it was ground under-heel and extinguished. A final plume of smoke issued tightly from his pursed lips as he stepped onto the pavement and into the downpour.

This was rain he knew. It was Glasgow, pavement-spattering rain; rain that could find weakness in the most protective of garments. McLeod had a short distance to walk before reaching the shelter of his red sandstone home in nearby Courthill Avenue but fortified

1

by the contents of a couple of bottles of McEwan's Pale Ale, he anticipated his imminent soaking with some equanimity.

Across the street, parked where an unobstructed view of the pub door could be obtained, a silver Triumph Acclaim sat parked; its powerful engine idling quietly, lights out, its wipers struggling to shed the still heavy rain. Two men inside affected disinterest in all that took place outside the comfort of their cabin, staring straight ahead as McLeod crossed the road and knuckled the roadside front window of the vehicle sharply, inviting attention.

Detective Sergeant Anderson Carnegie grimaced slowly to his partner and turning to face a stooped McLeod grinning outside, silently mouthed, "Fuck off!" Rain drumming on the car roof would have drowned out any attempt to communicate verbally.

More window knocking elicited a more measured response from the driver of the car, D.S. Bob Gall. "You might as well open the windae, Andy. That bastard'll chap away all night until you do."

"Aye, it's all right for you...but it'll be me that gets soaked!"

"Just open the windae! Ah'll get wee Sheila from forensics to towel you down back at the station."

A further scowl and a sigh of resignation prefaced a reluctant half-turn of the window-handle, opening the window some two inches. "Fuck off, McLeod. The rain's gettin' in."

"Sorry about that Sergeant Carnegie. Just thought you'd want to know that's me away up the road!"

"As if we give a monkey's, McLeod. We're just sittin' here havin' a break."

"You two have been up my jacksie all day. Just thought I'd be courteous and let you know that I plan to go home now, dry off and go to bed early. There's usually a free space across from my flat so you can park there until my lights go out and I'm in the land of slumber. Think I'll go for the morning papers tomorrow around eight. I'll see you then."

"Don't flatter yourself, McLeod. We've got more important things to do than spend our time wondering what you and your knob-head nationalist pals are up to. Now beat it...ah'm gettin' soaked here."

"*Saor Alba, boys.* Free Scotland!"

McLeod waved a comically theatrical, open-handed farewell to a closing car window and turning his shoulder to the gale, leapt lightly across a gutter puddle and started his walk home, the lusty wind at his back intermittently encouraging his brisk steps.

Chapter Two

THURSDAY 7TH MARCH 1985

London, England.

Her Britannic Majesty's Principal Secretary of State for the Home Department, the Right Honourable Leon Brittan QC MP had occupied the position of Home Secretary in Margaret Thatcher's Conservative Government for some twelve months and had established a routine to which he'd become accustomed on those occasions when he wasn't attending to constituency matters in affluent Richmond in Yorkshire or was otherwise engaged on political business away from London.

Given that Brittan had twice been elected some forty percentage points beyond the reach of his closest Liberal Party rival and that the Conservative Party had held the Richmond seat continuously since 1910, he had been able to devolve many of the troublesome local matters to his constituency staff, confident that not dealing personally with Mrs Higgins' planning problem wasn't going to see him challenged electorally. The notion that a thumping Conservative majority in Richmond could be taken as granted, could be taken as granted.

The House having voted earlier in the evening was now dealing with adjournment proceedings permitting Brittan to attend to his administrative duties in his grand office in Queen Anne's Gate in Petty France, a short street in the City of Westminster in central London, linking Buckingham Gate with Broadway.

A timid knock on his office door admitted Miss Elizabeth Warren-Coates, the elderly spinster who had run the outer office of whichever Minister had occupied the position of Home Secretary for the past eighteen years. She entered carrying a glass of iced water and a notepad. "Your water, Minister." She stood tentatively next to the backrest of the nearest of three seats which were positioned on the other side of Brittan's large mahogany desk. "And an urgent request to see you from Geoffrey Dickens, MP for Huddersfield West. He's seated outside now."

Brittan's brow furrowed. He spoke quietly. "What? Dear God! The man's a crashing bore. He'll only seek to lecture me on the reintroduction of hanging in that unintelligible accent of his. How was he ever allowed as far as my outer office without being intercepted?"

"He'd brook no interference, Minister. As you are aware he has rather a stubborn attitude and can be very direct!"

Brittan groaned. "When's my next appointment?"

"You're seeing the Prime Minster at ten o'clock this evening in Downing Street. You have the briefing notes in your red box, Minister. The purpose of the meeting is to discuss the prison service."

"She'll want to reintroduce bread and water for everyone including the prison officers, I shouldn't wonder," mused Brittan sufficiently audibly to have Miss Warren-Coates pretend not to hear.

He sighed loudly as he flipped open the lid on his box, satisfying himself that the papers he'd need were there. "I'd suppose you'd better let him in but I'll be lectured on something, that's for sure. No one's more confident in his political abilities than the Member of Parliament for Huddersfield West. So interrupt me after a few minutes, Elizabeth. I'll need to go over the brief one more time before I go round to Downing Street to make quite sure that I know just one scintilla more on the topic of prisons than she does!"

Miss Warren-Coates nodded and retreated before re-entering some moments later holding the door open for the large and ruddy-faced Member of Parliament for Huddersfield West who strode purposefully, taking several paces before reaching Brittan's desk which was located at the far end of the extravagantly sized room.

"Mr. Geoffrey Dickens, Minister," she announced somewhat unnecessarily.

Brittan rose from his desk beaming and extending a hand as if greeting a long-lost friend.

"My dear Geoffrey. How nice to see you. How's that delightful family of yours?

Dickens took his hand in cursory fashion, noticing almost subliminally how limp and sweaty was Brittan's grasp.

"They're fine, Minister. But I didn't come 'ere to exchange pleasantries."

"Of course you didn't, dear chap. Please have a seat but regrettably, you should be aware I've a meeting with the Prime Minister shortly so our chat will have to be brief!"

"I won't stand on ceremony, Minister. What I have to say is of cataclysmic...I say *cataclysmic* proportions."

"Then by all accounts it sounds as if I must give you my utmost attention, Geoffrey."

"Don't patronise me Minister. I know we're in the same party but we don't like one another, let's be blunt. Anyways, I have information that you, as Home Secretary must act on, and act on immediately...even though it affects members of our own blessed party."

Brittan smiled awkwardly. The conversation was proceeding exactly as he'd anticipated.

"I expect you're well aware that in the past I've made it clear that there's a paedophile network involving big, big names... people in positions of power, influence and responsibility not only within our House of Commons 'ere but also at the highest reaches of power in our country. People in the Intelligence Services are also involved. I've already used Parliamentary Privilege and named our High Commissioner to Canada, Sir Peter Hayman, as a child molester...a pederast... and now after a lot of work, let me tell you, I have a dossier on a whole lot more." He paused for emphasis. "Now, I expect you to deal with this properly or else I'll bloody name the lot of them in the Commons."

Brittan shuffled uneasily in his chair. "This sounds very serious indeed, Geoffrey. And you say you have proof?"

"Proof as far as I'm concerned Minister. It'll be for the police to nail these bastards but I've spent a lot of time speakin' with a solicitor like you who's taken an interest and with them people who's willin' to come forward and I'm tellin' you Minister, it's bloody cataclysmic! *Cataclysmic,*" he repeated for emphasis.

"I'm aware it's a cause that's close to your heart, Geoffrey."

"Bloody right, Minister. Young kids being interfered with... *raped* by them that should know better...them that's meant to be running our country! Bang out of order, Minister. They should be 'anged by the neck until almost dead then boiled in oil!"

"I'd be happy to look at what you have, Geoffrey. May I ask if you've gone public with these allegations?"

"I won't lie to you Minister. I've actually spoken with Mrs. Thatcher, our esteemed leader. I'd an opportunity at a bash she'd thrown in Downing Street last week but she 'eld 'er 'ands up in 'orror an' told me to speak with you direct. Didn't want to know. Seemed to me that she didn't even want to believe that them sort of things could go on."

Brittan gazed at the buff-coloured manila folder that rested on Dickens' lap.

"And beyond the Prime Minister?" Brittan raised his eyebrows.

"Just you, this evening."

"And may I ask which solicitor has taken an interest in your investigations'"

"'E's Scotch. Used to be Vice President of the Scot Nats. Fellah called William McRae. Done his own enquiries as well, I might say."

"And you say that your evidence is contained in the file you've brought with you?"

Dickens' grasp on the folder tightened.

"Before I give this to you, Minister, I have to tell you that things are a bit more complicated than what I tried to tell the Prime Minister."

"Really? How so, Geoffrey?"

Dickens' right hand stroked his chin. His eyes narrowed evincing awkwardness, his earlier brio deserting him.

"Truth be told, Minister, some of them statements...the reason I went to 'er rather than direct to you....some of the people that spoke with me...well, ah'm sure they're wrong...I certainly 'ope so Minister...but some of them...they name *you*!"

Brittan blanched. "I...I...Well that's just preposterous, Geoffrey. If the rest of your allegations are as accurate as the suggestion that I'd...I'd..."

Dickens interrupted a clearly embarrassed Brittan. "Well, like I say, Minister...let's hope not. It places both of us in a terrible awkward position. I know that." He looked uncertainly at the folder he held before proffering it gingerly towards Brittan and continued. "But you're the man with the formal responsibility to deal with this and no matter the cost to you personally, I expect you to see to it."

Brittan summoned a nervous smile as he placed a chubby hand on the file and pulled it slowly across his desk towards him. "My dear chap, you have my word. I assure you I am completely unconcerned about any ridiculous allegation concerning myself but I'll certainly see to it that the matter is given the attention to which it is entitled."

Dickens nodded and rose.

"I'll let me'self out. You have a look at *that*!" He pointed at the manila folder he'd just left.

Dickens reached the door just as Miss Warren-Coates was about to alert her Minister of his need to end the meeting. Dickens breezed past her, hardly acknowledging her presence. Once the door of the outer office had closed, she returned to the Minister's desk and waited a few seconds as he continued to scan the document he'd been left.

"You wanted to read your prison brief, Minister."

8

Brittan was roused from his thoughts. "Eh, yes, but would you be so good to invite Sir Kenneth Newman to join me here at eight o'clock tomorrow morning?"

"Certainly, Minister but the Police Commissioner will also be attending the meeting with the Prime Minister later this evening."

Brittan paused. "Even so, I want to see him alone. Eight o'clock here. Unless he has a second meeting with the Prime Minister of which I'm unaware, he's to drop everything and be in my office as I request."

"Certainly, Minister. I'll call Scotland Yard immediately."

Chapter Three

FRIDAY 8TH MARCH 1985

London, England.

Miss Warren-Coates showed the Commissioner of the Metropolitan Police Force, Britain's most senior police officer, into the Minister's office precisely at the time requested of him. Brittan rose and walked towards his guest, arm extended, his face wreathed in a smile.

"Ken! Thanks for meeting me at such short notice. I want you to know that it's *much* appreciated."

"Always a pleasure, Minister."

Accepting the invitational gesture by Brittan to be seated on one of the distressed brown leather couches which occupied the floor of his spacious office some distance removed from his desk, Newman made himself comfortable and flicked some imaginary detritus from his lapel as he spoke. "So, what's so important you couldn't just whisper in my ear last night as we left the Prime Minister?"

"I confess this is an awkward one, Ken." Brittan shuffled uncomfortably in his seat, the leather squeaking as he did so. "I wanted to discuss the matter of the undercover police officers; the Special Operations Squad we agreed with the Crown Prosecution Service could be used to infiltrate organisations presumed to be a threat to our country."

"What *of* them? As you know, that's an operational matter, Minister. Now that the political decision's been made? *My* business, not yours." A small reflection allowed him to offer a compromise.

"I could send you an anonymised list if you're interested."

"Indeed, that would be most helpful. In the strictest confidence of course."

"Of course, Minister. People's lives would depend on that list remaining completely dark."

"I genuinely appreciate that, Ken. I am well aware that there are very brave men operating in Northern Ireland who would be compromised immediately..."

"Compromised, Minister? That's political language...they'd be tortured and killed."

"Quite so, Commissioner," conceded Brittan, mildly irked that the usual courtesies normally afforded him in his position as Home Secretary never seemed to trouble his most senior police officer.

"Well, as you know, we agreed that we should limit the number of undercover police officers to one hundred and so arrange matters that complete deniability is afforded you and your political colleagues should questions ever be asked. For your information only, seventeen of them are women. Eighty-four have been allocated to obvious organisations such as Greenpeace, CND, the Communist Party, the Miners Union, trades unionists, National Front and so on. We're well on but are working on the final few deployments. Just had a meeting about placing an undercover officer in the Animal Rights mob actually." He laced his fingers together and cracked the knuckles of his left hand as he considered the probable purpose of the meeting. "Have you some recommendations you'd like me to consider, Minister?"

Brittan smiled oleaginously. "My colleagues and myself have a number of concerns we worry might have eluded your gaze. Now these people I've been asked to draw to your attention are not of concern to us politically, you understand, but we do wonder whether you might cast your net sufficiently widely to embrace certain groupings and individuals whom we view as potential threats to the nation."

Newman groaned inwardly and repeated his request. "Might you offer me some suggestions, Minister?"

"Well, it's obvious that you're already covered the miners' strike and so on but there were a couple of people...indeed people within Parliament itself who might merit attention."

Sir Ken Newman paid attention. "Within Parliament, you say?"

"Regrettably so, Ken." He paused, uncertain of Newman's reaction. "For example, Geoffrey Dickens, one of our own Conservative MPs, just to demonstrate that our concerns are not *party*-political...is behaving like a complete fantasist. He has no proof, certainly no apparent *written* evidence but is making the most extravagant claims against the propriety of sitting MPs. We believe he's getting his information from external sources, is merely using it recklessly to advance his profile and wonder if you might take an interest. He's a funny chap. A working class boy from London, a boxer and a goalkeeper for some insignificant football team but somehow found himself the Conservative Member of Parliament for Littleborough and Saddleworth just south of my own constituency up north. Most unusual fellow. Announced to the press he was having an affair of the heart without thinking to tell his wife first. My people tell me that he suffered for that particular act of thoughtlessness." Brittan spread his arms, palms upwards conveying bewilderment and shrugged his shoulders. "Of all things, he's been campaigning to have teddy bears banned for some reason but he shoots from the hip and it's important that we don't allow his eccentricity to blind us to the fact that he's a subversive and very dangerous man."

Newman pulled a pen from his chest pocket and scribbled Dickens' name on a small pad.

"What's he claiming?"

Brittan ran his tongue over the bottom of his upper lip, always a tell that he was anxious.

"He alleges sexual impropriety by some Members of Parliament with people below the age of legal consent."

"Yeah, we get stories like that from time to time. Usually groundless. Any others?"

Relieved at Newman's reaction, Brittan continued.

"Perhaps one. A Scottish radical. His name's William McRae. Like myself, he's a legal man... and he's been the main intellectual energy in Scotland opposing the safeguarding of nuclear waste. In 1980, he opposed the proposals by the Atomic Energy Authority to bury nuclear waste in a place called Mullwarchar in Ayrshire in Scotland. He won and it provided a major setback to plans for having nuclear waste buried, not only in Scotland but in the rest of the UK. I've been asking around. What little I know of him is that he's reputed to be mentally unstable, an alcoholic and a homosexual. Of some interest to you might be that he was both a lieutenant commander in the Royal Indian Navy following a commission with the Seaforth Highlanders and subsequently the aide-de-camp to Admiral Lord Mountbatten in India so he's used to dealing with senior people. Perhaps unsurprisingly given his Scottish separatist beliefs, he supported the Indian independence movement and speaks Urdu and Hindi fluently. He was also the legal brains behind the enactment of the maritime law of Israel. He was Vice President of the Scottish National Party, is their legal adviser, runs a law firm in Glasgow and, frankly, we're concerned that he's being manipulated from Israel. We have no proof but thought it prudent to invite you to keep an eye on him, particularly given the fact that in a few months there's another enquiry, into the prospect of a nuclear facility in Dounray in the north of Scotland. I'm advised he's already girding his loins for that fight. Another subversive. Now he *also* seems to have his hands on a list of senior people in and around Parliament whom he intends alleging are paedophiles."

Brittan paused and allowed a silence as Newman wrote, the better to have his information received. He continued, "Better safe than sorry, don't you think?"

"And you want me to add these men to the list of people we've identified as requiring undercover surveillance?"

"That, of course, is an operational matter which is entirely within your province, Commissioner. However, I did wonder whether investigating the activities in respect of each man might help determine whether there's anything going on which would comprise actions against the interests of the State?"

"Well, I'll look at it, Minister." He continued writing in his notebook and continued speaking without lifting his head. "I'll make my own enquiries but it has to be said that on the face of it, for different reasons, there's enough here on each man to warrant *some* kind of further understanding of their activities."

He tucked his notebook in his inside pocket and placed his palms on his knees as a prelude to ending the discussion. "That it, Minister?"

"Only with the rider that I'd appreciate it if you'd keep me informed of progress."

"I'll maybe speak with you informally, Minister if you don't mind. It can get messy if there's a paper trail that allows people to know we've discussed things."

"Which is exactly why I don't have any officials present this morning, Ken." He got to his feet. "Please give my regards to your lovely wife."

* * *

Glenmallan, Loch Long, Scotland

The corrugated roof of the old barn near Glenmallan had long given way to rust and its holed wooden walls showed obvious evidence of wet rot. Deserted now for some ten years, the MacLennan farmstead no longer operated and had fallen into terminal decline. Weeds and saplings now grew in and around its entrance.

Inside the barn, Kev Doran, a young Ministry of Defence Police Officer stood, arms bound behind him, his tongue feeling around the inside of his mouth to test whether any teeth had been loosened by the blow he'd taken to his left cheek.

A man wearing a balaclava with holes only for his eyes and mouth grasped him by his throat.

"Now, son. Allow me to introduce myself. I go under the moniker of Lone Wolf and you can call me Wolf. Lone would be a bit familiar don't you think? I mean we hardly know one another. But I don't want you to think we're kiddin' around here. I don't have much in the way of patience so I'm going to remove the bag over your head. I'm wearing a balaclava so you might still survive this if you can't identify me but I want you to think very carefully before you decide if you want to be a hero or to die here." He pulled the rough hessian sack from the head of the policeman and displayed a hand grenade some inches from the police officer's chin.

"Do you understand what this is, son?"

Doran eyed the device and nodded.

"Well, specifically, son, this is an American M67 grenade...a fragmentation grenade. Much more effective than the iron balls packed with gunpowder that were first used against the Jacobites in the Battle of Killiecrankie. Not a lot of people know that, eh? Another Scottish first! Anyway, this wee beauty has a steel body that contains about six ounces of composition B explosive, that's sixty percent RDX and forty percent TNT, very bad stuff and when I remove this pin here, it frees a spring-loaded striker. That creates a wee spark which ignites a fuse and in about four seconds it sets off an explosion that blows the grenade apart. Bits of metal from this metal casing take off, straight through anybody and anything in their road. But all *you* need to remember is that if I pull this pin out, your head will explode and wallpaper this room. So...I've a few questions to ask and the first is how long you think you can stand here tonight without your legs buckling. Eh? It's important, son!"

He stepped back to a raised wooden pallet behind him where he lifted a ball of string and threaded one end through the safety pin of the grenade, tying it. Holding the grenade in his left hand, he threw the ball of string over a rafter catching it on the fall.

"Now, no one knows you're here, son. You don't know where you are but I can assure you that you are somewhere that no one's going to walk in and wish you the time of day. So I'm going to ask you a few questions. I haven't the time or inclination to play games so you answer my questions and I go away. Sooner or later you'll manage to free yourself and you walk home to friends and family. You *don't* answer my questions and I also walk away...but before I go, I'll tie this grenade to your neck and tighten the string from that rafter above you. Sooner or later you'll no' be able to stand up any more. We all have to sleep sometime. You'll fall to the floor and when you do, you'll cover the walls here with what's left of your brains. When that happens, I'll be tucked up in bed. Now...am I clear?"

Doran swallowed and uttered his first word since earlier being knocked unconscious. "Yes."

"Good. Now...you're a Military Police Officer at Faslane Nuclear Submarine base and you're going to tell me everything I want to know about HMS Resolution. I am aware that she is due to complete a Polaris patrol during which she tested two Chevaline Improved Front End missiles."

Silent tears began to run down the young man's cheek. He shook his head. "I swear to God I don't know what you're talking about. We're not told that kind of stuff. I just look after the entrance gate."

His interlocutor collected a roll of masking tape from the table and wordlessly bound the grenade to the neck of the police officer. Satisfied, he eased the string so that it had only enough play to accommodate slight movement. Ignoring the weeping police officer, he tugged gently on the string so as not to disturb the safety pin but to ensure that he could if he chose."

"We're not doing so well, are we?"

Doran stiffened. "Look, I suspect you're going to kill me anyway so here's my end of the bargain. I'll tell you as much as I can. I'm young. I want to live. But if you make that string tight, I'll fall immediately and take us both out."

The hooded man hesitated and grimaced his understanding of the stand-off.

"Well, it's not as elegant but we'll maybe change our approach here." He stepped back and fed the string loosely through his fingers, walking backwards until he reached a space that used to accommodate a barn door, thumping an adjacent brick wall that used to hold hay with his fist, assessing its mass. "Aye, this'll stop any shrapnel. Certainly easier than your head. If I tug this string, son, you have four seconds until your head explodes."

Almost as an afterthought, he reached into his pocket and threw a card depicting a Saltire on floor of the barn.

"Now, about the docking of HMS Resolution..."

*

Sometime later, as twilight fell, old Mrs Aiton was putting the day's rubbish in her outside bin. She'd lived alone in her small cottage at the foot of the Glen for fifty years now and was used to the rhythms, peace and quiet that her rural existence brought her. It was a still night, far too cold yet for midges, but tranquil, which was why she was subsequently able to report quite confidently to the police of the muffled explosion she'd heard and of the orange flash she'd witnessed from the barn belonging to the long abandoned farm cottage previously owned by her neighbour old Gudgie MacLennan.

Chapter Four

MONDAY 18TH MARCH 1985

Hanoi, Vietnam

The British High Commissioner to Vietnam, Sir Michael Pike sipped at his coffee, the first of several that he'd take over a punishing fourteen hour day. Outside, a cold, grey autumnal day in Hanoi promised rain. He watched from an office window of the British Embassy, a sturdy whitewashed example of French colonial architecture on *Ly Thuong Kiet* Street, as the citizens of Vietnam's capital city went to work, most of them astride a scooter; the noise from their motorcycles sounding like a grand urban buzz-saw each time the traffic lights below him turned green. He turned his head as he heard his office door open midst the din outside.

"Morning Sir Michael. Looks like another cold day in my city."

Pike smiled. "'Fraid it does that, *Tha'ng*. Why can't you find me a reason to visit Saigon on days like this?"

"Saigon is raining today, Sir Michael. Water everywhere in the rainy season. Saigon only have two seasons...very hot and dry and very hot and wet."

Pike nodded the accuracy of his assistant's comment while placing his hand on a nearby radiator to ensure it emanated some heat. Hanoi did not share the same weather as Saigon.

"Hmm, well, let's get to it. What's first on my 'to do' list this morning?"

"First thing you wanted to see our security chief, Mr. Macmillan. He is outside."

"Ah, yes. Jock." He consulted his watch. "This won't take long, *Tha'ng*. Please arrange a car to take me to the Australian Embassy in half an hour. I want to be there by ten."

Tha'ng Linh made a note and spoke while still writing. "Certainly, sir. I bring in Mr. Macmillan now, Sir?" He looked up to receive confirmation and turned on his heel towards his desk outside the Ambassador's office door, returning with Macmillan.

"Morning, Jock." Pike finished his coffee and gestured towards two armchairs placed next to a wood fire that crackled in the hearth. "Come and sit down."

"Sir Michael," said Macmillan in acknowledgement.

Pike collected a green cardboard folder and brought it with him to the armchair. Both men sat as Pike glanced though the contents contained within the file before speaking.

"Been here a year, Jock?"

"Just over, sir. Thirteen months."

"Enjoying it?"

"Very much, sir. It has its quieter moments but I love Vietnam and its people. Staff here are great and the weather suits me. I'm from Stornoway so Hanoi's cold and rainy weather is just perfect for me."

Pike grinned. "Just talking to *Tha'ng* about that. Forgot you were from the northern wastes."

"I'll accept 'northern' but not 'wastes', sir. It's beautiful up in Lewis."

"Well," Pike clipped the file with the middle finger of his right hand as if flicking a crumb from a napkin, "It appears you might be rejoining your friends and former colleagues rather sooner than expected, Jock. I've a request here from your bosses in Special Branch asking that you return to London to undertake new duties as soon as possible."

Macmillan sat forward in his seat. "But sir, this is a three year tour. Diplomatic protection. I'm just getting the feel of the place."

Pike ignored Macmillan's protest. "You've a law degree from Edinburgh?"

"Scots law. Not much good here or London."

"And you've worked in Special Branch in London for five years, two in Belfast...promoted to Detective Sergeant with the Irish Joint Section and six before that as a police officer in the Met before some eighteen months ago being promoted to Detective Inspector and asking to be seconded to the Foreign and Commonwealth Office?"

"Correct. I wanted to see something of the world and I understood that my next two years at least were to be here in Vietnam.'

"Well, I'd be perfectly happy were that to be the case, Jock. We'll miss you. As you know, Vietnam's still at war with China but it appears that our country's interests might be better served were you to return with all possible speed to London. According to this dispatch you have a meeting with Sir Kenneth Newman, the Commissioner of the Met no less, three days hence."

"Have I incurred his wrath, do you know?"

"No indication of that, Jock and certainly nothing but high praise from this end of things. You're extremely able, detailed, tenacious and popular. My first and only appraisal of you was fulsome. So I can only imagine they have a task for you that's more important than looking after my skin."

Macmillan smiled. "Can't imagine anything more important to Her Majesty's Government."

Pike returned the grin. "I'm but a humble Ambassador. Looking after the Queen's Welsh Corgis ranks somewhat higher than saving my neck." He closed the file. "I'll be sorry to lose you, Jock but ours is not to reason why, so I'd suggest you speak with admin and get flights sorted out. It appears that you're destined for more adventurous things. Being pulled back to London from the other side of the world suggests they have in mind a new responsibility of some importance."

* * *

Glasgow, Scotland.

The Saltire flag flying over the Auld Smiddy was flapping briskly in the breeze. The pub, community based but often used by those of a Nationalist persuasion was usually quiet on a Monday evening and when Hector McLeod walked in, the only people drinking were the three he'd arranged to meet. A glass of McEwan's Pale Ale sat unattended awaiting his presence.

"Better late than never," said Sandy Tarbet, one of the waiting threesome.

McLeod wrestled his coat from his shoulders and hung it on the rear of a chair. He folded his bunnet, placed it in his coat pocket and chuckled as he shook the hands of each of his friends in turn. One of his preferred brands of cigarettes, Embassy Number 5 which he smoked almost mechanically, dangled from his lips as he spoke.

"I'm worth the wait!"

"Sammy!" Tam O'Neil, a stocky, powerful-looking man with tattooed arms, the most substantial of which was a Scottish Saltire, called the attention of the barman who was sitting reading a newspaper at the other end of the pub. "We're just moving over to the back table. Can we put a tab on and get another round in?"

McLeod paused the glass he'd just raised at his lips. "Jesus, Tam, I've not even had a sniff at this *first* pint!"

"That's what happens when you turn up late, Hector! The early bird and all that..." The group laughed.

The four men took their drinks over to a table at the furthest end of the pub. Tommy Docherty, during office hours, a builder to trade, re-opened the conversation the three men had had just prior to McLeod arriving. "So, Hector, Tam here tells us you were followed by the Special Branch on Saturday night."

McLeod's eyes crinkled while he took a large draught of his pint. "Aye, Butch and Sundance followed me all day but I saw them early on when I was having a coffee in Byres Road. They stayed with me all day then sat outside here in their souped-up Special Branch Triumph Acclaim in the pissin' rain while I had one for the road and the buggers never even offered me a lift home!" He placed his glass on a beer mat and wiped some foam from his mouth. "I imagine they were hoping I'd make contact with Willie McRae but I just wandered about all day up at the Barras. When I left here I spoke with them..."

O'Neill swallowed his Glenlivet whisky without savouring its peaty flavour as he usually did. "What the fu...you *spoke* with them?"

"Look, Tam. *We* know they take an interest in our politics. *They* know that *we* know...Pretending that we keep bumping into them by accident is a bit daft...a bit absurd...fatuous."

"Aye, very good, Hector. I got your meaning at daft! Anyway, did you meet Willie?"

"No but I'm seeing him tomorrow if I can do so without the cops following me. He's excited about some information that's come into his hands."

"What do you think it is, Hector?"

"No idea."

Docherty intervened. "Here boys...we were going to discuss what civil disobedience we could get up to when Prince Philip visits Fairfields Shipyards in Govan next week to lunch that new minesweeper."

Tarbet raised his hand. "I vote we stay in here, enjoy the wonderful gantry that sits before us, moan to each other about how the Establishment is a malevolent force that runs the country and how Queen Elizabeth the Second of England and First of Scotland is the devil incarnate!"

"Aye, that's going to change things here in Scotland, eh?"

O'Neill, always the most pugnacious in the small group, offered an alternative. "Why don't we blow up his fuckin' Rolls Royce?"

Docherty interjected. "Behave yourself, Tam. How's that goin' to bring about an independent Scotland?"

O'Neill considered an alternative. "Well then, maybe we could sneak up behind his Rolls and stick a potato over his exhaust pipe. That way the car'll no' go and it'll be great PR."

"Maybe if we stick a wee Saltire flag on the spud and let the media in on the joke," said Tarbet.

"D'y'know, Sandy, that's no' the *worst* idea..." said O'Neill seeking approval.

McLeod toasted O'Neill, raising his glass and interrupting him. "Right, Tam. We're agreed. You're in charge of spud acquisition and flag insertion. Problem solved. Independence for Scotland by the year end."

"Cut the nonsense, Hector. We've business to conduct." Docherty pulled a copy of the day's Scotsman newspaper from his small rucksack. "What's the story with this Ministry of Defence cop who got his head blown off? Was that any of our boys?"

There was a silent shaking of heads before McLeod spoke, "It does look a bit suspicious. Some of our people are getting frustrated at the lack of progress towards independence. Perhaps one or two of them have decided to play the establishment at their own game. Fight fire with fire and that kind of stuff."

"Well, who could blame them, eh? All they understand down south is bullets and explosions. It's been shown in Ireland that the only way to get your freedom is to fight for it." O'Neill again.

McLeod demurred. "For all we know, that young cop could have been as committed to Scottish Independence as we are. I accept that violence can be understandable but it needs to be thought through. Just because someone wears a uniform doesn't make them a government or unionist lackey."

O'Neill continued. "Well, it wasn't an accident and it wasn't suicide and you mark my words, Hector, the polis, the MOD boys, MI5 and Special Branch will leave no stone unturned to find out who did this and they'll have our names on a list somewhere."

"Aye, maybe so," agreed McLeod. He shrugged. "We'll see. I suggest we let Prince Philip have his visit to the yards without our intervention. Let him launch HMS Middleton. They've also just won a new order down in the yards and there'll be a feel-good atmosphere in Govan. We'd just look like we were just trying to spoil the party. In any event, it's the same day we have the big protest march from George Square a week on Saturday. Everyone still up for it?"

A murmur of agreement prefaced McLeod reaching into his hip pocket and bringing out a small map showing the route to be taken by a protest march against the Conservative Government.

"The organisers expect a big turnout especially since that over-the-top police response to the riots in Brixton and Handsworth. People are pissed off."

"They were bang out of order, they polis in London. Bang out of order," grumbled O'Neill.

"Well, we'll be there with our flags and banners and we've already printed some leaflets setting out our demands for a Scottish Parliament." His finger traced lines on the map. "The march leaves George Square and heads along Ingram street, into High Street and down past the Tolbooth to Glasgow Green. We expect about a hundred of our supporters and we also expect the cameras to be there. We reckon they'll take some crowd shots, do a piece to camera in George Square and then some more shots of the crowd as they pass the Tolbooth. They won't have time to do anything much at Glasgow Green if they want to have something ready for the evening news so our plan is that we try to get a bit of publicity at the Tolbooth. We'll be joined by Davy Asquith and his pals..."

"Christ, he's as mental as wee Tam here!" guffawed Docherty.

McLeod grinned his acknowledgement and continued." And we'll all take our flags and force entry to the Tolbooth Steeple. If we time things properly, we'll have the Independence banner displayed prominently just as the camera action starts. So," his finger followed the route on the map and tapped it where it showed Glasgow Cross, "as we pass the Tolbooth Steeple we force the door and run up the seven flights to the top..."

Docherty protested. "Aye, you, maybe. I'll be walking... slowly!" The group laughed.

Mcleod continued. "There are windows on each landing. We use them to display the Saltire and at the top behind the clock and the crown, we hang the banner for independence."

O'Neill nodded his approval. "Sounds fine but we need to do something to make more of an impact. A wee scuffle or something."

"Absolutely not. It's important we look dignified and passionate not boorish and violent. So, no stupidity boys. We only want good headlines." He caught O'Neill's attention. "You need to behave like a good boy scout, Tam"

O'Neill demurred. "Me? Behave at a protest march? I'd rather shite in my hands and applaud the Tories!"

"Aye, well 'a wee scuffle' is an insufficient action, Tam. It'll take more than that but we pick our time, we pick our place and we work to a strategy. We're not going to win the hearts and minds of our countrymen by acting like a bunch of neds on television while people are at their dinner."

"Where's the fun, Hector?" O'Neill attempted a smile that didn't reach his eyes.

"Look, in this china shop, we've a strict 'no bulls' policy. We agreed years ago that we'd make our case through civil disobedience and direct action. So we do it the way we've agreed. No violence."

Docherty and Tarbet looked at O'Neill who met their gaze. He shaped the three finger salute of the Boy Scouts, touched the right side of his forehead and mumbled unconvincingly, "Scout's honour! Fine by me, boys! Fine by me."

Chapter Five

FRIDAY 22ND MARCH 1985

London, England

Macmillan sat on a comfortable settee in the outer office of the Police Commissioner of Greater London Metropolitan Police Service scanning a National Geographic magazine disinterestedly, unable to shift his thoughts from the purpose of his visit. From behind him, a pair of strong hands grasped his trapezius muscles at each shoulder and began massaging them.

"Oh, there's tension there. I can feel the knotted muscles. Lot of work needed here...."

Macmillan craned his neck to see the smiling face of Nobby Clark.

"Nobby, you old bastard! How are you? It must be...six, seven years."

"That'll be Chief Inspector Clark, if you don't mind, you miserable piece of shit!"

"Chief Inspector? Who did you pay off to get a promotion like that?"

Clark clipped him playfully around the head and sat on an armchair opposite him. "Raw talent, Jock. Nothing other than raw talent and clean living."

"Christ, what are you doing here? Last time I saw you we were both hiding in a broom cupboard in a pub in Crossmaglen over in Ulster."

"Personal Assistant to the Commissioner of Police, Sir Kenneth Newman. Bit of a change, eh?"

"You? A personal assistant? I might be wrong but I can't think of anyone less suited to the humdrum life of a toady. I always figured that the next time I saw you I'd be in a church somewhere and I'd be eulogising your glorious life in uniform and promising to nail the bastard who shot you." Both laughed, Clark in a high-pitched whine that used to incur much teasing from Macmillan; 'a laugh only dogs could hear', he'd say.

"So you're here to see the boss?"

"Aye. But for the life of me I can't work out why. I've been out in Vietnam. Seconded to the Foreign and Commonwealth Office. Diplomatic Protection. I was given three days to get back here today. What can you tell me before I enter the lion's den?"

"You know I'd tell you, Jock but it's all very hush-hush. The old man is seeing you with Mo McGinnis, the Head of 'F' Branch in MI5...Counter Subversion. "

Macmillan pursed his lips. "And what conclusion would you draw from that?"

"Frankly, that they're going to involve you in some entertaining skulduggery."

A buzzer sounded quietly in the vicinity of Clark's desk.

"That's you being paged, Jock." He took a card from the breast pocket of his uniform. "Here's my number. If you want a chat afterwards give me a bell. I'm due to louse at six this evening. If you're free we could have a pint and catch up."

"Yeah, I'd like that Nobby...I mean Chief Inspector."

Clark spoke sotto voce. "Fuck off!"...then louder as he knocked and opened the door, "Detective Inspector John Macmillan, Sir."

Macmillan placed his magazine back on the coffee table and stood up, tightening his tie and re-buttoning his suit jacket before striding into the office with a confidence born of years of having had his talents affirmed by senior officers.

The Commissioner of Police stood with his back to Macmillan and was in close conversation with a woman in her forties as both of them consulted a file they had open on his desk. He turned his head momentarily and addressed Macmillan. "Have a seat. We'll be over in a minute."

After some further reading, Newman took off his spectacles, placed them in his shirt pocket and approached a now seated Macmillan without offering his hand.

He addressed the woman. "Well, I wish someone had advised me of this before we had this chap travel half way round the world to sit two feet from me."

Mo McGinnis took a cup and saucer with which she'd been provided earlier and sat in an adjacent armchair. She spoke confidently, apparently unconcerned about the Commissioner's dark mood. "These details came from Police files, Sir Kenneth, not MI5. I was only apprised of this as I was leaving my office this morning."

"Nothing's bloody straightforward in this operation," he growled before addressing Macmillan.

He rubbed his eyes and sighed as if attempting to summon another more positive demeanour. "Thank you for making arrangements to travel here. It was last minute and your efforts have been appreciated. Unfortunately I've just been made aware of circumstances that might make the deployment we had in mind somewhat more complicated..." He replaced his spectacles and consulted the file he'd brought over with him before continuing..."and might suggest you would have been better buying return tickets to Vietnam."

"Don't let that trouble you, Sir Kenneth. I'd be delighted to return to Hanoi. It came as something of a surprise to be ordered back to London."

Newman looked over the rim of his glasses. "You'll go where we have need of you to go, Detective Inspector." He gestured at his colleague. "Ms. McGinnis here...she's Head of MI5's Counter Subversion Branch ...she thinks you're ideal for an assignment we have in mind but it has just transpired that the operative we have in place to support you isn't exactly a kissing cousin." He waved the file he'd been holding and dropped it on a nearby table.

Mo McGinnis interjected and changed the subject. "I gather that we both come from the same island."

"I'm a Lewis man, Ms. McGinnis. You too?"

"Well, I'm a Lewis *woman*, but born and brought up in *Griais* within the Parish of Stornoway; attended the Nicolson Institute just like you did although I left just as you were arriving. Your file here says you were brought up in Garenin away up in Carloway."

"I was that," he smiled and employed the language of his childhood. "*Carson a tha am bodach ud cho diumbach?* Why is that old man in such a bad mood?"

She returned his grin. "Tha *e direach air faighinn a mach gu bheil droch bheachd agaibh air am fear a bh'againn air taghadh dhuibh*. He's just been told that you have a poor opinion of the support officer we'd chosen for you."

Newman intervened. "Right! Enough of that mumbo-jumbo. We speak English in this office."

Macmillan addressed him in English. "I must confess that I'm intrigued about what role is necessary that requires me to be flown across the world when there are hundreds of cops who must surely be able to fill whatever brief you have in mind...sir!"

McGinnis interjected again as Newman prepared to debate him. "You're a cop with pertinent experience. You have a wonderful set of assessments which paint you as an ideal fit psychologically, but importantly, you left school, went to Edinburgh University to study law and made your way in the Metropolitan Police force and elsewhere without troubling the denizens of Glasgow overmuch. You wouldn't appear to be known much in Scotland's industrial heartland...and you're unmarried without a partner unless you tell us differently. Finally, you were positively vetted only three months ago so you've an up-to-date security clearance."

"I live alone. No important relationship beyond my parents and a sister, all of whom live on Lewis. Been at a few concerts in Glasgow over the years but haven't travelled much beyond Queen Street Station. No friends there."

McGinnis frowned genially. "Everyone should have at least *one* Glaswegian friend, Mr Macmillan. They're an unusual breed!"

Newman tired of the banter and spoke directly to Macmillan. "Listen, Detective Inspector...you've taken an oath to serve the Queen in the office of constable. You've signed the Official Secrets Act. In the normal course of things that would be that but for this assignment I'm afraid I need to ask after your politics."

"Not very political, sir. I've always voted Independent. Up on the islands, we tend to vote the person rather than the party."

"That's true, Sir Kenneth," confirmed McGinnis.

"Have you a view about whether Scotland should be a country independent of the rest of the United Kingdom?"

"Well, I'm not too keen on the Secretary of State, George Younger. He seems a bit toffee-nosed for me. But like I said, I'm not very political. I'm happy with things as they stand. Never given it much thought."

Newman sat back in his chair, pondering his next move and directed his comment to McGinnis.

"Well, I suppose we should deal with this matter of his support."

McGinnis took over. "When you were in Northern Ireland, you worked with Detective Sergeant Melissa Rees. Your reports made it clear at the time that you disapproved of her conduct?"

Macmillan grimaced at the question posed but responded to Newman. "I *wondered* if she was the person you were discussing." He sat forward in his chair. "In my view sir, she's a hothead, she put people's lives in danger, she refused to listen to reason, she wasn't a team player and she has a temper...she's..."

"Alright, Macmillan, I get your drift. She'd be the person you'd be meeting from time to time in order to be debriefed. We want you to work undercover in Glasgow and you'd be cut adrift from all the normal supports. She'd be your lifeline."

"Blood would be spilled between us, sir. She's certifiable."

"And you're just an angel?"

Macmillan relented. "I have my moments, sir."

Newman sighed, suddenly wearied of the conversation. "This is an important assignment, Macmillan...a joint operation between Special Branch and MI5's Counter-subversion Branch. Its genesis comes from the very top of the tree. It can't be allowed to fail and in my view, if you're half the professional that I've been advised that you are, you're just going to have to suck it up and deal with Detective Sergeant Rees who's back in Special Branch for this operation. You'll have a lot more than your relationship with her to worry about once you go undercover." He turned to McGinnis. "Can I leave this in your hands, Mo?

"Of course, Sir Kenneth."

Newman stood as did the two others in anticipation of the meeting ending. "And Inspector...don't cut your hair until you get permission from me in writing. You look like a cross between a Grenadier Guardsman and a Marks and Sparks window mannequin. Loosen up a bit. You're shortly to enter civvy street in your undercover role as something approaching a hippy! Presently you look like a rather conservative estate agent."

Chapter Six

MONDAY 25TH MARCH 1985

Glenmallan, Loch Long, Scotland

T he small cottage was set back from Loch Long just off the narrow road between Arrochar and Garelochhead. Its peat fire was now settled and warming the kitchen within which an ancient, green Rayburn cooking stove that over many years hadn't received the care and attention it had been due, nevertheless worked hard to boil a kettle. Using the same heat source, a frying pan containing four slices of bacon and two sausages spat fat on its mottled surround. Nearby, three buttered, well-fired rolls on an unwashed plate awaited the removal of the frying pan from the range.

Content that his evening meal was coming along nicely, Jimmy Hancock returned to the kitchen table on which were assembled a battery-powered doorbell, some clothes pegs, a soldering iron and some fishing line. Tentatively, he removed the small circuit board from the bell section and soldered a substantial length of extension wire to the button terminals. These he attached to the open ends of a wooden clothes peg. Satisfied, he drilled holes in the closed end of the pegs and pushed metal rivets into each ensuring that a metallic connection was inevitable when the jaws were closed. He reached up to a dusty shelf and brought down some tent pegs. So equipped, he repeated the process a further twice, manufacturing three trip wires, each of which when placed on his ash path leading to his front door would trigger a bell in his croft.

He stepped into the front room which faced the road along the lochside and peeled back one of the drab pair of curtains that had hung there unmet and unwashed for the ten years that had elapsed since his mother's death. Nothing stirred. It was twilight now and a mist was beginning to form along the loch blending with the peat smoke from his fire. He narrowed his eyes and looked sky-wards at darker clouds forming overhead suggesting a wet evening to come. Hancock opened his front door which scraped along the flagstone floor due to its loosened, aged and rusty hinges and walked to the bottom of the compressed earthen path that led to his cottage. Taking the first of his trip wires, he fastened one end to a tent peg and at a height of one foot from the ground, eased back the fishing line which he affixed to a second to which was tied a clothes peg on the other side of the path and tightened it. Within the jaws of each peg was a small piece of wood. Anyone tugging the wire would remove the wood, close the jaws and set off the alarm in his croft. *I'll hear it, but anyone setting off this alarm wouldn't be aware they'd alerted me to their presence.*

Some minutes later, he stepped over the three almost invisible trip-wires he'd set, checking they were primed and would alert him should anyone approach his home from the front gate. Anyone seeking entry from the sides or rear might easily stumble upon one of the several disguised pits within which were a series of metal spikes that would be lethal in at least two of the deeper pits. These required to be checked daily due to their effectiveness in trapping foxes and other animals. Resetting them was simple although disposing of dead or maimed animals was more time consuming. Above and inside his rear door, a hinged and weighted spar, again sporting eight-inch sharpened metal spikes was adhered to the ceiling in such a way as to fall forwards like a pendulum should the door be pulled open, visiting terrible injuries upon anyone attempting entry.

Hancock was content that any attempt to engage him could be resisted sufficiently or set off an alarm which would at least allow him to arm himself.

Returning to his kitchen and having consumed his three filled rolls in as many minutes, Hancock lifted a floorboard in his small kitchen and withdrew an Enfield Pattern 14 Rifle, a bolt action sniper rifle made obsolete in 1947 but still useful. With a five bullet internal magazine and optimised for rapid fire, the rifle remained formidable despite its ageing. Hancock could forgive its tendency to overheat when fired repeatedly as he had other plans for this weapon. He checked that the two forward stabilising lugs moved easily then wiped the rifle with a rag to remove all fingerprints, not forgetting to wipe and replace the five bullets that would accompany it on its journey. Satisfied, he once again replaced it under the floorboard with the rest of his small arsenal, first removing then replacing his black balaclava to allow the Enfield to fit snugly. Before replacing the floorboard to conceal his weaponry, he first opened a small tin box and removed a business card which he placed in his pocket.

* * *

McGinnis's office was contained within an anonymous grey limestone block at 140 Gower Street. Rows of perfectly symmetrical windows looked across the street to University College Hospital in London. Internally, it was spartan and minimalist. Ensconced within the corridors that accommodated Military Intelligence 5, or the 'Domestic Service' as their cousins in MI6 called them, the suite of offices still didn't show any evidence of modernity in terms of furnishings although some very sophisticated electronics were buried within their confines.

McGinnis issued Macmillan into her office in more business-like fashion than that she'd exhibited in the office of the Commissioner. She hung her coat on a peg behind her door and bid Macmillan sit at a conference table while she collected a file from a rather ordinary desk. *No small talk now*, thought Macmillan.

"Well, Detective Inspector Macmillan, my job today is to brief you on the assignment we've allocated you. As was mentioned earlier by Sir Kenneth, this task is completely confidential and has been required of us from the highest levels of government. You'll be working undercover and will have only the most rudimentary of supports. We have in our sights a Scottish solicitor named William McRae. By all accounts a very brilliant lawyer and a very average politician but we require to reassure ourselves that he and those around him pose no threat to the good order of the United Kingdom. It's all here in the file and you have the afternoon to read and remember its contents. Your job is to get close to him and your law degree might be useful here. You have to be in Glasgow a week on Saturday but will move into your new rented apartment in the city's west end immediately in order to get to know the place rather better than you do now. You travel north on the 11.00pm Caledonian Sleeper train to Glasgow Central from Euston tonight."

"You guys don't hang around!"

McGinnis ignored his intervention. "There's a large protest march being organised on the thirtieth of March and you'll be arrested for some minor violence you'll perpetrate on some unsuspecting bobby. We also intend to find reason to arrest a man called Hector McLeod who is a confidant of McRae. You'll spend the weekend in a cell with him awaiting court. During that time you're to befriend him and convince him that your politics are aligned with his."

"And his politics are?"

"He's a nationalist but not a member of the Scottish National Party although he seems to act as a sort of lieutenant for Willie McRae. We're open-minded about his relationship with the Scottish National Liberation Army and we're rather persuaded that he seemed to have had a hand in organising their "Oystercatcher" operation to frustrate what they saw as illicit test-boring for nuclear storage in Glen Etive. Both McRae and McLeod seem to have a hand in Dark Harvest Commando operation. It's all in the report."

"I've heard of the SNLA. Are they still active?"

"Last year they sent letter bombs to Lady Diana Spencer and to the Prime Minister. Fortunately, although the device sent to Mrs. Thatcher was active and was opened in her office, there was no explosion. The head of the SNLA, a man called Adam Busby, a former soldier, fled to Dublin after the letter-bombing campaign and remains at large... we think McLeod was involved. He's smart and keeps his cards close to his chest. We keep tabs on him but we can't get close to him. Also, as you'll have seen in the news, a young Ministry of Defence police officer had his head removed from his body by means of a grenade taped to his neck. A grizzly end. The local boys are investigating and haven't ruled out a nationalist action but they're not particularly close to tying things up."

"And I've to find a way into this tight circle of ultra-nationalists?"

"You have, D.I. Macmillan. And your cover is as simple as we could make it. You retain much of your own identity lest you require to use your legal background to serve the interests of McRae. Your registration with the Law Society of Scotland would be easily checked."

"I have a law degree but I've never been a practising solicitor."

"Nevertheless, your legend is that you retain your name but following university in 1970, you decided against practising law, opened a shop in London where you sold low grade *objets d'art*... we haven't time to have you become an expert...and after the ending of hostilities in Vietnam in 1975, travelled there where you set up a shop in Hanoi selling local pottery, becoming a bit of a back-packing hippy. You can wing that part of your back story. It's all detailed in a note I'll leave with you, but nothing leaves this room. "

"Straightforward enough, I imagine. Although I don't look much like a hippy, do I?"

"Do your best to blend in. Grow a beard. Paint your face in blue woad. Whatever! You returned to your native Scotland to set up a business and you're happy to become involved in nationalist politics. In the meantime, you bought into a taxi business. Black cab. It's a legit taxi and you rent it currently on a twenty-four hour basis from a retired cop. We recompense him, but not much as it's an ancient taxi. He's been using it to make pocket money rather than as a business."

"Just a normal taxi?"

"Unusually, perhaps because of its age, it's a petrol-driven vehicle. Modern ones tend to be diesel but it's a regular taxi other than the fact that when you're driving, everything said in the cab will be recorded. You also have a radio that's solely for your use. A simple switch allows it to become a normal taxi radio. The taxi's also how you meet your support officer, Detective Sergeant Melissa Rees."

Macmillan groaned, "God, I'd almost forgotten that part of the job."

"She'll be fine. She's been on secondment to MI5 from North Wales Police Authority but she's being returned to the auspices of Special Branch for this work. I've spoken with her. She's up in Glasgow already. It'll be simple for you to pick her up in the cab and share information without raising suspicion. If you require to access any items such as weaponry or telephony, you do so in the cab." She handed him an envelope. "If you seek cash, we'll need to know in advance what you intend to do with it."

"Sounds interesting. Does Strathclyde Police know I'm operating behind enemy lines?"

"No they don't. No one does. We have an ability through Special Branch to make arrangements such as you sharing a cell with McLeod but you're pretty much on your own other than D.S. Rees who will report to me on your progress."

Macmillan acknowledged her support. "I think I could make all of that believable."

"You'll have to. Now...take this file next door and start reading! You leave here at 10.15pm and cross the road to Euston Station to catch your train north to Glasgow." McGinnis closed the file she'd been consulting and laid it before her on the table. "Look, Detective Inspector, I'm following a hunch here. I need this to work out well and I've checked your background to satisfy myself that you're the kind of man I want to see poking around in this. I want you to know that I've given very careful thought to who might best meet my objectives here. I didn't bring you half-way across the world on a whim, I assure you. I'm happy that you're ethical, tenacious and bright...and you have a sufficient disdain for authority. You'll do the job that needs to be done. That job is twofold; first, infiltrate the group of people who surround William McRae. Secondly, and the *purpose* of that infiltration, is to secure information pertinent to the security of the state. I would expect you eventually to withdraw in a way which does not give rise to speculation as to your role here. However, if you uncover circumstances that require you to protect yourself or to act in order to protect the best interests of the state, you have permission so to do. You are authorised to use lethal force if necessary, as is D.S. Rees. I intend writing these instructions and permissions in the case notes for this assignment. You'll be protected." She rose. "I hope that's clear...Coffee and sandwiches are available at any time from my secretary, Janice outside. I'll be working at my desk. Don't interrupt me." *Sealbh ort*. Good luck."

Smiling inwardly at the still soft tones of McGinnis's Hebridean accent issuing forth such formal command, Macmillan took his leave and opened the file on McRae. Within it, neatly pinned in sequence were surveillance reports and copies of newspaper cuttings but his eye was caught by several photographs of the man in question. A large man, bulky, with jet black, slicked-back hair stared out at him. He wore a crisp white shirt, dark tie and sober suit, obviously a photograph taken for some professional or political purpose. Behind it were more of him in action. In one, he stood behind a lectern obviously fulminating about something, his left hand grasping the edge of the lectern, the right arm gesticulating aggressively. *Unusual for a politician,* thought Macmillan as he noticed the wide grin on McRae's face as he was caught by the cameraman. *Usually these people are deadly boring. He looks like he's having fun!*

Chapter Seven

THURSDAY 28TH MARCH 1985

Glasgow, Scotland

Glasgow publican, John Waterson, the owner of the Pot Still bar in Glasgow's Hope Street, wearily climbed the five steps to the upper gallery of his pub and approached a table where was seated a large man aged in his early sixties whose bleary eyes suggested a surfeit of whisky obtained from the famous gantry behind the bar. He drank alone.

"Have you no' had enough for one night, Willie?"

A slow smile spread across Willie McRae's face. "I never have enough, John. There's not enough whisky in this fine establishment of yours to satisfy my appetite."

"By heavens, I know that well, Willie but you've work again in the morning and you'll have some heid on you if you keep sipping away at that Glenmorangie."

McRae placed the lit end of his Gold Flake against a fresh cigarette, drawing its smoke into his lungs, stubbing the dead one in a single movement. Before answering he removed a loose piece of tobacco from his tongue, spitting air to ensure removal. A phlegm-generating coughing fit delayed his response.

"Aye, well it's the eighteen year old with just a wee splash of water to release its flavour and it's not to be resisted, John."

He consulted his watch. "The night's yet young. I'll maybe have a go at your twenty-five year old. I can never make my mind up which of the two is superior. And to finish with a flourish, I might have a wee Islay Mist to see me up the road. "Lifting his glass, he gestured at a pile of paperwork he'd been dealing with." Anyway, I've this to finish and I've a friend meeting me before I head up the road. So, thank you for your concern and thank you for the excellent management of your fine hostelry. I'll have a big twenty-five year old Glenmorangie please." As Waterson levered himself slowly from the wooden balustrade to fulfil his request, McRae added, "You'd better pour me a glass of McEwan's Pale Ale as well, John. My young friend has no taste for the whisky."

Draining the glass, he turned his attention again to his paperwork until Waterson returned with his Glenmorangie and the glass of Pale Ale placing them on the table simultaneously with the arrival of Hector McLeod.

"Good to see you Willie." He looked at the scattered paperwork and offered his hand to McRae who shook it warmly after placing his cigarette in his mouth to free it.

"You're looking busy."

"Never too busy to see you, Hector. I have your favourite tipple just poured."

McLeod toasted his health wordlessly and looked around the bar approvingly. "What a great gantry they have here, Willie. I can well see why you use this as your evening office."

"Famed throughout the land, Hector. They have rare whiskies here that were on the big boat with Noah. And it's quiet of an evening except the weekend when it's more boisterous. I can get work done and I write better when alcohol encourages my inner devil."

"God alone knows the mischief your inner devil causes the British Establishment. So keep up the good work."

"Well, it's the mischief of their panjandrums I'm looking into tonight, Hector. Not satisfied with the Atomic Energy Authority taking a beating over their plans of to dump nuclear waste beneath the feet of the good people who like to wander Mullwharchar in our Galloway Hills, they now want to attempt simply to pour the nuclear waste from the Dounreay nuclear facility into our seas. Anywhere so long as it's not in England."

"Might they succeed this time?"

"Not if my name's Lieutenant Commander, Professor emeritus William McRae esquire, legal maestro and all round good egg. I'll have them store it where Guy Fawkes put his gunpowder before I'm done." He took a sip of his whisky and changed the subject. "We have important business to discuss tonight, Hector. Can you be sure you weren't followed here?"

"I've done my best. I bought a ticket to see that new James Bond film, 'A View To A Kill' in the Odeon round the corner in Renfield Street, went to the toilet after ten minutes then left. No one followed me out. I'm sure of that so I think we're safe."

"I have need of your services. My home was burgled again last night. That makes five occasions on which Special Branch or MI5 have broken and entered my abode looking for evidence of whatever they imagine I'm up to. In consequence I find myself keeping all of my important paperwork in my briefcase at all times. They're a tricky bunch and I'm sure they wouldn't hesitate to cook up some cock and bull story about me in order to have me in front of the beak on some trumped up charge to discredit me and to give them due cause to search my belongings with more leisure than is possible when it's a cloak and dagger opera-tion." He patted the leather satchel that sat at his side. "If they don't steal my briefcase, they don't have due cause."

McLeod frowned his displeasure. "We must do something to offer you more protection, Willie."

"Ah, Hector, you're a good man. However, I fear that the forces of the Great British Establishment would conspire to over-come whatever brave and innovative measures you might put in place. We must be careful but we must also be realistic. The forces of the Crown are mighty and we are small. That they are feart of us is in little doubt so we must redouble our efforts to give them cause to be even *more* feart of us and that, my young friend is to make our case in the court of public opinion."

41

"Well, that court is in session...but its opinion at present is not to have anything to do with Scottish Nationalism. Presently we're a bit of a busted flush!"

"Regrettably you're right, Hector." His mood darkened momentarily. "But things change...things change." He lifted his empty whisky glass. "By Jove, the whisky in this glass appears to have evaporated."

"Then let me get you three fingers of a wee malt so it'll take longer to disappear into thin air, Willie. A Glenmorangie or an Islay Mist?"

McRae preferred the Glenmorangie and busied himself with his papers, this time tidying them and placing them inside his briefcase. McLeod returned with a large Glenmorangie and a whispered request from John Waterson to see Willie home soon before he fell down.

McLeod sat on a stool opposite McRae. "Here, Willie, I'm no' having any of your pessimism. That last election was bad for us. There's no getting away from it. Two MPs elected. But who knows how things might have turned out if Labour hadn't elected that eegit Michael Foot as Leader, if Thatcher hadn't sent her Task Force to the Falklands, if the Labour Party hadn't fractured and created the SDP...we must remember that some four hundred and ninety-odd thousand people voted for the SNP in Scotland..."

"Aye, Hector, but the Tories now have three hundred and fifty-nine MPs to our two. We have a harridan of a Tory Leader who thought nothing of sinking the Belgrano three years ago despite the fact that it was outside her illegal 'exclusion zone' and was steaming away from the Falklands at the time. Her state is up to all sorts of skulduggery in Northern Ireland. Operation Countryman demonstrated beyond peradventure only some months ago that her police are corrupt and up to all sorts of illegal mischief. Do you not think she would hesitate to act with extreme prejudice against the likes of you and me if it suited her purpose?"

"I'm sure she would, Willie." He placed his hand on the pin-striped shoulder of his friend and grinned at him. "But I'm just as sure that you and me don't give a tinker's cuss about that old bugger!"

McRae was slower in his responses now but he manufactured a smile. "No, we don't, do we?"

"You said you had need of my help?"

"I do, Hector." He poured some water into his glass, diluting its contents and continued. "I find myself being careful whenever an opportunity presents itself, my friend. I have to be sure that it's not the forces of darkness attempting to lure me into something that might limit my ability to conduct myself as I do today." He contemplated the whisky, took a generous mouthful and placed the glass carefully upon the beer mat, measuring his words. "I received an interesting letter this morning at my office. It bore no postage stamp and had obviously been hand delivered. It was anonymous but spoke of providing me with information that would be what they described as politically explosive. It was signed '*Alba*'. It's author insisted that they must protect their identity at all times and that it would be too dangerous of them to meet directly with me but that they'd consider meeting with an intermediary of my choice if they were confident that they'd be safe. They want to meet in the multi-story car park at Buchanan Bus Station on a night of our choosing within the next five days. It's open all night so they want to meet at eight o'clock sharp when it's dark and quiet. All we're asked to do is to place a small ad in the Evening Times under the heading 'Red carpet for sale'. The cost in pounds we seek shall be the date we intend to meet him or her. We simply drive in, park and wait with our side-lights on. They'll contact us."

McLeod sat back in his chair and sipped at his beer, mulling over the *tête-à-tête* with his friend.

"Wow, this is more like the story-line I expected to see in the Bond movie I'm meant to be attending." He placed his beer on the table and offered his hand to McRae. "But I'm up for it!"

They shook hands and McLeod continued. "Now Willie, is it no' time you were away up the road?"

"Nonsense my young friend. I happen to be in fine fettle. I'll drive home shortly."

"Willie, I don't need to remind you that you've been convicted twice of drunk driving and you've another case pending. If you want to give the authorities an excuse to throw the keys away and be rid of you, it's your affection for the drink that'll do it, not a political mistake. You know fine that Special Branch have you under surveillance."

"It's the fascinating enticement of a fine Glenmorangie malt, Hector. She's an evil temptress and I confess it's a weakness that blunts my judgement from time to time."

"So you'll catch a 'fast black' home?"

"You're a fuss-pot, Hector McLeod but I suppose I could leave the car at the office. A taxi might be useful I imagine if once again I return home to find yet another brick through my window or a fourth break-in in as many weeks. Taxi drivers are usually good enough to summon the polis on their radio although I confess it wouldn't surprise me if that was the intention all along... to get the polis into my house so they can do their nosey."

"It troubles me, Willie. I mean you live in a lovely, posh apartment in a quiet street overlooking a bowling green and a park. I mean, there are perhaps twenty apartments in your street but yours...on the top floor, mind you... is the only one broken into... the only one selected by the brick throwers."

"Och, it'll probably just be some wee ragamuffins with a catapult."

"Aye and it's just mere coincidence that they invariably pick your windows." He placed his hand on his old friend's arm. "Willie, we have to face facts. You're vulnerable."

❧

Chapter Eight

FRIDAY 29TH MARCH 1985

Glasgow, Scotland.

The red sandstone apartments in Broomhill Road in Glasgow's west end; tenemented dwelling houses as the local estate agents called them, were in high demand as domiciles for professors and lecturers at nearby Glasgow University, medics from the Western and Yorkhill Infirmaries and the sizeable coterie of luvvies who populated the nearby and substantial BBC Scotland building at the other end of Byres Road. One or two properties were also occupied by friendship groups of three or four students where the landlord hadn't minded the occasional damage to furnishings brought about by high-spirited drinking.

Macmillan gazed from the first floor window of his two bed-roomed apartment onto the quiet street below him whereon his ancient black Hackney Carriage taxi was parked. *I'll say this about undercover work*, he thought to himself, *so far it's bloody lonely and bloody boring.* He retreated, sat on the beige linen couch that had been rented for him within the furnished apartment, lifted a yellow cloth and dabbed it in a tin of Kiwi Parade Gloss Prestige boot polish. Carefully he drew his finger in deep, tight circles, dulling the leather until after some effort it began to shine more brightly than before. As had been taught when at police college, he sprayed a little water and buffed further before applying yet more polish, inverting the shoe and igniting a small cigarette lighter beneath it, the flame gently melting the polish he'd applied before polishing until the shoe had a mirror gloss. He placed the brush upon the floor. *Jesus, would you look at me? Some undercover cop I am,* he mused before gathering the contents of his shoe polishing kit and placing them in a nearby plastic bag, ready for disposal. *Once a cop, eh? I'm meant to blend in as a radical hippy-type and I'm ready to wear shoes that wouldn't be out of place at a society wedding!* He made a mental note to purchase a pair of second hand shoes from a charity shop after lunch and to make sure they were scored and muddied before wearing them in the context of his new duties. Tonight he'd dine with his old adversary from his time in Northern Ireland. Wearing highly polished shoes to the meeting would give her all the ammunition she'd need to pronounce him the idiot she'd always known him to be.

Back at the window he rehearsed his back story; an Edinburgh law degree but no interest in practising law, a London period selling curios and *bric-à-brac* before heading off to Hanoi in Vietnam after the cessation of hostilities there, backpacking then opening a shop selling local ceramics to the few tourists who didn't mind the restrictions imposed by a nation still at war with its neighbours. Now back home with a part-interest in a taxi while working out what to do next. Always a man with nationalist politics but also one who'd never yet given voice to what he saw as Scotland's unalienable birthright ... independence. *That'll do,* he reckoned. *I'll wing it if the conversation ever goes beyond that.*

Another tour round Glasgow was needed, he decided. *Not much of a taxi driver if I can't convince people I know where Sauchiehall Street is.* He lifted the bag containing the polish and accoutrements, left his new home and walked down the flight of stairs to the street. His taxi had been altered to permit recorded conversations and its rear seat had been modified so as to carry items within its depths in relative safety but other than that, it was a perfectly ordinary fifteen years' old Glasgow taxi, older but identical to hundreds of others on the city's streets. In an act of creative ingenuity he assumed must have derived from MI5 and not the unimaginative and pedestrian Special Branch he knew better, his four taxi doors had been laminated with the St. Andrews' Cross; Scotland's Saltire, advertising a plumbing firm which had chosen that background to advertise its details.

He drove around the west end, stopping to buy a pair of second-hand shoes from Oxfam in Byres Road, then on to the city centre, venturing into the city's east end, deciding to leave his education regarding the south side until the following day. Passing a large skip outside Celtic Park in Parkhead, home of Celtic Football Club where workmen were re-laying some paving, he exited the cab and surreptitiously placed the bag of boot polish and a pair of inexpensive if highly-polished brogues in its depth.

He looked at his watch. *Home time! I'll park up then walk up to Byres Road and have a couple of beers. I'm not meeting Melissa Rees without a wee straightener in me. Dinner with her tonight will be interesting. Let's hope we make the sweet course without her stabbing me with her fork!*

* * *

As darkness fell, Jimmy Hancock parked his rusty white van and sat for some minutes at the wheel observing his misty, brumal surroundings. Although the district of Govan in Glasgow had witnessed some redevelopment in recent years, it hadn't reached the core of the place. Govan Road near the old Lyceum Cinema still reeked of poverty. Its grubby pubs still offered violence to anyone who wished to enjoy some with their pint. Dogs nosed around upturned litter bins and graffiti still spoke to the existence of disaffected youth.

Minutes passed while Hancock satisfied himself that there was no one aware of his presence. He checked his watch, pulled a pair of rubber gloves normally used for washing dishes from his pocket and wrestled them on to his stubby hands. Withdrawing the keys from the van's ignition, he stepped out and opened its rear doors. Leaning in, he dragged towards him a small rug which he gathered under one arm, locking the door whilst looking around to see if he had been noticed. The street door to the sandstone flats where he'd parked was meant to be locked and openable only by those resident in the close but mischief had been done to the lock and it lay closed only because the last person exiting had pulled it shut. One push and Hancock entered, taking each of the three levels of stairs two at a time.

Breathing heavily, he reached the front door of the apartment he'd rented three weeks earlier under an assumed name. He entered and closed the door behind him, stepping over months of unopened mail, content that the first part of his plan had gone well. He switched on the dim light in the hallway and used its low lux to find his way into the living room where the table he'd earlier placed three feet back from the bay window remained in place just as he'd left it.

Wiping his forehead with the back of his hand, he unwrapped the rug, revealing the Enfield rifle he'd cleaned and primed in his cottage. He pulled down the two lugs at the front of the barrel and positioned the bolt-action sniper rifle on the table where it pointed towards the window. Leaving it, he stepped around the table and opened the soiled net curtain before raising the sash window, lifting it some two feet, allowing a chill draught of air into the already cold room. From his vantage point he could clearly see the road below him and looking to the left could see where the entrance to Fairfield Shipyards would allow Prince Philip access the following day. Stepping back into the room, he ignored the Enfield and walked through to the adjacent bathroom where he inspected the green, stained enamel bath which looked as if it hadn't been used to clean the occupants of the apartment for some time. The bath had been boxed in using cheap painted hardboard and Hancock took some time to reassure himself that nothing in the bathroom was different to the last time he'd visited, running the edge of his thumbnail along the length of the tub. A visit to the kitchen, the only remaining room, persuaded him that his rented apartment hadn't been interfered with.

From his hip pocket, he took a card which on one side was embla-zoned the Scottish Saltire and on the other a depiction of a lone wolf howling at the moon. This he left in the dry and mottled stainless steel sink. Leaving the rug on the sofa where he'd thrown it, he left, closing the door behind him, noticing as he did so the splintered and much-repaired wooden door-frame indicating attempts that had been made over the years to break in. As he descended the stairs to the street below, he noticed that all of the door casings on lower floors had had similar injury.

He made his way down the stairs quietly, his rubber-soled boots almost soundless, returned to his car and prepared to drive off. Before he did so, he checked his watch again. Seven minutes. Precisely as he'd calculated. Mission accomplished.

* * *

Only a mile away as the crow flies, but on the other side of the Clyde, Macmillan sat at a table on his own in the crowded Tennent's bar in Glasgow's exuberant and bohemian Byres Road. Two pints of Guinness had already been consumed. He consulted his watch. *Seven thirty-five. I could be a gentleman, drink up and be across the road in the Ubiquitous Chip early in order comfortably to greet my dining companion when she arrives at eight...or I could order another swift one and make it just seconds before she gets there.*

He rose from his seat, raising his empty glass to the young barman indicating a request for another Guinness.

She's always late anyway, he rationalised.

* * *

Just at the time that Macmillan was finishing his third pint, McLeod turned into the car park at Buchanan Bus Station and drove to the first level. Several cars remained, their owners either working late or enjoying the hospitality of city centre bars. Either way, he was disappointed that he was not the only customer using the gloomy facility that evening. He found an empty line of free parking spaces and manoeuvred his Vauxhall Cavalier against the wall. Adjusting the rear-view mirror so he could see the door leading to the stairs, he waited.

* * *

The Ubiquitous Chip had first seen the light of day ten years earlier where, as its name implied, it catered to a largely student clientele which sought plain fare. Since then its reputation as a fine restaurant had grown and now, amidst leafy indoor trees and shrubs, tables with fine linen tablecloths and silver cutlery, it sported food and drinks menus incorporating a wine list matched only by the finer watering holes and eating houses in London.

Macmillan groaned inwardly upon entering as he noticed his host already seated at the table. He glanced at his watch and comforted himself that she'd arrived earlier than their eight o'clock appointment. She hadn't been aware of his arrival and as he awaited an attendant to show him to her table, he was able to observe her unnoticed through the bowery. *She's an unexploded time-bomb but she doesn't half brush up well,* he thought. He watched as she rolled the stem of a glass of white wine between her thumb and forefinger before draining it and signalling to the sommelier that she'd like another. Macmillan smiled. *She's as bloody anxious as me,* he thought.

A waitress took him to the table just as her glass of *Bougrier Sancerre* 1973 arrived and was announced as such by the sommelier. "Still enjoying expensive wines then, eh, Detective Sergeant?"

Rees removed the glass from the tray presented to her and sipped as she recognised her interlocutor. "Now, I might be mistaken but it seemed to me that you just slurred your words, Detective Inspector Macmillan."

50

Macmillan addressed the sommelier. "I'll have a Gin and Tonic, thanks. Gordon's will be fine

"Of course sir," said the sommelier as he left.

"You didn't think I could turn up to meet you sober did you? I had two pints of Guinness before I arrived."

"*Shit*...I had three glasses of wine. This is my fourth!"

"Then if I'm being honest, I had *three* pints of Guinness...the equivalent of *six* glasses of wine!"

"*Shit*! I knew it would be like this! I warned McGinnis that it would be like this!"

"Well, for what it's worth, I warned her too...*and* Sir Kenneth Newman! And had it been permissible, I'd have taken out a full page advert in the Times of London and warned the populace of the United Kingdom that my involvement...indeed, *anybody's* involvement with crazy person Melissa Rees could only end in tears!"

"*Shit*! You're still the misogynistic, pompous, overbearing, cocky jackass you were in Northern Ireland!"

They lapsed into a silence as they considered the menu, each barely able to understand its contents as they considered their next insult.

The sommelier returned. "Your gin sir. Are you ready to order dinner?"

Macmillan sat, his mind trying to fashion a response to each of the last two communications at the same time. His voice rose, suggesting incredulity. "Eh...misogynistic?" And to the sommelier in a more modulated tone, "Eh...no...not yet, could we have five minutes and bring me another...make that a *double* G&T, would you?"

Without waiting for a response, he launched into a further tirade. "Overbearing? If it hadn't been for me you'd have been killed and you'd have got me and Nobby Clark killed as well!"

"*Shit*..."

Macmillan interjected, reaching across the table and placing his hand on Melissa's arm. He looked around at nearby diners. "Look, do you have to start every sentence with '*shit*'? You're frightening the lieges."

"*Shit...*"

Macmillan held out his hands, fingers facing towards the ceiling, at his dinner guest. "Whoa, whoa....Look, let's order dinner..." He placed the menu before Rees. "We'll order dinner, take a breath and start again. I'm sure the people who need us to work together wouldn't be happy at us bickering. And I suspect we'd end the evening being thrown out of this really rather nice restaurant...so, whatdyasay? A ceasefire until we order dinner?"

Rees lowered her voice to a whisper. "Bloody jackass!"

"Excellent," responded Macmillan, "A truce!"

* * *

McLeod had been seated in his car for less than five minutes when the rear door of his vehicle opened and a man slid into the rear bench seat, closing the door behind him.

"Are you 'Red Carpet'?" asked the man.

"Well...yes, I suppose so."

"Are you an emissary from Willie McRae?"

"I am."

"Then keep facing the front and listen. I have four messages from *Alba*."

"Are *you* not *Alba*?"

"Your job tonight is to listen and report back to Mr McRae."

"Fine...fine..."

"*One*...tell Mr McRae that his suspicions about Dounreay are well-founded."

"*Two*..."

"Are you saying that..."

"*Two*" repeated the man..."Tell him to continue his investigations into child molesters in government."

"I don't know about this investigation can you...."

"*Three*...a top secret report on the value of oil to Scotland's economy was commissioned ten years ago by Prime Minister Edward heath. It was written by Professor Gavin McCrone of the Scottish Office in St. Andrew's House in Edinburgh and would be of significant interest to Mr. McRae. Everyone will deny its existence so he must be subtle but it is incredibly important to his cause. If the establishment knew Mr. McRae was aware of its existence it would cause a panic so I repeat my warning of the need for subtlety in enquiring after it. *Four*...tell Mr McRae to be very careful. There are people who find him inconvenient."

"He had his house broken into again last night, his windows have been broken...I've warned him..."

The car door opened and closed a few seconds later and McLeod attempted to reposition the mirror to catch a view of the departing messenger. In this he was unsuccessful.

* * *

Macmillan and Rees had considered the menu and had just ordered but had yet to speak directly to one another, confining their remarks to the young waitress dressed, as were all other staff, completely in *burqa* black.

Macmillan decided he'd better break the ice. He smiled his best smile. "Well, Melissa...Mel...you're looking lovely tonight and I apologise profusely for any untoward remarks I may have made earlier in the evening."

"*Shit...*"

"Jesus...I'm trying to be concilliat..."

"No, it's not that. I think I must have downed those glasses of wine a bit too...*shit!*"

Placing her napkin over her mouth, she rose urgently from the table and headed in what she presumed was the direction of the ladies' bathroom, being redirected by a waitress who noticed her plight and realised she was heading towards the kitchen.

Macmillan smiled at nearby table guests who'd noticed the kerfuffle. "Irritable bowel syndrome. She practically *lives* in the toilet!"

* * *

Willie McRae poured some water into his whisky glass, removed his spectacles and rubbed his weary eyes with thumb and forefinger. He lifted a sheaf of papers he'd been working on from the table and replaced it in his briefcase.

The Station Bar had served the thirsty denizens of Glasgow's Cowcaddens for well over one hundred years but, in McRae's view, wasn't as exquisite as his other city centre bar, the Pot Still. That said, the McHugh family whose generations had owned and managed the premises over that time had still kept a rather impressive pub whose clientele included some of the more hardened local drinkers along with the bow-tied and dinner-suited musicians who enjoyed a glass after their orchestral performances in the Theatre Royal and the Pavilion Theatre. It was also the watering hole enjoyed by members of Strathclyde Police Pipe Band who practiced nearby. Regulars anticipated that newspaper reports of the building of a new international concert hall across the road and the relocation of the Royal Scottish Academy of Music and Drama to Renfrew Street just round the corner would further encourage a musical patronage. Not that this was any cause for concern as it merely increased the likelihood of informal sessions once some strong drink had been consumed, as was often the case.

The busy Station Bar had an exemplary gantry and a fine selection of fine ales but McRae chose to drink there that night as it was the closest hostelry to the car park at Buchanan Bus Station.

McLeod arrived, tousling his long hair in a bid to remove the rain that had caused it to cling to his scalp and neck in the short journey from the car park to the pub. Breathlessly he reported faithfully to McRae the messages he'd been given, causing the solicitor to remove a pen from his inside jacket pocket and make some notes.

"Of everything he told me, the most worrying was the warning that there are people out there who find you 'inconvenient'!"

"Aye well, they would, Hector...they would...but I can look after myself." He glanced round the quiet bar to ensure he wasn't being observed and widened the opening of his briefcase, displaying sheaves of paperwork and between them and the leather innards, a small, pearl-handled Smith & Wesson .45 calibre revolver.

"Jesus, Willie. Are you still carrying that antiquated piece of junk around with you? It's not registered and it's a bloody antique. If you ever try to use it it'll take your right arm off...and if the forces of law and order catch you carrying it, not only will you be eating porridge for breakfast for a long time but you'll be struck off as a practising solicitor."

"Usually it's in my office safe. Because of recent break-ins I thought I'd carry it on my person for a bit,"

McRae closed his briefcase, and reviewed the notes he'd written. "But think on, Hector...I didn't need to be alerted to the work I'm doing on paedophilia in government circles. I'm on pretty solid ground there."

"More than I am, Willie. If it's true, it's dynamite!"

McRae produced a pack of Gold Leaf from his pocket and raised two cigarettes from its ranks, offering one to McLeod who shook his head and took one from his own Benson &Hedges carton. They both lit their own cigarette and drew heavily before commencing.

"I'm not ready to share anything yet, Hector." He flicked the notepaper with the back of his fingers. "Nor do I require affirmation that the Dounreay coastline is about to be made awash with nuclear waste if we don't oppose it. Many people know of my work on this. And I'm all too well aware that the powers that be would happily see me side-lined so that my enquiries on these matters come to nothing. I'm confident that they find me a pain in the tonsils."

"Pain in the arse, more like."

McLeod considered his notes one more time. "As you say, Hector. As you say. But this report...this...have I the spelling right? The *McCrone* Report on Scottish oil?"

"Don't know, Willie. He just spoke the word. No notes."

"Well, at first glance, this seems likely to have been the real message they were attempting to impart." McRae realised his young protégé was without a drink. "Here, Hector...one of those

Pale Ales of which you're so fond?" Without waiting for his answer, he hailed a passing barman. "Andy, a Pale Ale for my friend here and another big Islay Mist." He turned to McLeod and spoke in lower tones. 'We have to look very carefully at everything we're offered, everything we unearth, everything that's happening around us and consider whether it's a manoeuvre by the state to unsettle us or worse. This government's just settled the miners' strike...a strike that started in the Polmaise Colliery up near Stirling over a year ago before it spread across the UK. Now it's ended with the National Union of Mineworkers returning cap in hand to a blessed handful of pits after a vicious campaign by Thatcher and her private police force. Don't be mistaken, this mob isn't only brutal, they're cunning and they've had centuries of experience so let's not presume we've found a benefactor. It could just as easily be a fifth columnist."

"But it might merit a wee, quiet investigation?"

"So long as it's wee and quiet...and not a word to another living soul. Let's be clear, Hector. Scotland's politics are designed to bring about bland acquiescence. Our land is owned by robber barons. The entire apparatus of state is corrupt. Our media encourages blind obedience to the ruling classes while the Establishment picks our pocket." He took a deep drag of his cigarette and coughed heartily. "We need to tell the story of Scotland, Hector...the real Scotland. Any democracy such as ours that doesn't come to terms with its history isn't able to make sense of its present or mould its future...but the patrician elite who populate perfidious Albion are sleekit buggers and we have to be wise to their blandishments and suspicious of their gifts."

"Aye, Willie, we know all that...but you'll look over your shoulder now and again?"

"Only to order another drink!"

* * *

Dinner had evolved in more conciliatory fashion, both Macmillan and Rees maintaining a measure of composure even if some of their communication was somewhat forced.

"If I'm being honest, I'm a bit pissed off that you're getting the interesting part of the assignment and once again I'm nothing but the message girl."

"Well, neither of us asked for this assignment, Mel. When I heard I was being recalled from Vietnam I was never as disappointed since Dylan went electric. But we'd better just get on and deal with the task in hand."

Rees sighed and sipped gingerly at her glass of still water having earlier decided to eat nothing and sip only water. Macmillan was now on his third gin and was enjoying with some relish a course of Caramelised Coconut Rice Pudding and Rum Soaked Baby Figs.

"And tomorrow you've to engage with McLeod during this protest march?"

"I'm told I'm to get involved in a manufactured fracas then spend the Sabbath in the pokey with him in an attempt to befriend him. He's the route we've to take to access Willie McRae."

"Well, I'm keen to find out what nonsense McRae's up to. Stopping the Atomic Energy Authority from dumping nuclear waste in Ayrshire or up in Dounreay seems like an example of an able man performing a civic duty!"

"We won't know until we get closer to him, Mel. Once I'm released I'll contact you and meet you in the taxi for a debrief. You can report our findings to McGinnis."

"Do you think they're connected to that awful killing of the military policeman?"

"Who knows? Strathclyde Police are all over that incident. We'll know soon enough. When you brief MI5 you should ask McGinnis for information on the case. She'll be being briefed by Special Branch."

"Why don't I start making discrete enquiries up here in Glasgow? It'd be quicker and more useful than getting information from London."

"And more interesting, I'm sure. But you can't just manufacture an operational role that wasn't given you. This is Belfast all over again. You must accept the notion of teamwork and of the role you're assigned. Don't go trampling all over the work of others."

"This is just typical of you. You think that a woman's work is only to do the back-up, the admin, the support roles. I'm as good as you any day of the week."

Macmillan began a protest but thought better of it. "Sure you are. But just do as you're told for once! Otherwise you're not a support, you're a liability!"

* * *

At McRae's insistence, McLeod saw him into a black taxi and waved him into the dark of Port Dundas Road before walking back to collect his car and driving to the south side and to the Auld Smiddy. His three friends had occupied the same table as previously and had had a few drinks under their belts prior to his arrival. McLeod raised his arm in salute, hailing his group across a more crowded Friday night bar than was the case on his last visit and made his way through the crush towards them, stopping every so often to chat briefly with regulars, before accepting the spare chair offered him by O'Neill.

"And where have you been Mister Mcleod? This is our drinking night. It's not like you to be late," rebuked Docherty affably.

"I've been busy," replied McLeod deepening his jacket pockets to unearth his cigarette lighter. "Just some background stuff".

"Well, spill the beans, Hector. We're all ears here," insisted Sandy Tarbet.

"Not tonight boys. I'm tired. Like you say, it's our drinking night and I've not had the benefit of a gallon of beer like you three."

O'Neill wouldn't be put off. "You've been meetin' McRae, haven't you? You and him are up to somethin' eh?"

McLeod looked at O'Neill with a serious demeanour. "Tam! Hear me. When I have something to tell you, I tell you. When I don't tell you, it's because I've nothing to tell you or because I *won't* tell you."

"And what is it tonight?"

McLeod decided to defuse matters. "Tonight...it's because there's nothing to tell you. I've been up at the Tolbooth checking that we can force the door easily enough when we're on the march tomorrow."

O'Neill followed McLeod's ruse. "Well, after watching Thatcher's police deal with them miners, on TV earlier, I'm taking my old baton with me. It'll be up my sleeve to protect me if they have a go but if things get serious, it'll be on show. And you'd better believe that I'll give as good as I get."

McLeod lit his cigarette and dragged at it deeply, allowing a silence while he exhaled. "I thought we were clear, Tam. No violence. We act responsibly. Now if you can't accept that, you don't show tomorrow. And if it matters to you, then you'll need to bugger off. There'd be no hard feelings. We can all understand the need to fight fire with fire but Willie McRae insists that we support independence for our country in a non-violent way. Given the political situation at present, we do not give our opponents the reason they need to characterise nationalists as violent extremists. We are activists and propagandists, not soldiers. That might change, but not at present. Now leave the group if you wish. We'll still drink together on a Friday evening but you'd play no further part in our plans."

O'Neill laughed nervously. "There you go again, Hector. Goin' all serious on us. I was only pissin' about. I'll be grand for tomorrow." He looked at his friends for confirmation. "We're *all* grand, eh lads?"

McLeod smiled at his three friends. "Then mine's a glass of McEwan's Pale Ale."

O'Neil lifted his glass and invited a toast. *Alba gu bràth.* Scotland forever!

Chapter Nine

SATURDAY 30TH MARCH 1985

Glasgow, Scotland

The morning of Saturday 30th March brought with it blue skies and unseasonable sun although a frosty chill still permeated the city. Special Branch Detective Sergeants Gall and Carnegie were seated in their unmarked police car fretting over the arrival in Govan of His Royal Highness, The Duke of Edinburgh.

"God only knows why we're babysitting this big Greek fucker, Bob. We should be over in George Square keeping an eye on McLeod and his troops."

"There's people living in villages on the island of Tanna in Vanuatu think Prince Philip's a God, Andy. The traffic boys'll get him here for ten o'clock. After he's safely in the yards we can get over to the square. No one'll have arrived there by that time. Relax."

"He'll only insult the workers in the yard. He's no' exactly one of nature's diplomats."

"Aye, but then, neither are you!"

"I'd be better at the job than him, Bob. How difficult can it be launching ships and shaking hands?"

Gall smiled, "I'm sure there are people living in villages all over the West of Scotland that think you're a God, Andy. Wee Sheila from Forensics, for one!"

"Aye, ah wish!"

The two Special Branch police officers fell into a silence, every so often consulting a watch to gauge the arrival of the Queen's consort. The radio crackled into service, white noise requiring Gall to adjust the settings in time to hear that the aircraft carrying the Prince had landed on schedule and was taxiing towards the terminal.

* * *

Standing at the entrance to Central Station, McLeod's three drinking companions of the previous evening had gathered and were waiting on his arrival.

"That big get's always late."

"He'll be here in a minute. The train might be running slow."

Sandy Tarbet nodded in the direction of the platforms. "There he is now. Looking like an ageing rock star; long hair waving in the wind."

Docherty joined in on affable descant. "Aye, the sun's splittin' the trees today and he's still wearing that big daft coat."

The light-hearted banter of the group continued as McLeod joined them, each taking some of the armful of placards and flags he carried with him. Mcleod retained a canvas bag within which was a substantial jemmy designed to permit him access to the Tolbooth Steeple. More jollity accompanied the group as they walked the short distance to George Square having earlier arranged to meet with other like-minded nationalists in the Horseshoe Bar in Drury Street prior to the commencement of the march.

* * *

Hancock's white van had been parked close to a slip road in Govan that led to the Clyde Tunnel. Between the van and the flat rented by Hancock was positioned Elder Park, an enclosed green swathe established prior to the beginning of the twenty-first century by Mrs Isabella Elder as a monument to her shipbuilder husband John who had founded Fairfield Shipyards. Her noble ambition at the time was to provide for the people of Govan 'healthful recreation by music and amusement'; objectives that persisted if only by somewhat unsteady members of the fortified wine club which convened each morning at one of the park benches. The park ran the length of the frontage of Fairfield Shipyards much of which was occupied by imposing red sandstone drawing offices designed in part by a young Charles Rennie Macintosh.

Hancock walked its length until he reached its exit at Govan road. A red phone box stood empty at the corner of the road. He entered and looking round to ensure he could discern nothing untoward, pushed the 9 button three times and was connected to an operator asking him which emergency service he required.

"Police," he spat down the line.

Another voice took his call almost immediately asking his location and the nature of the emergency.

"Listen! I'm looking up at an open window of the top flat of number 915 Govan Road. I just saw a man with a rifle and realised that Prince Philip was meant to be passing here soon to launch a ship. I thought you'd better know in case there's something wrong!"

The operator sought further information but Hancock countered abruptly, telling her that he was scared in case bullets started flying. He placed the phone on its receiver and left, crossing the road to a newsagent where he pottered around, eventually buying a newspaper at which point three police cars, one unmarked, swept up Govan Road, sirens blaring. They came to a halt outside his flat and four uniformed police officers, tailed by Sergeants Carnegie and Gall entered the close-mouth and hurried up the stairs as Prince Philip's entourage sat, guarded by outriders awaiting instruction, in the car park of Ibrox Stadium, home of Glasgow Rangers FC one mile away.

Hancock looked upwards and waited until he could see movement in the room where he'd left the Enfield rifle. Scanning the road for any further arrivals, he folded the newspaper and felt inside his coat pocket for a small radio-controlled device. He checked the window again to confirm the police presence in the front room and moved a switch on his electronic transmitter from 'off' to 'on'.

The four uniformed police officers had attended the property, crashing the fragile door open after a perfunctory attempt to request entrance legally. Both Gall and Carnegie were hurriedly calming a neighbour on the floor below, each grateful for the opportunity for a brief respite following their race up the first two flights of stairs. The amatol high explosive, a mixture of 80% ammonium nitrate with 20% trinitrotoluene earlier removed from a land mine, had been concealed within the casing of the bathtub and exploded instantly having been triggered by Hancock's transmitter. The concussive power of the shock wave and its blast-induced overpressure of 100 PSI travelled with a velocity of 1500 mph and shredded the wall separating the bathroom from the living room, its masonry construction comprising stone bedded in lime mortar acting as shrapnel. In a nano-second, as their flesh was punctured and torn from their bodies, each of the four police officers in the adjacent room suffered lethal injuries as their eyes, ears and internal organs ruptured, killing them instantly.

The front door of the apartment, never a particularly secure portal, blew outwards knocking over like skittles the two Special Branch officers on the floor below and seriously concussing the pensioner with whom they'd been in conversation. The front windows of the apartment shattered sending shards of glass to the pavement below.

Satisfied with his morning's work, Hancock rolled his folded newspaper, lightly slapped his thigh with it and walked through Elder Park to his van to begin the journey home to his loch-side cottage.

* * *

Macmillan had parked his taxi close to Stewart Street Police Station where his colleague Melissa Rees had advised he'd probably be held over the weekend with Hector McLeod. Macmillan had calculated in advance that he might offer him a lift home. Following a steadying pint of Guinness, coincidentally in McRae's favoured Station Bar which was nearby, he stopped outside a shop window in Renfield Street and observed the dress decisions he'd made that morning in its reflection. *Hair's still a bit too short but the denims, casual shoes and woolly jumper quite set off the stained anorak,* he decided. A three-day eschewal of his razor also assisted his desired appearance.

Walking downhill to George Square, he mingled with small knots of protestors, mostly left-wing supporters of the Labour Party and the noisier Militant Tendency supporters as they began to congregate at the assembly point. A flag seller took a pound from him and sold him a Saltire flag on a stick which he waved self-consciously as he attempted to rehearse the shouted slogans being chanted by his fellow protestors.

His research over the previous few days had given him confidence that he'd recognise McLeod when he saw him but still it took him some time before he determined that he'd found him, the proximity of numerous Scottish flags and an authoritative demeanour marking him as the leader he'd anticipated. As the march moved off, Macmillan manoeuvred himself as close to McLeod as seemed possible without appearing too intrusive. The large group supporting Scottish independence were vocal but in good mood as they sang and chanted their slogans, waving enthusiastically to onlookers who gestured their goodwill from the sides of the roads, jeering good-naturedly at those who remonstrated their participation in the march.

***

Deputy Chief Constable Russell Laurie entered a room illuminated by fluorescent tubing wherein sat several senior police officers in animated conversation. "Right, people, let's call this meeting to order. Four officers dead. His Royal Highness the Prince Philip,

Duke of Edinburgh is heading back to his fucking palace and I've journalists and politicians kicking my door in. I need an accurate situation report immediately." He sat on a leather swivel chair with a headrest higher than the others, signifying his seniority. "Barnes!"

Chief Superintendent Jim Barnes consulted a sheet of paper before him. "Sir...as you say, Officers George McCuthbert, Gary Eaglesham, Donald Brendan O'Herlihy and Graham Elliot Ewington have all been killed by the bomb blast in Govan Road. Detective Sergeants Bob Gall and Anderson Carnegie of Special Branch were slightly concussed but are still operational."

"Where are they now?"

"According to Inspector Maxwell who's on the scene, they took off at speed in their car. It doesn't appear to have been hot pursuit but we're still trying to make contact with them."

"Find them and get them in here. I want to speak with them personally." He redirected his enquiries to Chief Superintendent Seamus McGrattan, "Seamus...What the fuck happened here?"

"Early days sir. There was no gas supply to the property so we've ruled out a gas explosion. There was an anonymous 999 call from a male caller intimating a man with a rifle was observed in the property and three cars attended. All officers were unarmed. An Enfield rifle has been found at the scene but no individual. At first glance it would appear that officers have been lured to the scene and that an explosive device was intended to detonate upon their arrival causing death or injury...and it kind of looks that it might be linked to the recent killing of the military policeman. Forensics has just called to say that they've found the same calling card we picked up at the Doran crime scene. Different explosives used by the looks of it."

"Was it the card with the Saltire?"

McGrattan nodded, "...and the wolf depicted on its rear, sir."

Laurie looked around the room. "What's this telling us?

Barnes interjected, changing the subject. "The call was made from a local call box, sir. We've forensics out there now checking for prints. We're also looking for prints on the card."

There was silence in the room as Laurie considered his options.

"Right. We meet again here at two o'clock. Full report then. I'm leaving to visit the families of the four officers." He directed his next comment to McGrattan. "Seamus, you take the wheel. Have Personnel contact me in the car with details of the officers' families. Throw every resource necessary at this incident. I want results here."

* * *

Macmillan decided the Scottish flag he was waving was too contrived a device and removed the cane, folding and tying the flag loosely around his wrist. *Bit more informal,* he thought. *Don't want to be seen to be trying too hard.*

The Independence contingent had almost approached the Trongate steeple and was on High Street. Police sirens grew in intensity until a silver Triumph Acclaim passed them, its blue flashing light adhered temporarily to one side of its roof, the only visible intimation of its police credentials. It came to a sharp halt and, as if synchronised, both front doors flew open and Gall and Carnegie emerged making directly towards the cluster of Scottish flags and banners.

Seeing them approach, McLeod waved a welcome and raised his flag higher in salute. Taller than most in the company, he was easily identifiable and the two Special Branch officers walked briskly towards him, pushing their way roughly past the first few marchers in order to reach him.

Carnegie grabbed the lapel of McLeod's coat and elbowed him in the face for good measure. "You're coming with us, McLeod. You and your pals have fuckin' done it this time."

McLeod remained genial. "Sergeant Carnegie, behave yourself. You'll be giving Strathclyde's finest a bad..."

Carnegie placed his forehead aggressively against McLeod's, drawing him closer. "Shut it, McLeod. You're lifted!" He brought his head back some few inches and head-butted him roughly to emphasise his point. Mcleod buckled momentarily.

From his waistband Carnegie produced a set of handcuffs and set about placing them on McLeod's wrists. Macmillan saw his opportunity.

"Leave him alone," he shouted. "He's marching peaceably. Away and pick on some auld granny that's not been picking up her dog shit."

Gall entered the fray. "Shut it pal. This doesn't concern you."

Years of policing allowed Macmillan to understand the consequences of his next move and he shoved Gall backwards before attempting to impede Carnegie's attempts to cuff McLeod. Other marchers began to remonstrate and scuffles broke out as uniformed officers joined what was fast becoming a brawl. A police vehicle pulled up and four marchers were hauled aside and handcuffed, McLeod among them. Pushed roughly into its interior, Macmillan looked through the side window of the van and noticed that McLeod had been placed in the rear of the Triumph next to Gall while Carnegie drove the vehicle away, its blue light and siren clearing a path made more distinct by march organisers and police.

Oh, *this is excellent*, Macmillan thought sarcastically; *don't tell me I'm going to spend a weekend in a cell on my own!* A lone policeman seated across from him provided a health and safety warning. "If you boys just sit quiet till we get to the station we'll all be just fine. Any nonsense and there'll be an accident when you're leaving the van. It'll hurt!"

* * *

Hancock steered his van into a lay-by and waited for five minutes to establish the likelihood of his having been followed. Satisfied that he was not under surveillance, he lowered the handbrake and set off the remaining few miles to his cottage. On arrival, he parked and made his way up his garden path ensuring that he did not tread on any of the three trip wires that would trigger his home-made alarm, an alarm set off occasionally by a wandering fox, reassuring him of the efficacy of his device when it did.

He unlocked the front door and entered, making his way directly to the front room where an ancient television took its time to warm sufficiently before providing him with the images he sought. A BBC reporter stood against the blue and white chequered police tape that kept all but the authorities from the crime scene. Behind him the carnage was clearly evident as he spoke into an unseen microphone and described the horror for viewers, speculating on its cause and attempting to find something novel to say beyond the fact that four police officers had been caught in the blast and had been killed.

"*Four*," murmured Hancock to himself. "*A decent day's work.*"

* * *

An exasperated Anderson Carnegie placed his palms on a table separating him from Hector McLeod and leaned his upper body towards him; face red, eyes narrowed, neck bulging. "Four fucking officers! Men with wives and children." The force of his denunciation was now spittle-flecked. "Murdered by you and your mob of nut-job nationalists. For what? How does this help your fucking cause? Innocent lives..."

McLeod interrupted. "Sergeant Carnegie. I can only repeat that I know nothing of this. I'm as shocked as you are and want nothing to do with violence."

"I want fucking names, McLeod. I want the name of the bastard or bastards who did this and I swear you're going nowhere until you start telling me what you know. We know you spend most nights in the Auld Smiddy with K.C. and his fucking Sunshine Band of head-cases. *One* of you knows what's going on here!"

McLeod sighed and lowered his chin towards his chest, considering his response.

"Look sergeant. This is getting us nowhere. I understand you're upset but shouting at a man who knows nothing of the offence committed and who shares your disgust at the event isn't going to have you catch those who did plant the bomb. Now either arrest me and allow me to call my lawyer or let me walk out of here."

Carnegie held his gaze for some seconds before pushing back and standing erect.

"You're going fucking nowhere."

The door of the interview room opened and Gall entered along with the bar sergeant.

"Andy, the boss wants to see us. We've to head on up to Pitt Street."

Carnegie held McLeod's gaze. "This bastard goes nowhere. Lock him up until I get back."

The two Special Branch officers left and McLeod was taken along a corridor to cells where even at that early hour in the afternoon, drunken shouts and insults flew at everyone and no one in particular. He passed an open office door and had he but looked, he'd have noticed the slim form of Melissa Rees leaning against a filing cabinet, watching observantly.

A key attached to the officer's chained fob unlocked a cell door and McLeod walked through to find Jock Macmillan lying on one of two raised surfaces that were meant to act as beds.

The door was locked behind McLeod and both men eyed one another.

"You're that guy in the march who got lifted for being nice to that plain clothes cop," offered Macmillan.

"And *you're* the eegit that started the rough stuff!"

Macmillan sat up, swung his legs to the floor of the cell and placed his elbows on his knees. "Frankly, I thought the cops started the rough stuff. It wasn't my intention to cause trouble. I just thought these guys were out of order."

McLeod considered Macmillan's response before conceding. "S'pose."

Macmillan allowed a silence. "Well, this is a first for me. I've never been locked up before. I'm assuming we're here until court on Monday."

"We'll see. This bombing has thrown everything off kilter."

Macmillan allowed his surprise to show. "What bombing?"

"That's why these guys lifted me. They think I might know something about it. They think it was linked to nationalist sympathisers."

"Jesus...Where? Anyone injured?"

"Four cops dead. Down in Govan. Strathclyde's finest are somewhat preoccupied."

"Christ, no wonder." He played up his new persona. "Here, I hope they've not put you in here because they think that I know anything about it. I just took a walk down to George Square on a notion."

McLeod was circumspect. "Who knows what they think?" He sat down on the *palliasse* opposite Macmillan. "Have they treated you well?"

Macmillan grimaced. "Aye...I can't complain. I shouldn't have interfered. They've been pretty polite. The bar sergeant just stuck me in here. I'm assuming they'll bring me up before the beak on Monday morning and because I've no previous, the most I'll get is a fine and a finger wagging unless there's a big *stramash* about this bombing and everyone is seen to be connected with it."

"It's a real possibility. Their heads'll have gone on this. Four cops dead." He shook his head resignedly. "That's got nothing to do with nationalism I'm sure but they'll chase down that presumption, I imagine."

Macmillan affected concern for his position. "Christ...I bought a flag, joined the march and expected to be back behind the wheel of my taxi by mid-afternoon. Didn't realise I'd be sharing a cell with a guy suspected of killing four cops."

"I killed no one," said McLeod evenly. "But I'm not unaware of the ability of the state to prove something against me if they need a body!"

"Maybe I can help you. I'm a lawyer."

"Thought you drove a taxi?"

"Well...I do...and I'm not a real lawyer. Read law at Edinburgh before deciding it wasn't for me. Travelled the world but I'm home again, got a wee two-bedroomed flat in the west end and I'm driving a taxi until I decide what to do next although now it'll need to be something where they don't mind previous convictions."

McLeod smiled. "Well, I'm covered legally, thanks."

"Got your own lawyer?"

"Yeah. A big noise in the legal world. He'd be down here demanding my release if he knew I was locked up but the police won't let me make a phone call yet."

Macmillan decided to try his luck. "Sounds like you're going to need a big beast to call off the dogs on this one. Will I have heard of him?"

"Not if you've been travelling the world you won't. But he's a top man in Scottish politics and a brilliant solicitor. Couldn't ask for anyone more effective in my corner." He decided to close the matter. "Still, maybe they'll turn the key in the lock and tell me it's just been one big mistake."

Macmillan picked up the cue and pursued his line of questioning no further. "Aye...and pigs might fly!"

* * *

Later that afternoon, Willie McRae strode into Stewart Street police station and, introducing himself as Hector McLeod's lawyer, asked to speak with the Divisional Commander. Some minutes later Superintendent Eric Ronald appeared and bid McRae enter through a hatch and follow him into an office adjacent to the main room. Cursing under his breath, he cleared four empty mugs and some half eaten pizzas, now cold and still within their boxes. The scent of stale cooked food caused McRae to wrinkle his nose upon entry.

"Sorry about the mess, Mr McRae. My memorandums inviting the back shift to clean up after they gorge themselves on this inedible junk appear to have been ignored. They like a bite before they head off on duty."

McRae, looked around for an ashtray and finding one under an empty pizza box, stubbed out his half-smoked Gold Leaf cigarette. "It's of no consequence, Superintendent. I've been known to indulge myself on occasion."

"So...you represent Mr McLeod?"

"I do, and I want him released immediately. I've been provided with testimony to the effect that he committed no offence whatsoever. Indeed if any blame is to be laid, it should be at the door of your officers who provoked a...let's call it a *situation*...in High Street today."

"I don't need to tell you that four officers were..."

"Look, Superintendent, we're all aware of the tragic killing of these young men but that doesn't give you the right to go detaining people with absolutely no cause beyond the ill-temper of your understandably flustered officers."

"Mr McRae..."

"Superintendent, under Scots' law, the purpose of arrest is to bring the suspect before a court for examination. Arrest is not permitted merely to take a suspect into custody for the purposes of further investigation or questioning by your officers."

"Aye, but a police officer has the power to arrest where there is a reasonable suspicion of a person having committed an offence."

"And what offence did you have in mind, Superintendent? My client was clearly elsewhere when the blast occurred...as indeed were the other three people you took into custody. He committed no offence on the march and any incident that occurred at that point was clearly caused by bellicose attitude of your two officers. I gather there's film of the event. Now, I'm minded to overlook their behaviour given the terrible circumstances just prior to their assault on my client and the three other protestors but I must remind you that a suspect should not be detained unless it is necessary and proportionate." He drummed his fingers on the formica-topped table. "My suggestion is therefore as follows, Superintendent. You release Hector McLeod immediately...and while you're at it, there's no reason to detain the other three...and I won't call for the immediate apprehension of the two officers.

Nor will I cause an almighty stushie in court on Monday morning and I'll cancel any plans I may have been making to call a press conference denouncing you and your intemperate boys for overreacting..."

Ronald held his hands up in surrender. "Okay...you make your point...you make your point...I've viewed the film," he confessed. "I've also phoned the high heid yins...So..." He leaned back in his chair so as to permit himself a view of the Bar Sergeant but noted instead his duty inspector. "Inspector Young...are Sergeants Gall and Carnegie back here yet?"

"No sir."

He allowed his forward chair legs to return to the floor. "I'll deal with them later. Let's go spring your client."

"And...?"

Superintendent Ronald sighed philosophically. "And the other three peaceful protestors, as you'd describe them."

Melissa Rees stepped backwards from her position just outside the door where she had listened keenly to the conversation between McRae and Ronald. As they exited the room she turned to face an opposing wall and appeared to busy herself with some paperwork lying on a convenient desk. Superintendent Ronald guided McRae towards the cells and Rees approached the figure of Inspector Shona Young. "Thanks, Inspector. I'll ensure that your helpfulness will be noted where it matters."

"My pleasure, Detective Sergeant."

*

McRae, Ronald and another officer walked along to the door behind which Macmillan and McLeod had spent the afternoon getting acquainted. The worn lock of the cell surrendered easily to a key which had been used to trigger its spring-latch bolt several times a day over decades of use.

McRae entered first hailing his friend. "Hector, my dear chap, apparently the police have no more use of your services and you're free to leave with me!"

"Willie! By God, you're a sight for sore eyes. How did you know I was in here?"

"Tommy Docherty phoned me. A few phone calls soon found your place of incarceration."

McLeod stood and shook McRae's hand warmly. He turned to Macmillan. "Well, Jock. Nice meeting you. Perhaps next time we'll constrain our conversations to a march rather than a jail cell."

McRae interrupted. "Superintendent, is this one of the four who were arrested on the march?"

Ronald consulted a piece of paper he held. "Aye, this is John Macmillan. One of the four."

"Then you, too, are free to go Mr. Macmillan." He turned back to Superintendent Ronald. "Where are the other two?"

"They're in cells in our Govan station. No room at the inn here, I'm afraid...but I'll make the call and have them released immediately."

"Aye, well, that would be just fine." He offered Superintendent his hand which was taken. "Thanks for being practical, Superintendent. It's saved a lot of tears."

Out on the pavement, McRae looked skywards. "It's beginning to spit," he said as the blue sky of the morning gave way to more typical Glaswegian weather.

Macmillan interjected. "Listen; let me pay you back, sir. I'm a taxi driver and my cab is just round the corner next to the Station Bar...I had a beer there before joining the march... and I'd be delighted to take the two of you wherever you wanted to go. It's the least I could do for getting me out of that cell."

"And might this journey home be free of charge Mr Macmillan? I live in Balvicar Drive in the south side, Hector's in Cathcart and you taxi drivers are not known for your generosity," he teased, smiling at Macmillan.

"Not only that, but if you've time, I'd love to buy you a drink in the Station Bar before dropping you off afterwards."

McLeod demurred whilst trying to ignite a match. He spoke with an unlit cigarette bobbing between his lips. "Well, Jock... that's very generous but..."

McRae intervened. "It's more than generous, Hector. It's the closest I've come to Highland hospitality in Glasgow." He placed his arm around McLeod's shoulders. "Now...one wee drink won't hurt...will it?"

Chapter Ten

MONDAY 1ST APRIL 1985

London, England

The London clinic that Rosemary Roberts had attended for several months still brought its anxieties each time she approached its portals. Today she took the six steps that took her upwards from the pavement in Hampstead as ever she did; one at a time, very slowly and deliberately but no longer requiring the reassuring habit of ensuring that both feet were on the same step before proceeding to the next. Upon being admitted she seated herself in the well-appointed antechamber just off the foyer and waited.

Some minutes later, the deep pile of the expensive Axminster carpet muffled the steps of the receptionist as she approached the small waiting room. Only one person awaited her arrival.

"Miss Roberts? Doctor Müller will see you now." She opened a door leading from reception, smiling as Roberts passed her at the door frame and entered the psychiatrist's office.

She removed her coat and took her usual seat as her therapist rose from behind her desk and seated herself opposite her smiling a fixed smile that Roberts had decided months previously must have been handed out along with her professional qualification some thirty years earlier.

"Well, Rosemary, it's nice to see you again. Now tell me, are you still committed to terminating our work together? It's been almost a year you've been coming to see me but two weeks ago you seemed sure that you could bring closure to the issues that brought you here."

Roberts was diffident in her reply and some time passed before she spoke, slowly and in a whisper. "I want to thank you for spending so much time with me, doctor. Last year I felt very down and my attempted suicide began a process that saw me begin a long period of reflection. I couldn't have done it without you and I'm terribly grateful. However, I now understand the burden I've been carrying and I'm now resolved to remove this load from my shoulders."

Müller placed the small notepad on a table next to her chair and clasped her hands around her knees. She leaned forward and spoke in tones infused with friendliness and concern.

"I know from your files that your work has been in areas of the civil service that are classified. But I want to repeat that every-thing we discuss...and that's *everything* we discuss...is confiden-tial. I would tell no one and I couldn't be asked to reveal anything of our conversations, even in a court of law."

"You don't underst..."

"If it helped you, I wouldn't even make notes."

Roberts wept quietly and was silent for some moments. "I know you're trying to help, Doctor but I believe I understand the issues that brought me here. I no longer feel the need to end my life and I know it must be frustrating to you that I don't reveal the thinking behind my decision. I'm asking you to accept my word that I've worked things out but I truly have...and part of my reasoning involves not telling you anything of the motives that drew me to the overdose I took." She dabbed at her eyes with a tissue removed from a box placed next to her chair, thoughtfully placed there and replenished each day by the receptionist who had shown her in. "I've been on sick leave now for eleven months and although my job remains open to me, I propose to leave formally and seek employment in other work, perhaps in a library or a bookshop... anything that's quiet and undemanding. I just want to forget my troubles and start afresh."

"And you're sure you can't confide in me?"

"Thank you Doctor, but no. My mind is made up."

Doctor and patient spent a further period discussing future plans and the ability that Rosemary would have to return for further consultation as a consequence of the special civil service contract she had. Some further pleasantries followed as Müller walked her to the front door.

"Goodbye, Rosemary. It's been lovely getting to know you. Good luck for the future and remember that I'm always here if you need me."

Closing the front door, Doctor Müller returned to her office, nodding approval as she entered at the suggestion of a coffee by her receptionist. Seated behind her desk she opened a file and pressed against its spine to flatten the page on which she proposed to write. Hesitating, she laid her pen on the desk and lifted a phone, dialling a number not to be found in any phone book available to the public. It rang three times before being answered in an office within the Personnel Division of MI5.

"Hello Henry. It's Helena Müller. I've just finished interviewing Rosemary Roberts. We've concluded treatment and she's stoutly refused to divulge any information to me despite a number of invitations over a period of many months. She wants to move on to other work...quieter work involving books. She's damaged but I don't think she's likely to offend the Official Secrets Act. You might want to keep an avuncular eye on her if and when she takes up new responsibilities but, for now, I don't think she's a threat to the state."

The voice on the other end of the conversation expressed gratitude and agreed the suggestion of a light touch going forward.

"Thanks, Henry. I'll send my fee invoice to you as usual.
She replaced the phone on its cradle just as her coffee arrived.

* * *

London traffic was as busy as ever as Rosemary Roberts took her seat on the red bus which would return her to her small rented flat above the Duke's Head pub in nearby Highgate High Street. Memories of merry evenings spent in its rear jarred with her mood of recent years during which she'd attempted suicide. Even yet, a dystopian blanket of depression consumed her but therapy had at least offered a possible solution to her melancholy. She'd considered the options...'put up or shut up'...or 'shut up' had reduced her to an attempt on her life. So, logically, she determined that 'putting up' might hold potentially more rewarding outcomes. And if it didn't? Well a warm bath, the quiet cello sonatas of Johann Sebastian Bach played by Rostropovich & Richter, an overdose of pills and a nice red *Rioja* as she drifted off also held attractions.

Oblivion had yet some appeal.

Instead of climbing the stairs to her flat, Roberts walked instead to a red phone box four streets away. The door of the phone box was heavy and took some effort to open. Entering, she fumbled in her coat pocket for a piece of paper and withdrew it, lifting her spectacles to her forehead the better to view the number written there. It was a Glasgow number. She thumbed more coin than was necessary to reduce the likelihood of the call being aborted and, taking a breath, dialled. It rang for a while during which Roberts considered replacing the phone on its receiver. Eventually a Glasgow accent spoke to her.

Her confidence fast failing her, she nevertheless summoned the words she'd rehearsed."
    "I'd like to speak with Mr. McRae, please."
    "I'm afraid....oh wait a minute...he's just come back in. Who may I say is calling?"

"Eh...my name is Brown...Miss Caroline Brown."

"And are you known to Mr. McRae?"

"No...I'm not known to him. But it's very important I speak with him."

"Please hold while I connect you."

Perhaps a minute passed while the connection was made, McRae having taken that time to climb the two flights of stairs to his office. When he picked up the receiver he was still breathless.

"Willie McRae here, how can I help you, Miss Brown?"

Roberts swallowed nervously before speaking. "Mr. McRae, Caroline Brown isn't my real name but I need to speak with you under conditions of complete secrecy. I've been following newspaper accounts of your political work but can't reveal anything over the phone in case your calls are being traced. However, if you find a call box and call me at my present number...also a call box...I'd be able to reassure you that in speaking with me you'd be made privy to information that you would view as crucial to your efforts in Scotland."

"Well, that sounds very melodramatic Miss Brown. And how long might I have before you give up and leave your call box?"

Roberts hesitated. "I hadn't thought, Mr. McRae. How long would you need?"

"Heavens, an old man my age? I'd need fifteen minutes, and that would depend upon finding a call box that hadn't been vandalised." McRae hesitated. "And you're sure it'd be worth my while to run down two flights of stairs, walk uphill to the top of Buchanan Street and phone you back?"

"It would be important for *both* of us Mr. McRae."

"Then I'll take you at your word, Miss Brown. What's your number?

* * *

Glasgow, Scotland

Macmillan's taxi turned right from Jamaica Street underneath the rail bridge that straddles Glasgow's Broomielaw. He indicated left and pulled into the side of the road where Melissa Rees was standing in the shadow of one of the huge granite pillars that supported the arch. Almost as he'd stopped she pulled at his passenger door handle and stepped inside the vehicle, seating herself in the rear seat so she might see his reflection in the rear view mirror while they spoke.

"Welcome aboard, Mel."

Let's cut to the chase. Turn the recorder on and make your report."

"Patience is a virtue you've not got, eh, Detective Sergeant Rees," he mocked as he steered the cab along Broomielaw towards Lancefield Quay and on to the docks along the River Clyde.

"Well, don't test what little of that commodity I have. How did you get on with McLeod and McRae?"

Macmillan fell in line. "Got on well with Hector McLeod while we were locked up. He came across as a sincere guy. He was condemning of the bomb that killed the policemen and seems quite authentic when he spoke of his preference for peaceful means to secure independence for Scotland. He has three friends with whom he deals in his local action group, Thomas O'Neill, Thomas Docherty and Alexander Tarbet."

Do they seem like they're terrorists?"

"Not really. They all live in and around the Cathcart area of Glasgow's south side. He seemed to know nothing about the bomb and fretted that it might set back his cause. He's a self-employed accountant and does the books for a variety of voluntary organisations. Very much a mild-mannered Clark Kent. Stays alone in Courthill Avenue in Cathcart. Near the Auld Smiddy pub that he calls his local."

"What about McRae?"

"Now, *he's* quite a character. He consumes alcohol in quantities that would stun the average Clydesdale horse and when he's had a few, he veers between being the life and soul of the party and slitting his wrists with a rusty razor. He's clearly brilliant and shared McLeod's views of the bombing. Unless these two are carrying Equity cards, their denunciation of violence seemed genuine."

"Did McRae speak of the nuclear plant at Dounreay?"

"No."

Did he speak of any political matters pertaining to Westminster?"

"No."

"Anything of import beyond the bombing?"

"We stayed for six drinks. I bought four rounds. I drank only soft drinks but McLeod and McRae drank beer and spirits respectively. McRae drank doubles. The conversation tended to surround the march on Saturday, the bombing and the general political situation. They are not fans of the Prime Minister, Margaret Thatcher but then, here in Glasgow, few are. McRae's a very amusing *raconteur* when he gets started and he has stories that go all the way back to Indian independence and his dealings with Lord Mountbatten, Gandhi and Nehru as well as senior Israelis like David Ben-Gurion and a young Golda Meir. But then he'll become melancholic before a glint in his eye returns him to another funny anecdote."

"A bit of a comedian!"

"He's not a thump the table barrel of laughs. More wry humour. He's a wee bit hubristic, lots of ten dollar words, a wee bit exotic but he's got much to be self-confident about. A charismatic and frankly, a very likeable man."

"London will be delighted that you've made contact."

"That's *exactly* what they'll be, Mel! It's given me access to the two guys most likely to provide any information London wants. They're aware I have a law degree, seem content with my back story and McLeod proposed a drink tomorrow evening to repay what he saw as my over-generous supply of drink on Saturday. Who knows how this might develop but my overarching sense was that these two guys are men of integrity. McRae appears to do a mountain of work at no charge for people in difficult straits. If every enemy of the state was as apparently benign as these two there'd be no need for MI5!"

"Is that it? No arrangement to meet again with McRae?"

"My main point of contact at present seems as if it'll be McLeod but it's early days. I still have McRae in my sights."

"Anything you need?"

"Triple my expenses budget if I'm to keep pace with McRae's alcohol consumption."

Rees ignored his tongue-in-cheek request. "Okay, give me the tape of our discussion and drop me off at the next lights. I'll report to London." She observed the flow of traffic outside on the dockside as Macmillan retrieved the cassette tape from his dashboard. "Pull over. Now'll do!"

* * *

McRae made his way to a call box and phoned the number he'd been given by Roberts. A quiet voice answered.

"Am I speaking to Miss Brown?"

"Eh...yes. Is this Mr. McRae?"

"Indeed so. Well, Miss Brown, I'm speaking to you from a phone box so we stand a fighting chance of being able to speak without being overheard by Special Branch operatives or other ne'er-do-weels. Now, you mentioned that you might have information that would interest me?"

"I'm afraid I have to ask you to trust me Mr. McRae. You don't know me and have no reason to imagine that what I say is true...I've already confessed to having used a pseudonym to protect my identity...but I promise you that my purpose is to help...and in so doing to help myself."

"Honesty rings from your every word, Miss Brown," said McRae, bordering on the disingenuous.

"I'm afraid I need to meet you face to face, Mr McRae. I must show you a piece of paper that I hope will verify the information I want to share with you but I can't take the chance of posting it to you. Not only might *your* mail be being read, but my own letters may be being intercepted by forces of the crown. I have no proof of that but I've signed the Official Secrets Act and if I'm found to have violated its purpose, I'd suffer the consequences."

"And they can be grave," agreed McRae..."So let's work on the principle that we protect your identity from the word go. Can you give me an idea of the significance of your information?"

"Well, perhaps a hint...I don't want to speak too long in case...well I don't know how these things work...but I just want to make an arrangement to see you privately so no one knows we're meeting." She hesitated. "Perhaps if I tell you I have access to information on a secret report written for government which shows the true value of North Sea oil to the economy of Scotland and..."

"Permit me to interrupt, Miss Brown." McRae pondered a moment before continuing. "Might this be a report written by Professor Gavin McCrone of the Scottish Office?"

Roberts gasped at his question, her hand flying to her mouth in puzzlement. "But how could you know...I mean how...?"

McRae weighed the import of his intervention before speaking. "Miss Brown, you must forgive me but while you have an honesty about you and there's a certain authenticity about your message, there's a tidiness here that disturbs me slightly. You see, I have as much to lose as do you if the state proves that I'm up to no good. Only recently I learned of this report and..." He paused and spoke aloud the words he was thinking. "Have you heard the name, *Alba*?"

"Well, I know it's the *Gaelic* name for Scotland but beyond that..."

"You know no one who would use that name as a pseudonym?"

"No one."

He thought further. "Then I'm either dealing with a surprising and highly advantageous coincidence or a very convincing deception and if that, the prospect of walking into the duplicitous schemes of perfidious Albion, much to my probable material disadvantage."

"I can only promise you..."

"Indeed, Miss Brown." McRae assembled his thoughts. "Alright, Miss Brown. Let me make a few observations and a couple of suggestions. I don't know you but you know that I am among other things, a respected and fairly well-known solicitor and am unlikely to attempt to deceive you. You also know my politics and that the information you have is very likely to excite my interest." He paused as he calculated his options. "Can I ask where you're phoning from...in general terms?"

"I'm in Lon...I'm in England...in the south," she finished lamely.

"Do you have the wherewithal to travel to Scotland...To Glasgow or Edinburgh?"

"Yes I do. I have no commitments and could travel north to meet you as long as I was guaranteed complete secrecy."

"That would be assured. Well...let me see. This is Monday." He thought out loud. "I've court in Edinburgh tomorrow and on Wednesday morning. Could you catch a train to Glasgow arriving at about four o'clock on Wednesday....in the afternoon or thereabouts?"

"Certainly."

"Then when you arrive at Central Station, carry a copy of the National Geographic magazine under your arm with the title page observable. Leave the station by an exit immediately to your right upon leaving the platform and turn right again. Keep walking towards the river. You will be contacted and identified by your pseudonym, 'Miss Brown'. I will arrange overnight accommodation in a safe place and will return you to the station the following day. You should expect to catch a train south around noon if that helps you book something."

"So, Wednesday, four o'clock, magazine, turn right and right again and keep walking?"

"That's it."

"I look forward to meeting you Mr. McRae."

McRae placed the phone back on the receiver and pursed his lips in thought. He lifted it again, inserted more coins and phoned Hector McLeod who answered immediately. "Hector, it's Willie. We need to meet. Eight o'clock tonight. Not one of our usual haunts...how about..."

McLeod interjected. "Make it half past. I've some work I need to complete. Eh...what about the Three Judges pub at the bottom of Byres Road."

"Aye, fine...and let's try not to find ourselves followed and overheard by the forces of darkness."

* * *

Glenmallan, Loch Long, Scotland

That evening, Hancock sat at his kitchen table, an ancient angle-poise lamp the only source of light in his darkened kitchen. Carefully, he placed a trigger switch in a small box whose contents he'd assembled earlier and pushed a detonator on top of a small amount of Semtex explosive as if it were putty. Satisfied that the device was armed and ready for final packaging, he manoeuvred the switch in such a way as to adhere it to the lid of the box once closed. From his pocket he took a card depicting a Saltire and placed it inside the box. Removing the detonator from the Semtex, he ensured that it had clearly left its imprint on its putty before laying it loosely but attached in a separate compartment in the box. In its current configuration, the device could not explode. Slowly he placed the lid on its box and held it to ensure that there must be a connection between the lid and the switch.

Having addressed then retrieved an identically weighted box from his Govan address a week previously, he was confident that the value of the stamps he'd bought would be commensurate with the appropriate charge rate. Content that the device was as he intended it should be, he took a padded envelope and in capital letters addressed it to The Right Honourable George Younger M.P., Secretary of State for Scotland at his home at Leckie House in Gargunnock near Stirling. Carefully he inserted the box into the envelope and sealed it before removing his thin rubber gloves. *This'll cause a stir.* He laughed as he stood from the table and stretched his athletic frame to ease a cramp in his shoulders.

* * *

Glasgow, Scotland

Gall and Carnegie commiserated one with another.

"That old fucker doesn't know what he's talkin' about", complained Sergeant Anderson Carnegie. "We were first on the scene, brought in McLeod and his cronies but our esteemed Deputy Chief Constable decides to focus on the way we lifted the bastard?"

"Well, to be fair, Andy, it didn't look good on film, eh? Thank Christ it was CCTV and not a film crew. We'd have been crucified for manhandling peaceful members of the public if it'd been on the telly."

"Aye, well fuck'm anyway."

Gall changed gear. "You going to any of the funerals?"

"I knew O'Herlihy a wee bit. Met him and his wife at a social so I'll go along to that one on Thursday. You?"

"Nah! I know I should but I've always hated funerals. I'll say a wee prayer for him next time I say a wee prayer," he suggested, implying that it may be some time before he would act on that thought.

Gall swilled the remnants of his coffee in his mug and drank its contents.

"So, what next given the boss's mild suggestion that we'd better not annoy these people again without good cause?"

"Well, *I've* got good cause. I know in my bones that McLeod and his pals are up to no good with thon Willie McRae and one way or another I'm going to prove it. Starting tonight."

Gall demurred. "Andy, calm down. We've done McRae's house. Found nothing. We've tapped his home phone. Heard nothing. We've tapped his business phone. Heard nothing. We've interrogated his lieutenant McLeod, got nothing. Maybe...just maybe, we're barking up the wrong nationalist!"

"Well, *somebody* blew the heid off that young cop at Faslane and *somebody* killed those four cops and my guess is that if it wasn't McLeod and McRae, they'll know who did it."

"This is just guesswork, Andy. Your gut instinct!"

"Well today my gut instinct is to tan the house of one Hector McLeod."

"Here we go again...and I'm presuming that you won't want to bother with a warrant?"

"As soon as he leaves his house, I'm going in."

"And I'm assuming you want me to haud your jaikit?"

Carnegie smiled. "If you do, I'll say a wee thank you prayer for you next time I say a wee thank you prayer."

Gall returned his grin and shook his head resignedly. "Bugger it...Lead on McDuff!"

* * *

Melissa Rees opened the door in Tennant's Bar and narrowed her eyes, trying to spot her colleague Jock Macmillan. A waved arm drew her gaze to him seated against the wall with a half-finished pint of Guinness in front of him. She made her way through the afternoon drinkers and joined him. In front of him on the table lay copies of some of the day's newspapers, each opened at the page dealing with the killing and consequent investigation of the death of the four officers. Nothing had been mentioned of the apprehension of himself and McLeod.

"Hi Mel. That taxi's great but meeting in a pub is better, eh?"

"How many drinks have you had? That Willie McRae's a bad influence on you."

Macmillan laughed. "I'm not meeting McLeod until tomorrow night. If I don't meet my support officer I'd just be at home staring at the wall. I've given it a lot of thought and having a drink with you is marginally more entertaining."

"Ha ha...Well, I was about to have root canal treatment without anaesthetic and decided that meeting you just shaved it."

Both smiled despite themselves. Macmillan bought a round and they spoke more convivially together than either might earlier have thought possible, even jointly entertaining the affable intervention of a mildly intoxicated retired university lecturer at a nearby table who presumed them husband and wife.

Rees was first to bring the conversation back to business having decided that using her feminine charms might produce better results than her usual aggressive approach.

"Jock, you know how you said that undercover work was pretty boring?"

"Well, I'm sure it has its moments but there's a lot of down time which is why I'm pleased that my colleague is prepared to spend some time with me in the pub in order to deal with what I view as crucial operational matters that arise from time to time."

"Sure...but the thing is. If you think undercover work is boring, being your message girl is *infinitesimally* more tedious." She sipped at her wine. "I was wondering..."

"Eh...before you start, *Message Girl...Support Officer*...you don't get involved in..."

"Of course not...there's no way I'd compromise this work... we've been over this...but I did wonder if I couldn't be more helpful to you. I mean you can't be in two places at the same time and there must be occasions when having another pair of eyes could be helpful."

"And if and when that circumstance arose, I'd be first to ask your assistance."

"Excellent! Because what I was thinking was that when you were meeting with McLeod tomorrow evening, I might keep a watch on McRae. Even just if it was to follow him from his office to his home. He might have contacts other than McLeod you know. You can't be sure."

Macmillan sighed loudly. "This is what happened over by in Crossmaglen. You decide to involve yourself in something that's not your responsibility and before long..."

Rees became heated despite herself. "I used my initiative..."

"Your *initiative*?" Macmillan shook his head wearily, conceding her request. He sighed resignedly. "Okay...okay...you follow McRae from work to home while I'm with McLeod and we'll compare notes. You do not engage directly. You do not speak with a living soul. You do not do anything I've not thought of telling you not to do." He finished his Guinness. "Do I make myself clear?"

"Apart from that last bit of tortured English...Another Guinness?"

The late afternoon passed into early evening and Rees and Macmillan continued their conversation. After his fifth pint of Guinness – Rees had changed to spritzers then further eased back to water following her recent reaction to too much wine consumed too quickly – Macmillan found himself looking at her while she spoke, hearing nothing. *God almighty, she really is a beautiful creature. If only she wasn't such a headstrong pain in the butt.* Rees's cheeks dimpled as she smiled, showing her even teeth to perfection as she spoke.

"...and that is proof positive, Jock, that my Wrexham (she pronounced it *Wrexhaaam*) is much more beautiful than your Edinburgh!"

Macmillan rallied. "Sorry Mel. I was miles away for a moment. That last sip of Guinness took me over the top...unless it was you talking about your love of Wales!"

Rees's cheeks dimpled once more. "Then you've probably had enough for one night. Let's get you home. We've an important day tomorrow. You deal with McLeod and I deal with McRae."

Macmillan remembered his bargain. "Yeah, but Detective Sergeant Rees, you have to promise me that you'll stick to the agreement. No direct contact with McRae. Remember what Yogi Berra said, 'You can observe a lot by just watching!' Just observe!"

"Absolutely, Detective Inspector Macmillan."

* * *

McRae made his way to the Three Judges bar by taxi, his bulging leather briefcase tight by his side; the usually phlegmatic taxi driver raising his eyebrows only imperceptibly as McRae invited him to circle a roundabout three times to ensure that no one was following.

McLeod left his home, having noticed Carnegie and Gall's Triumph sitting at the corner of his street trying to be discrete. He walked to the Cathcart Railway Station, left immediately by another exit and caught a taxi on Holmlea Road, emerging at Bridge Street Subway Station. He remained seated and allowed two underground trains to pass leaving a deserted platform before being satisfied that he wasn't followed by the two Special Branch officers, and boarded a third train. He exited at Kelvinhall Station and crossed the road to the Three Judges just as McRae's taxi arrived. They entered together and McRae urged McLeod in the direction of an empty table while ordering and collecting a couple of drinks at the bar.

"Followed?" he asked McLeod as he placed the drinks on the table.

"Hope not. I saw Abbot and Costello in their car outside my flat but, if they tried, I don't think they managed to follow me beyond the railway station. Anyway, we'll be able to see anyone suspicious from here."

"Well, thanks for coming. I've some important information to share that I don't want to trust to the telephone. You'll remember your conversation with thon representative of *Alba*?"

"Aye."

"Well, I took a call this morning from a woman with an English accent called Caroline Brown...although she confesses that's not her real name. She seemed frightened...but that might have been put on. She won't tell me the detail of her concerns over the phone...she phoned from somewhere in England...but wants to meet me to share information to do with this McCrone Report you talked to me about."

McLeod started. "McCrone? Willie, this smells of MI5 or Special Branch. Who knows what they might be cooking up?"

"My concerns exactly. But maybe we can arrange things so we're not as exposed as we might otherwise be. I've arranged for her to come by train to Glasgow on Wednesday afternoon and upon arrival, to walk down Jamaica Street towards the river until she's contacted by us."

"Willie, if it *is* a police or security services operation, we'd be walking right into something."

"Aye, we would that, Hector. But I've been thinking. Your taxi man, Jock Macmillan. You spent time with him in the jail on Saturday. What did you make of him? Trustworthy?"

McLeod drew his lower lip over his top lip as he pondered the question, measuring his response. "Seemed okay. Didn't seem much involved in politics beyond attending the march on Saturday. Seemed like a nice guy. Certainly bright enough. A law graduate."

"Aye...and didn't he say in the Station Bar that he lived in a two bedroom flat in the west end and that he didn't share it with anyone?"

"Aye. He did that! I'd say he was a supporter if not a particularly active one."

"But he was offering us all sorts of assistance. Seemed anxious to thank us for our help in getting him out of the jail?"

"Well, *your* help!"

McRae accepted the amendment. "Well, Special Branch and MI5 won't have him on their radar screen so I was wondering whether he might help by collecting this woman in his taxi and taking her to his flat. If we are satisfied that she's not being followed, I could meet with her and see what she has to say for herself."

"D'you want me there with you?"

"I've agreed with her that there will be a guarantee of confidentiality...indeed complete secrecy. She seeks total anonymity. So I'll need you looking after the street outside the flat to make sure no one visits us once we're together in Macmillan's flat. I'll also need him to help in that regard as well as him putting her up for a night and taking her back for the train south the following day."

"I'm seeing him for a beer tomorrow night."

"Then might I rely on your discernment to engage him in our proposition as you deem it safe so to do?"

"Of course. But if I smell a rat or if he has the slightest doubts about getting involved then we return to the drawing board. Agreed?"

"Agreed, Hector." McRae drained his glass. "Now, a wee malt to toast our possible good fortune?"

"*Alba gu bràth,* Willie. Scotland forever!"

Chapter Eleven

TUESDAY 2ND APRIL 1985

Gargunnock, Stirling.

Diana Younger placed the telephone on its receiver having bid her husband, who had phoned from his office in the House of Commons in London, much love and good luck for his contribution at that morning's Cabinet Meeting. A whistle signalled a boiling kettle and drew her back into the kitchen where she began preparations for a morning cup of tea and a short break from household duties. As she opened the door of the refrigerator seeking milk, the doorbell sounded and the cheery daily welcome of Alan, the local postman could be heard intimating to the household that Her Majesty's Mail had been delivered and now lay in a pile on a shelf in the entrance hall.

It can wait, she decided. *I'll read it at the kitchen table once the tea is poured and the scone is buttered.*

Some minutes later, preparations having been concluded, she collected the mail and returned to the kitchen where she bit into a toasted scone, the butter dripping onto her chin occasioning a brief grunt of annoyance. Her spectacles hung on a lanyard around her neck and she raised them and placed them atop her nose, reading disinterestedly unless an envelope indicated its origins. Sifting them into piles obviously intended for her husband's political and constituency interests, she furrowed her brow at a Jiffy bag which showed no indication of its source. Although addressed to her husband, George, she opened it as she usually did his mail given her unofficial role as his personal secretary up in Scotland. The envelope yielded a small thin box of a type usually containing handkerchiefs. Opening it she realised almost immediately that it was a device intended to kill or maim. Terrified of its potential to explode at any moment, she dropped it rather harder than she might have thought wise on the table and stepped away from it, backing quickly towards the doorway and into the hall. Her first thought was of relief that each of her four children were out of the house. Hurriedly she closed the door and slid her body behind the substantial sandstone wall that hinged the door, hoping that it might offer protection against any blast. She was conscious of a suddenly pronounced heartbeat but gathered herself, edged away from the wall and moved anxiously towards the hall telephone where, with tremulous fingers, she dialled 999.

* * *

Glasgow, Scotland

Hector McLeod sat immobilised on his wingback chair and gazed again at the top drawer of his cabinet wherein he usually kept his socks. No black edging could be seen. The sock he'd left protruding slightly had been returned tidily to its drawer. He sat squarely on the padded cushions that formed its seat and stared again to make sure his eyes weren't playing him tricks. Satisfied, he turned his gaze to a pencil he'd left precisely at a right angle to a pile of accountancy papers he'd left atop his desk. It was almost straight... but it had been moved, it had certainly been moved.

Standing, he began an audit of his belongings. Nothing obvious was missing. Whoever had visited his house the previous evening had not been bent upon theft. Money raised by rattling cans and asking for CND donations in the city's Buchanan Street; possibly some thirty pounds, remained very obviously intact on his desk.

His business cheque book lay apparently untouched beside the cash and an expensive watch bought him by his mother ticked precisely where he had left it.

Whatever they were looking for it wasn't for financial gain. He pursed his lips in slow recognition of the clandestine but enterprising entry to his apartment. *This looks like the work of Gall and Carnegie. No evidence of entry, nothing missing but I'd bet they've searched thoroughly when I was out. Photographed stuff, I'd imagine.* Suddenly alert he stood erect. *Jesus, I'd better check they haven't planted anything that would cause awkwardness.* He stepped forward and pulled the top drawer of his dressing table from its mountings and emptied its contents on his bed. *It'll take a while but this house gets checked from top to bottom!*

* * *

Gargunnock, Stirling.

It wasn't until about half past two when Sergeants Gall and Carnegie's Triumph pulled into the driveway of George Younger's sizeable country pile. Carnegie killed the ignition and turned to his colleague.

"Remember, Bob, our jaiket's on a shaky peg at the minute so no annoying this woman. Her husband's in charge of Scotland and just might have a bit of influence over our future careers."

"I'll be the very height of diplomacy, Andy. But this'll be the third of three cards from this wolf guy. Three very different *modus operandi*, three very different targets but after five deaths, it's the first time he's fucked up so this'll be the first time forensics might be able to give us something to go on."

They each cursorily furnished some identification to the uniformed policeman at the front door and entered to find half-a-dozen Scene-of-Crime officers in white overalls painstakingly assessing items of potential interest in the investigation. Diana Younger sat on a large leather settee, her fingers toying nervously with the remains of a paper handkerchief. Next to her sat a man dressed in the garb of a clergyman, introduced to them as the local minister, the Reverend Rob Calvert.

Following some early courteous exchanges and a description of Younger's discovery of the parcel bomb, Gall made his excuses and spoke with the Senior Forensic Examiner, leaving Carnegie to charm the wife of the Secretary of State for Scotland.

"Mrs Younger's been very lucky. There was enough Semtex in this device to kill. We'll have to do some further work in the lab but an educated guess would suggest it's the same batch that was used to kill the four officers in Govan."

"He left his card?"

"He did...another Saltire with a wolf on the reverse. A bit surprising as it'd have been shredded in the explosion."

"And it failed to detonate?"

"Yes. The detonator had loosened itself from the Semtex and failed to set it off when she opened it."

Gall peered at the box, noting the imprint of the detonator on the surface of the putty-like Semtex and shook his head. "Something about this isn't right. His calling card would have been shredded so why put it inside the box? And in any use of plastic explosive I've seen, the detonator is pushed inside the wax not placed on top of it." He thought for a moment. "Not unless it was designed specifically not to explode?"

"I see what you're getting at Sergeant. But what would be the purpose of that? It would have been a dangerous operation assembling the bomb. Let me be clear. If the detonator hadn't been shaken loose, the explosion would have certainly have caused limb damage, probably facial and chest injury and could easily have killed."

"Sure...but one possible scenario is that this guy wants us to know it's him but didn't want to have the bomb explode."

"And another is that he didn't care much about his card and that he intended to kill the Secretary of State for Scotland."

"Aye, well your job is to do the clever science stuff and my job is to work out what it all means."

"Precisely so, Sergeant. Precisely so."

Gall allowed his gruff riposte to pass before returning to his questioning. "However we're talking about a cheap, homemade, improvised device?"

"It is. The military these days drop bombs that cost more than the buildings they destroy. In retaliation, the state faces deadly kitchen-manufactured bombs that cost the price of a pint of beer." He picked up the now harmless device and reconsidered. "Perhaps a half-pint at today's prices!"

* * *

Glasgow, Scotland

Macmillan returned to Tennents' pub in Glasgow's Byres Road. Elbowing the swing-door open, he entered to the instant and noisy thrum of conversation. Immediately he knew the smell of it. It took him back to student pints in Edinburgh's Rose Street and to the Clachan Bar of his youth in Stornoway when he'd drink his full on a Saturday night before the Sunday Observance Society ensured that all enjoyment ceased in pursuit of collective Godliness. He made his way through drinkers to the busy bar, removed a ten pounds note and leaned forward, seeking service.

"What's your Guinness like in here?" he asked affably.

A barman hard-pressed and unused to anything but basic orders involving precise numbers of pints or whiskies, placed both hands on the counter, palms down and looked at his shoes before raising his gaze to someone he clearly viewed as a trouble-maker or a *poseur*. He found it hard to conceal his scorn. "Fair to middlin'."

"Hardly a ringing endorsement," said Macmillan.

With a sigh of irritation, the barman growled, "Do you want a ringin' endorsement or a pint of Guinness, pal?"

Recognising that the bartender was unlikely to place customer primacy above customer throughput that evening, he returned a thin smile and ordered a Guinness along with a Pale Ale in anticipation of McLeod's arrival.

Glasgow's Subway system creaked not unreasonably at the seams, given its status as the third oldest underground railway in the world but nevertheless, McLeod having again left early in order to allow two trains to pass in order to ensure that no one was following him, stepped aboard the third which delivered him timeously at Hillhead Station in the city's Byres Road. He climbed the stairs to its frontage and exited into a dark and rainy streetscape where passers-by walked with umbrellas pointed into the wind or with their chin tucked into their coat collars in an attempt to mitigate the downpour. Tennents' Bar was close by on the other side of the road and pulling his bunnet tighter about his head, McLeod made his way across the busy street and headed for its bright lights.

Macmillan was seated at the same table he'd used the previous evening with Melissa Rees.

"Good to see you, Hector", said Macmillan shaking his hand warmly. "I took the liberty of ordering you one of the Pale Ales you enjoyed when we were in the Station Bar."

"Good man, Jock. I could do with a couple of beers tonight."

"Busy day?"

McLeod took a long draught from his pint and nodded wordlessly at the muted television pinned to the wall whose subtitles scrolled along the bottom of the screen as the newsreader mimed the words before film of the frontage of Leckie House in Gargunnock replaced his image.

"Strathclyde Police today announced that a parcel bomb was sent to the home of the Secretary of State for Scotland, George Younger. Mr Younger was in London attending a Cabinet Meeting but his wife was at home and she opened the device which did not explode. Police would not confirm that it was connected to either of the two recent incidents which have resulted in the deaths of five police officers but say they are pursuing a definite line of enquiry."

"Here we go again," said Macmillan. "I saw it earlier. Am I to assume that Strathclyde's finest will be battering the door of this pub down any minute now?"

"Who knows, Jock? But what the idiots who are doing this don't realise is that they do irreparable harm to the cause of Scottish independence."

Macmillan reduced his pint by a third. "But you insist that it's not you and your boys?"

"Absolutely not. Willie McRae is a senior politician and a good man. He wants independence as much as anyone but his approach is to uncover the unfairnesses that are bestowed upon our country by an uncaring Westminster Government...of whatever colour...and offer alternatives. The British Establishment is a corrupt and prejudiced operation based upon entitlement and privilege and our country won't prosper as it could do unless it is replaced by an independent, modern Scottish institution that serves the interests of its own people. But we'll never win a ballot if people think we're no better than the IRA. None of us wants to see tanks on the streets of Glasgow but that'll be the outcome if this continues."

"Maybe it's the Establishment itself that's behind all this? Perfidious Albion and all that?"

"Don't think we've not considered that, Jock. The old false flag malarkey. These people have had centuries of experience of getting their own way. Only sixty years ago, they ruled over a fifth of the world's population and controlled a quarter of the world's land mass. They didn't achieve that by presiding over a host of vicar's tea parties in order to persuade the natives of the benefits of British rule. They're ruthless and vicious and capable of most things if it suits their purpose."

"So you don't support the IRA?"

"That's Ireland's business. They've suffered as we've suffered. They chose the way of the bullet. We choose the way of the ballot. Plus, in the century before the Easter Rising, Scotland was one of the richest areas in the world due to tobacco and our geographical position and Ireland was one of the poorest....so we're in a different situation."

"And you speak for your pals on the march on Saturday?"

"Absolutely." He paused. "Look, the guys I drink with are the kind of people who give unasked-for advice to people playing the puggy in the pub. They're innocents...well-meaning innocents. They're not front and centre players, they're the three daft guys, four horses back in John Wayne's posse." He took a sip of his beer and acknowledged the essence of Macmillan's question. "But there are nut cases in every movement. Over in Northern Ireland one of the leaders urging violence is a clergyman. How do we explain *that*? Not every leader is *Mahātma* Gandhi. In Scotland just now we don't have that leader, that personality who transcends politics, the William Wallace who can appeal beyond the narrow objectives of party politics. I have friends who are left wing. I have friends who are right wing but they all believe in independence for Scotland. We can sort out the politics afterwards. That's democracy."

"Christ, I wasn't expecting all that. You bring your soap box with you?"

McLeod smiled. "Sorry, Jock. I get carried away...Look, Scotland needs its troublemakers but these killings are anathema to the independence movement."

"Okay. I'm almost persuaded...as you know I've a legal background and I don't mind telling you that my apprehension at the march on Saturday shook me up more than a little. Yesterday I spent some time in the Mitchell Library and did a bit of reading around the splinter groups that also believe in independence for Scotland."

"I'm aware of them."

"Aye, but are you and Willie *involved* with them? I read of *Sìol nan Gàidheal*... 'Seed of the Gael' to you Lowlanders. It's been alleged that they stole the Dunkeld Lectern from St. Albans..."

McLeod interrupted attempting to conceal his intemperance. "It was *liberated* Jock. It was plundered by the English in 1544."

"And there's the Scottish National Liberation Army; bomb threats and parcel bombs sent to Margaret Thatcher, Norman Tebbit, Michael Heseltine, Malcolm Rifkind...even the Queen..."

"Allegedly..."

"I made a list...there's the Scottish Separatist Group, Scottish Patriots, the Scottish Republican Socialist Party, Settler Watch,

Dark Harvest Commando, the Scottish Citizen Army...Now I can understand why these people operate as they do but..."

"Every day's a school day, eh? Look, Jock, I won't lie to you. Of course these people are known to us. Like I say, Scotland needs its troublemakers...and Willie has given them advice in the past but we do *not* condone violence. We are entirely comfortable with civil disobedience; happy to take on the powers-that-be in court courtesy of Willie but...presently...we draw the line at violence, happy to march, happy to protest, happy to offer our political views to the media...."

"You say 'we'...do you mean the Scottish National Party?"

McLeod paused. "Not really. Willie and my pals are members of the SNP. One is also a member of *Sìol nan Gàidheal* but I'm not affiliated to anyone. I'm...well, I suppose I'm just a friend of Willie's. I know I'm well regarded within the independence movement but I don't want to be accused of bringing the party into disrepute by having them associated with anything impolitic. I'm used as a handy, all-purpose functionary who carries, I hope, the trust and respect of many within the movement. I'm happy that it remains that way. I kind of look after Willie...try to keep him out of pubs that sell madness by the bottle." He took a sizeable draught of his beer. "Look, Willie's different from most politicians. He's like a sort of political beaver who dams the river and changes the flow of events. He doesn't just talk the talk. I mean, look at the kind of eegits who oppose him in the press. Someone once said that when a true genius appears, you can know him by this sign; that all the dunces are in a confederacy against him." He raised his glass in an informal toast. "That's our Willie."

"I have the sense of him that he's a complex man really."

"Well, he's that for sure. Sometimes drinking with him is best reserved for pubs on the ground floor in case he throws himself out of the window...but it's usually a game of two halves. Ten minutes later and he's singing *'The Road And The Miles To Dundee'* and people are wishing he'd *take* them rather than sing them."

"Well, if he has emotional or psychological problems, Glenmorangie certainly isn't going to resolve them."

"Aye, but neither's Irn Bru! He's an unusually gifted man and sometimes he gets a wee bit downhearted but so do we all. Scottish Independence isn't just round the corner at present."

Macmillan rearranged two beer mats, giving himself a moment. "Well, I'm impressed by both of you. Anything I can do to help the movement as you describe it I'll do. I'm not educated in politics like you but I'd like to see Scotland looking after its own affairs. I'm no fan of the Westminster Establishment as you term it. I've seen the world and now that I'm home I'd like to be involved in something, even supposing it's just sticking stamps on letters to voters."

McLeod finished his beer and nodded at Macmillan's glass, still a third full. "Another Guinness?"

"Dear God, you and McRae can drink! I'll have to work harder to keep up with the two of you."

*

For the next hour McLeod and Macmillan discussed football, politics and religion, the three subjects most likely to cause a bar-room rumpus in Glasgow but smiles and laughter peppered their conversation. Five pints each having been consumed, McLeod leaned into the purpose of his meeting.

"Jock...you seem like a good guy." He raised his glass in an informal toast.

"Thanks, Hector. I appreciate that."

"Willie likes you."

"Then I'm honoured. Don't know him well, of course but he seems like a really genuine bloke...if a wee bit fond of the Glenmorangie and the Islay Mist."

"Aye, we're all a bit worried about his appetite in that regard."

"Christ...*you* can talk," teased Macmillan.

McLeod ignored the light barb. "Listen, Jock. There might be something you *could* do for Willie...it's very secret...and it'd just involve you picking up someone in your taxi."

"That's hardly a favour, Hector. I'd happily do that."

"Well, I need to be honest. We don't know if this person is a genuine individual seeking Willie's help or a stooge from MI5." He shifted in his seat. "I'll be straight with you, Jock. We're trying to organise this in such a way that if it *is* a set-up, you can claim you just picked up a fare from the side of the road and plead innocence. If not, you could convey her to a safe place where Willie could talk with her out of range of any listening devices. MI5 and the Special Branch don't know you beyond Saturday's incident. You'd be perfect if it was a lure."

"I'd appreciate that. I'd rather avoid another arrest."

"You'd be wise to, Hector. All the cards are stacked against us. Not only do we fear being set up by the security forces but we know that if and when they *do* get us in the dock...well, let's just say that the British Establishment has a way of ensuring that their fingers press down on the scales of justice so that it's not quite as impartial and equitable as they'd claim."

Macmillan took another swig of his Guinness. "Okay, I'm in. Where and when?"

"Tomorrow afternoon....the Broomielaw."

"That's no problem, Hector. I can't see how that could get me in trouble. And where do you want her dropped?"

"Your flat?"

* * *

Melissa Rees sat in the bay window seat of the rather expensive bistro/cafe immediately opposite Willie McRae's office in Buchanan Street awaiting his departure. She'd made her glass of mineral water last longer than she'd anticipated and had relaxed her evening's inviolate rule not to drink alcohol by ordering a glass of house white which she'd followed with another larger draught. *How long's this bugger going to work tonight?*

Eventually, one of the double doors guarding McRae's office opened and he emerged, his leather briefcase, as ever, tucked under his left arm even as awkwardly he locked the doors, his left knee balancing his heavy satchel as he did so. Rees rose, considered the half empty glass of wine placed on the table before shaking her head, lifting the glass and draining it. She collected her handbag and left, following McRae to his favourite hostelry, the Pot Still only a matter of a couple of hundred yards or so away.

She entered behind him to hear him declaim, "A big Glenmorangie, Mister Waterson and don't spare the horses. Eighteen years old, if you would. I'll pour the water myself. No ice, thank you. I abhor the Americanisation of our national drink!" She positioned herself at the bar while he organised his whisky which he took to a table in the upper gallery, otherwise empty of customers. His heavy briefcase accompanied him and was levered unceremoniously on the cushioned bench next to his seat. At that moment, more care was to be lavished upon his drink.

Rees commenced one of the approaches she'd been rehearsing since having been debriefed by Macmillan following his drinking session with McRae and McLeod. She spoke tentatively at the bar with the pub owner, John Waterson.

"Hi...I'm up in Glasgow from Wales and was told how important this public house was because of the range of whiskies you had available to buy. I'm told some of them could set me back a week's wages."

John Waterson prided himself on his comprehensive knowledge of anything to do with the water of life. He placed his drying towel near the sink below the bar surface and gazed at the miscellany of whiskies that adorned the deep shelves from bar-top level to the ceiling of the pub.

"Aye, we have a few rarities. But there are many others which would be within everyone's price range."

"Well, I've two Scottish friends in Swansea who argue repeatedly over which is the best, the eighteen or twenty-five year old Glenmorangie whisky. I'm told they're both malts?"

"Och, they're connoisseurs both, your friends! The two drinks are the very nectar. They have the same debate that another of my customers has each time he orders his tipple. That's him up there," he signalled to the gallery where McRae was taking his first sip, his eyebrows raised in rapture as if contemplating the music of the heavenly choirs.

"Oh, I don't want to trouble anyone...but I *would* like to tell my friends that I'd tried both and had formed a judgement. Do you think your customer would give me his advice?"

"He's a busy man but hold on..." He shouted to the gallery. "Willie, there's a young lady here asking me whether the eighteen or twenty-five year old Glenmorangie is the best."

McRae looked up somewhat startled from his opening drink of the night. The Pot Still wasn't a pub wherein shouting was the norm. On early weeknights it was usually a haven of peace and quiet and it took a moment before the question registered but he entered into the spirit of the conversation, spreading his palms on the table and looking towards the ceiling of the pub in contemplation.

"Well now, in my completely amateur opinion...although formed over some many years of attempting to unravel the truth of this matter...the eighteen year old is somewhat light and fruity but so drinkable the taste memory has stayed with me throughout the years and sustains me in troubled times. It is a simply wonderful construction, distilled from water drawn by the sixteen men of Tain from the Tarlogie Burn that flows from the hills above the distillery on Morangie Farm." He raised and jutted his jaw, while his left hand clutched the lapel of his suit jacket in a fashion used many times in courts of law when approaching a devastating assessment of the Crown's case. "The twenty-five year old, on the other hand, has similar antecedents but is sweet with notes of potpourri, almost floral oakiness. If the Lord God Almighty put a pistol to my head and had me choose, I'd invite him to pull the trigger were it not for the fact that I'd never be able to taste either vintage of my wonderful Glenmorangie again."

Rees offered a thumbs-up in McRae's direction and turned again to Waterson.

"I'll start with the eighteen year old, thank you."

"And just reveal the flavour with a wee drop water," counselled the barman.

Twenty minutes passed as Rees sat at the bar sipping at a whisky she swore she'd never drink again. *Dear God, this is something of an acquired taste.* Her reflections were somewhat interrupted as McRae stood beside her, a twenty pound note in his hand, addressing the barman.

"And again, John." He turned his attention to Rees who took a sip of her whisky; to any disinterested observer, appearing to enjoy the experience thoroughly. "Well, young Miss, are your first instincts to spit it back in the glass? It can take some time to appreciate a great whisky."

Rees swallowed and smiled despite the burning in her throat. "It's perfect, thank you. Can't see how the twenty-five year old could top *this*!"

McRae smiled at her timid consumption. "You don't appear to have the appetite that I do...but then, there are camels in Timbuktu preparing to cross the Sahara that don't have the appetite that I do. I see you're still to finish your eighteen year old but would you permit me to buy you a twenty-five year old? You might find it more to your taste."

"Thanks, but I didn't come in here tonight for company, I just wanted to help settle a silly bet."

McRae laughed. "You must trust me, young lady. Those who know me well would find it amusing were I to be accused of attempting to befriend a young lady in a bar." He smiled at her. "You must believe that my interest is merely in promulgating the virtues of the finest whisky known to man."

Rees appeared to relent. "I'm sorry. I misunderstood." She drained her whisky with great, if concealed, forbearance. "Thank you. I'd love to try the twenty-five year old."

A further aged malt having almost been consumed, Rees insisted on repaying McRae's generosity although he subsequently insisted that they repair to his gallery seat in order to protect his briefcase. He was now garrulous if not drunk. Rees was drunk if not garrulous.

"I carry in that briefcase, important information," he exclaimed somewhat portentously.

"Some legal analysis of the case you're working on?"

"I'm in court today and tomorrow and I've completed my notes. My client will be found not guilty, of that there's no doubt. He's an innocent man!" He gathered and rebuked himself as he appreciated his drunken proclivity to speak unwisely of the contents of his briefcase. "But the hard work's done. On the train to Edinburgh tomorrow morning, I'll add the poetry. The law without poetry is a boring thing."

The evening progressed and McRae was in gregarious mood as he encouraged his new friend, Miss Rees, to attempt an Islay Mist.

"It's a wonderful whisky, Miss Rees..."

"Please call me Melissa...Mel, Mr McRae."

"And you must call me Willie..." He pulled his pack of Gold Leaf from his jacket pocket. "Smoke?"

"No thanks. I don't indulge but please go ahead."

McRae lit his cigarette and commenced a mild coughing fit.

"If you don't mind me saying, that's a peculiar brand you smoke. Not one I recognise."

"I got a taste for these when I was in India." He coughed again. "They're a big brand over there, designed to appeal to the *Brahmin* and *Kshatriya,* the top two classes of social order in the sub-continent. I now have to import them from Ireland because they're not available in the UK. It's one of my two weaknesses. If you give me a bottle of Islay Mist or Glenmorangie and a few packs of Gold Flake, I'm as happy as a sand-boy. So...my cigarettes from Ireland and my premium spirits from the fine people at Inverarity Morton, one of Scotland's most prestigious companies. It would appear that I have tastes that cannot be satisfied by most corner shops."

"Why were you in India?"

"Och, it was a long while ago. I was a Lieutenant Commander in the Royal India Navy before working with Lord Mountbatten when he was busy trying to make sense of the relationship between India and Pakistan."

"What a fascinating life you've led, Willie."

"Well, the law is my mistress now."

"And perhaps Islay Mist and Gold Flake?"

"And independence for Scotland, Melissa. My other great passion."

Rees saw an opportunity. "Oh...wasn't it dreadful that these poor police officers were killed?"

McRae grimaced his agreement. "These deaths were nothing to do with the independence movement. A tragedy for them and their families and an outrage in a civilised society."

"Well, the BBC news speculated..."

"Aye, just that, but you'd expect nothing less from the English Broadcasting Corporation."

"But don't you approve of independence by any means?"

McRae gathered himself, determining that he was more comfortable talking with a stranger about whisky. He ignored the question.

"Here...if *you're* not having an Islay Mist, I'm not going to deprive myself."

"Perhaps an orange juice for me this time, Willie."

He smiled and extinguished his freshly lit cigarette. "We'll educate your palate yet, Mel." Another sip of his whisky saw him switch the questioning. "So you're up in Glasgow on holiday?"

"I'm a nurse. No dependents and I just needed a break. Had to get away from the mayhem."

"A public servant! An angel in white!" McRae was now slurring his words. "And what's your specialty?"

"Front line...Accident and emergency."

"Then I toast you and I toast you again. You deserve the respect, affection and every reward a grateful nation can bestow on you." He lifted his glass, drained it and placed it on the table before him. "Mel...I have a thirst for the drink that dwarfs yours. Would you mind terribly if I enjoyed another glass before you've had time to finish yours? It's not the done thing in polite society but, then...no one's ever accused me of being polite society."

"Fill your boots, Willie. I'm enjoying your company. You're a fascinating man."

McRae drew his lips tight as if rebuking himself, allowing a brief silence before responding, shaking his head in contradiction. "I'm afraid I'm not much more than a *drunk* man, my dear! Little more than an old, drunk man."

Chapter Twelve

WEDNESDAY 3RD APRIL 1985

Glasgow, Scotland

Deputy Chief Constable Russell Laurie raised his eyes from a paper given him by Chief Superintendent Seamus McGrattan and removed his spectacles. "So let me get this straight, Chief Superintendent McGrattan, we've four police officers, an MOD cop murdered and a letter bomb posted to George Younger. No finger-prints on the cards, the phone or the letter-bomb. No witnesses. Two different explosive materials but with the same batch of Semtex being used in both the Govan site and at the Secretary of State's house. In each case we have a fucking business card depicting a Saltire on one side and a lone wolf howling at the moon on the other. We've not been able to establish any information from known associates of Nationalist or terrorist movements. We know he has a Scottish accent but can't identify which region beyond 'probably West of Scotland' which cuts our suspects to about half of the entire population of Scotland..."

McGrattan stood at attention on the other side of Laurie's expansive desk. Beside him stood a man in his forties wearing a tweed jacket who peered at the Deputy Chief Constable through glasses with thick lenses. The frame was taped together at the bridge. His hands were clasped in front of him.

"I think there's an interesting finding in respect of the rug, sir. I've brought along Doctor George Abbey. He lectures in horticulture at the University of Strathclyde."

Laurie acknowledged Abbey's presence with the merest upward tilt of his head. "Have a seat, Seamus. You too, Doctor Abbey." He replaced his spectacles and read an aspect of the report to himself once again.

"And what do you make of the contents found on the rug, Doctor? It was covered in detritus normally found on the forest floor?"

Abbey was nothing if not evangelical about his subject matter. "Yes, Indeed. It might suggest that the rug was introduced to the crime scene in Govan."

"Probably disguising the Enfield rifle, sir, "interjected McGrattan. "And that it was probably brought from a place known to the killer, possibly his home."

"Which might suggest that he's not based in downtown Glasgow?"

Abbey continued his monologue. "The contents of the rug included many remnants of needles, cones and resin deriving from *pinus sylvestris,* the Scots pine. It also provided evidence of the Olive Oysterling which is a saprotrophic fungus whose task is breaking down dead wood and plant material on the forest floor. Now, being honest, these particles might be found anywhere in rural Scotland... parts of England too for that matter...but there might be one finding of keener interest to you. I found traces of a species of invertebrate known as the black tinder fungus beetle. Its Latin name..."

"Never mind its Latin name, Doctor! What's its significance?"

Abbey looked surprised at Laurie's outburst but continued, if with a new hesitancy.

"Well...in case you ever need to know, it's *Bolitophagus reticulatus...*" He smiled slightly in consequence of his small victory. "But its significance...is that it is a beetle that has now become extremely rare as a result of loss of habitat."

"So?"

"It tends to be found only in Glen Affric and in some of the forests of Argyll and Bute."

Laurie nodded his appreciation. "And what square mileage might we be looking at here, Doctor Abbey?"

"Well, there are about seven thousand square kilometres in Argyll and Bute...we don't do square miles any more. Glen Affric forest is about twenty-two thousand acres."

"So whether we calculate it in square kilometres, square acres or square fucking sausages...it's still like looking for a pine needle in a forest?"

Abbey's grin faded at the senior officer's blunt language. However, he acknowledged the policeman's bleak summary. "There you have it, Deputy Chief Constable! I'm happy to have been of assistance."

Having dismissed McGrattan and Abbey, Laurie walked to his window overlooking Pitt Street in Glasgow and mulled over the information just imparted to him. A sharp knock on his door prefaced his secretary announcing the presence outside of Detective Sergeants Carnegie and Gall.

"Send in the clowns," said Laurie uncharitably.

Both officers entered the office of the Deputy Chief Constable and stood rigidly to attention as Laurie took his seat. Before speaking, he organised his desk items neatly while he thought. Finally, placing his pen at right angles to his desk blotter, he addressed the two men quietly but angrily.

"You two have tried my patience. You're a pair of blithering idiots. You've successfully buggered up an operation where the public were supportive of the police following the deaths of four of our officers and turned them into at best neutral, at worst hostile because you can't control your temper." He looked directly at Carnegie. "Especially you, Carnegie." He looked away as if seeking counsel. "I should have you both disciplined...but I won't. At the end of the day, we're all upset about the men who died. But I'm curtailing your activities. I'm not returning you to uniform... although I've considered it...but I'm splitting you up. I've just been advised that there was evidence from forensics that suggested that the person who planted the bomb may have come from either the forests around Glen Affric or the forests around Argyll and

Bute. You, Carnegie will co-ordinate the searching of vehicles in and around the southern part of Argyll and Bute. You, Gall, the northern areas. Check all vehicles. Ask for information in the small post offices, pubs and cafes, petrol stations around the areas. The bastard who did this might be hiding out somewhere there. I want to know of any rumours, spiteful gossip…anything. Speak to village idiots like yourselves but get me information. Go now!"

* * *

Macmillan had ignored repeated attempts by Rees to contact him, telling himself he'd be more comfortable briefing her after the event to avoid any helpful advice she might care to offer. As he eased his taxi into the flow of traffic outside his flat, he also chose to avoid answering his cab radio as Rees made a further attempt to get in touch.

Twenty minutes later, his taxi sat in Glasgow's Jamaica Street as he watched the ebb and flow of people using the station entrance. He consulted his watch which showed the time as five past six in the evening just as a middle-aged woman carrying a copy of National Geographic stepped out of the station and turned right towards the river. Macmillan waited until she had disappeared from sight before moving off and following her anticipated route towards the Clyde. He saw her cross Argyle Street and continue her course down Jamaica Street.

Reading a newspaper outside Woolworths' store as she passed was Hector McLeod whose eyes scoured the street for evidence of anything untoward. Satisfied that all appeared well, he folded the paper, a sign to Macmillan that he should collect Miss Brown. A parking space ahead of her was available and MacMillan manoeuvred into the bay, waiting until she was abreast of him. He leaned from his driver's window.

"Caroline Brown? I'm a friend. You're safe. No one has followed you." His right arm reached out and behind as he pulled at the rear door handle. "Please get in."

112

Roberts did as requested and sat motionless and silently in the rear of the taxi.

Macmillan had been asked only to put her at ease while transporting her to his flat in the west end.

"You're very brave in meeting with us, Miss Brown," said Macmillan insinuating himself as an integral member of McRae's inner circle. "I want you to know that you're in safe and experienced hands. No one knows you're here. After you have a chat with Mr. McRae, I'll look after you in a safe house tonight before delivering you back to Central Station. You'll be home safely in no time." He attempted what he imagined was a reassuring smile for consumption via his rear-view mirror, but could see that his passenger was holding a handbag in her lap and that her knuckles were as white as his taxi was black.

Taking care to ensure he wasn't being followed by stopping three times and by travelling through the Clyde Tunnel in each direction, Macmillan reached his flat some twenty minutes later and escorted Rosemary Roberts, aka Caroline Brown up the stair and into his apartment where McRae was waiting, a pot of tea ready to pour.

"Miss Brown, you are very welcome." He placed the teapot on a placemat and offered her his hand. "Please allow me to introduce myself. I am Willie McRae. I've been looking forward to meeting you."

"And I, you, Mr. McRae."

"You'll be tired and parched after your journey. How do you take your tea?"

"Milk, no sugar, thanks."

"And have you eaten?"

"A sandwich on the train. Quite sufficient, thank you."

McRae gestured in the direction of Macmillan. "Your taxi driver is called Jock. You'll have met obviously. He'll be your host this evening and will look after your every need once we've had our little chat."

"That sounds most thoughtful."

As agreed earlier, Macmillan left and took up a position in his taxi, joined shortly by McLeod. They kept watch outside while

McRae attempted to have his guest tell her story. After some small talk concerning her journey north and some encouraging words from McRae about the complete confidentiality she'd enjoy upon relieving herself of the information she had to impart, Rosemary Roberts began to talk.

"I've recently taken the decision to retire early from public life, Mr McRae. I've not had great health of late and it's been a great unburdening just deciding to walk away. During my working life I was a fairly nondescript civil servant. Fetching and carrying... event organisation...report writing...clerking meetings...the typical faceless bureaucrat."

"So you feel it's appropriate to provide me some information now that you've retired?"

"Only partly, Mr McRae. I've signed the Official Secrets Act and I take that very seriously. So seriously, it's damaged my health...my mental health...over the last decade. You see, my accent belies my nationality. To your ears I must sound like an Oxbridge graduate born of good Home Counties stock, all jolly hockey sticks and public school giddiness. And you'd be partly right in that it does describe an important part of my life." She hesitated. "But you see, my parents, both now deceased, were from Kilmarnock...both GPs and both dedicated to Scottish Nationalism. I was told stories of Bruce and Wallace with my mother's milk. I was schooled in the immorality of the British Empire and the obscenity that is the British Establishment, the Royal Family and its hangers'-on."

"Aye, well you're in good company tonight, Miss Brown."

"I hadn't given it the measure of importance that they did and initially was quite happy building a fairly unexceptional career as a competent, likeable and invisible civil servant in Whitehall."

Roberts shifted uncomfortably in her chair and drained her cup. "Do you think I might have..."

"Of course, dear lady." McRae topped up her cup and added milk. "Please go on,"

"What changed things was a role I was asked to play supporting Professor Gavin McCrone, the Chief Economic Adviser to the Secretary of State for Scotland." She sipped again at her cup of tea, obviously ill at ease. "In 1984, Prime Minister Edward Heath asked for an assessment of the impact of North Sea Oil on the economy of Scotland should Scotland become independent." She ventured into her handbag and withdrew a single sheet of paper. "Professor McCrone was asked to compile it and I was asked to manage its production for the Cabinet Office. There were only a very few civil servants involved and it was made clear that this was top secret work and that was anything of it to leak there would be the most almighty row with hanging, drawing and quartering being the likely outcome for anyone offending the Act. MI5 were brought in to monitor matters. I thought little of it as maintaining confidentiality was second nature to me but as the report was written it became obvious that it was a complete vindication of the arguments of the Scottish National Party and shredded the arguments being put forward by Westminster."

She spread the single sheet of paper in her lap. "Everything that we produced was accounted for and I remember there being quite a kerfuffle when a copied contents page of the report went missing. We searched high and low. It was never found until about a year ago, I decided to get rid of a lot of bits and pieces I'd retained from my days as a civil servant. Pinned to the back of a report on fisheries policy in Scotland was the missing contents page. I brought it with me to demonstrate the veracity of my comments here today." She passed the paper to McRae who placed his Gold Flake cigarette on the side of an ashtray to give the document his full attention.

He read aloud. "So...we have here a single sheet of A4...no identifying marks...only eighteen pages it appears. Heading; the Economics of Nationalism Re-examined, Chapters...Executive Summary, the Implications of North Sea Oil, the Case Against Nationalism...bit political from a supposedly neutral civil servant, eh?...A Policy for Development, Construction, the Pace of North Sea Development, Inflation, Income Policy and Training, The European Community and Conclusion. It goes on to commence the report with the Executive Summary...only a few lines mind you...which reads, 'This paper will show that the advent of North Sea oil has completely overturned the traditional economic arguments used against Scottish nationalism. An independent Scotland could now expect to have massive surpluses both on its budget and on its balance of payments and with the proper husbanding of resources this situation could last for a very long time into the future.'..."

McRae turned to Roberts. "And this is all you have?"

Roberts gasped, "But Mr McRae, I've offered you this in good..."

"Oh, please, Miss Brown. I'm grateful to you for this but it's so...tantalising. I meant, don't you have any more?"

"No. But if it's any help, I know the report backwards."

"Then please feel free to give me the key details...I'll make notes."

"But first, Mr McRae, so you understand. What prompted me ultimately to come to you today was me watching the death of my parents, each of them *sure* in themselves that North Sea Oil was being squandered by Westminster Governments, each of them becoming more frail as the years passed. During that time I cared for them but put my career before their understanding...the satisfaction they'd have got by being proved right. They each died not knowing that they were correct in their analyses...correct that Westminster politicians lied and deceived the Scottish people. The Prime Minister slapped a Top Secret label on it and then asked his own tame civil servants to assess McCrone's report...I was also asked to help out on that...and *they* found that the report was accurate in all its particulars. It sent Heath and his Ministers into a spin."

"Heavens, I could well understand that...but before you continue, what were the given names of your parents?"

"Andrew and Megan. But why?"

"Andrew and Megan Brown?"

Roberts stiffened. "Why on earth might you have an interest in my parents?"

"Miss Brown. I must have a small measure of reassurance that you're not merely telling me a story. It would be a simple task for me quietly to establish that there were two general practitioners operating in Kilmarnock in the period after the war. A gentleman should never attempt to guess the age of a lady but if you'll forgive me, I have you as a woman in your mid to late forties. Now, you mentioned in your initial phone call to me that the name of Brown was a pseudonym and that you didn't want to be identified. I respect that and have no interest in anything other than establishing your *bona fides* and therefore the veracity of your information."

Roberts hesitated. "I see. But if I reveal my surname, I effectively concede my identity to you. I'd feel rather tricked after your reassurances, I must confess."

"I'll write nothing down. Your parents' names will remain locked in what is left of my brain. I'll ask of their existence quietly, *à propos* of nothing, and we can proceed in the knowledge that we can trust your information. If what you tell me is true...and I'm confident it is, ask yourself what your parents would have you do. My guess is that they'd invite you to be bold."

She considered McRae's request silently at some length before replying. "I may be trusting you with my life, Mr. McRae...but... my name is Rosemary Roberts and what I've told you about my family history and the McCrone Report is true in all aspects. I can only ask you to be discreet."

McRae smiled comfortingly. "If I may, I'll continue to refer to you as Miss Brown."

"Well, the key point from Professor McCrone was that were Scotland to be independent, the North Sea oil revenue would make the country as rich as Switzerland, giving the country a large tax surplus, on such a scale as to be embarrassing. Professor McCrone also surmised that this surplus revenue would make the Scottish pound the hardest currency in Europe with the exception of the Norwegian krone."

McRae sat back in his chair, his notepad on his lap, his pen suspended in mid-air.

"I need a drink!"

*

Following additional probing and copious notes taken by McRae, the evening ended in handshakes and Roberts was invited to make

herself comfortable in Macmillan's spare room while McRae left
to join his two lookouts in the taxi outside.

He settled into the back seat. "Thank you very much, Jock.
That was most interesting and your offer of the taxi for Miss
Brown and your spare room has been invaluable. Now, it's very
important that you escort her back to Central Station tomorrow
morning in time for her to catch the nine-thirty train south. It's
imperative that she retains anonymity so please check to make
sure you're not being followed. She's tired and will doubtless just
want to sleep tonight – even at this early hour. You'll look after
her?"

"That I will, Willie."

"Then maybe you'll join me for a glass around six o'clock
tomorrow evening in the Pot Still to permit me to thank you
properly?"

"I'd love that. Thanks, Willie."

* * *

Both McRae and McLeod exited the taxi and walked towards
Crow Road in order to hail another cab back into town.

As they stood close to the traffic lights that governed vehicular
movement between Crow Road and Broomhill Drive, McRae
spoke to McLeod in hushed tones despite the general absence of
another living sole on the street. "Hector, that was remarkable.
I have some thinking to do. I'll share our conversation later but
in the meantime, do you remember Bill and Betty Craigen down in
Kilmarnock? They're auld stagers and they've been members of
the SNP since Christ left Dumbarton in a sail boat."

"I do, Willie. They live in Riccarton."

Would you mind contacting them and asking them discretely
if they were aware of two SNP members, both GPs, who were
members of the Kilmarnock branch back in the late forties early
fifties? Doctors Andrew and Megan Roberts. If they ask why, tell
them that you're thinking of writing an article for a future edition
of the Kilmarnock Standard about people who've been members of
a political party for their entire life. If they confirm this, just ask

them a few questions as you would were you actually going to write the story. Then let me know once you've established the facts."

"Will do."

* * *

Macmillan returned to his flat where Roberts was standing at the bay window, looking down at the street below.

"Willie was most impressed by your conversation, Miss Brown. And he's most anxious to protect your identity. I've been tasked with getting you home tomorrow morning without any drama."

"I'm most grateful to you, Jock. Mr. McRae was most encouraging of your abilities to do just that."

Macmillan was about to suggest a nightcap when his phone rang. He lifted it knowing that only one caller had his number. As anticipated, it was Melissa Rees.

"Jock Macmillan! Where the hell have you been? I've been trying to contact you all day."

"Peter! It's good to hear from you. Haven't spoken to you in ages...but listen, I'm in the middle of a plumbing problem. Would you mind if I phoned you back tomorrow? There's water everywhere."

"Peter? *Jesus*! Macmillan. You'd better not be holding out on me."

"I suspect it's just a loose valve or something but I'd better attend to it. Say, tomorrow about eleven! I'd be clear by then."

"You are without doubt, the biggest..."

"Then that's fine, Peter. Speak with you soon."

He replaced the phone on its cradle saying in redundant explanation to Roberts, "That was my friend, Peter."

Roberts smiled. "If you don't mind me saying so, Jock. Your plumbing fiction suggests you lie easily!"

Macmillan feigned embarrassment. "Well, like Willie, I've a legal background so extemporising, comes naturally."

He opened a cupboard door wherein was a half empty bottle of Gordon's Gin.

"I've been asked only to make sure you get some shut-eye and not to bother you but would you like a gin and tonic as a night-cap? It's only gone eight o'clock and I know you'll want to get some sleep after today but one wee glass won't hurt. I've no ice and no lime, mind you."

"Actually that would be lovely, Jock. I could do with something stronger than tea. Your Mr. McRae was looking for a drink after I shared my information but your gin went unnoticed."

"He's very particular about his choice of poison, Miss Brown. He'd have choked on a gin."

Macmillan poured two drinks and sat down opposite Roberts. "Well, did you deal with things as you'd hoped?"

Roberts nodded. "He seems a nice man. And he was as interested in what I had to tell him as I'd imagined."

"With an accent such as yours, I'm maybe a wee bit surprised that you're caught up in the cause of Scottish Nationalism."

"Brought up English but born of Scots parents in Kilmarnock. Proud of my mixed heritage but compelled to right a wrong I saw frustrate my parents."

Macmillan measured his questioning, anxious not to probe too deeply and risk troubling his house guest but keen to establish as much as possible about her conversation with McRae. Later, Roberts agreed a second gin and they talked comfortably until ten o'clock when she yawned, signalling an end to the evening. She left to attend to her ablutions before sleep, promising to rise at seven-thirty. Macmillan had two further gins and sat until midnight reflecting on the day's events.

Chapter Thirteen

THURSDAY 4TH APRIL 1985

Glasgow, Scotland

McRae's office was furnished simply, an SNP calendar the only wall-hanging on otherwise unadorned beige wallpaper. A sturdy bookcase screened an entire wall, its contents mostly leather-bound law books bulked up by a section comprising brochures and papers dealing with the Scottish National Party. His desk was hidden beneath several piles of paper as were a series of filing cabinets whose locking mechanisms had been breached on more than one occasion following night-time burglaries. A black push-button office phone on his desk claimed space denied his paperwork and was characterised by one worn button that connected McRae to his Secretary, Ann Mahon.

McLeod's lunch-time phone call to McRae was short, to the point and coded. "Made that call you asked of me and your information is accurate. They even remembered your contact as a baby."

"I thought that'd be the case but it's nice to have it confirmed. See you as arranged after work?"

"As arranged."

"*Saor Alba.*"

"*Saor Alba,* Hector."

The call ended and McRae returned to his desk work. In front of him was a buff folder which contained details of a paedophile ring operating at the highest reaches of political power in the United Kingdom, listing names of prominent politicians – both Scottish and English. Beneath it were notes he'd prepared on the McCrone Report following his conversation with Rosemary Roberts the previous evening which presented the Conservative administration in London as duplicitous in regard to the value of North Sea oil. A green folder was thick with papers he'd assembled dealing with proposals being made by the Atomic Energy Authority to dump spent nuclear fuel in the seas around Scotland's northerly shores and at the bottom of the pile was a miscellany of papers dealing with drug smuggling in the West of Scotland.

Well, that looks enough to be going on with, he thought as he removed his pistol from the briefcase, stuffed the files inside it, replacing the Smith & Wesson beside them before buckling the two leather straps which closed the satchel.

*

A busy day dealing with a series of legal problems saw McRae tired and anxious for his first drink of the day. He looked at his watch and realised that the office had now closed. *I'll just tidy up here and head off to the Pot Still.* Given that his office was closed and now silenced, he called his secretary by shouting her name rather than by use of the phone. She made her way to his desk. "Ann, would you mind clearing this stuff up? I've noted down a few names and numbers of people I need to speak with tomorrow. If you could get them on the phone between appointments, that would be wonderful. When's my first appointment?"

"You've a Mr. Graham…" She consulted her notepad. "A Mr. Neil Graham, at nine-thirty. Something about a complaint against a bookmaker."

"Complaining about a bookmaker? Tell him to form an orderly queue!" He thought further. "Perhaps we could deal with some of the calls before he arrives." He stood and heaved his now weighty briefcase to its standing position on his desk, crushing a pile of correspondence as he did so. "I'm off for some refreshment and some good company, Ann. See you tomorrow. I'll be at my desk by eight."

*

McRae was first to arrive in the Pot Still. Being a Thursday evening, the pub was busy but an empty table in the gallery area was free and he shuffled his bulk into one of the green leather benches that sat against each wall and organised himself just as Macmillan and McLeod came through the door, each greeting the other as they did so.

"Ask Willie what he wants and I'll get a round in," urged Macmillan. "What's your preference?"

"A Pale Ale. I'll ask Willie," said McLeod as he headed up the short flight of stairs to the gallery.

A bar crowd two deep seeking service required that Macmillan await a free bartender. He was surprised some moments later when a hand on his shoulder seeking his attention wasn't McLeod's but McRae's.

"Jock, the drinks are on me all night tonight. I couldn't thank you properly last night and wanted to do so tonight with genuine gratitude. You can have no idea just how valuable was the service you rendered."

"Don't be daft, Willie. I was more than happy to help. In fact I...."

Macmillan's protestations were interrupted when a young lady addressed McRae at his elbow.

"Well if it isn't Willie McRae. You must *live* in this place!"

McRae's eyebrows descended from their quizzical position as he recognised his intruder.

"Well, if it isn't young Melissa. Are you here to attempt the Islay Mist tonight?" He turned to Macmillan whose mouth had remained agape since recognising Rees. "Jock, this is a new young friend of mine...a nurse called Melissa...but she wants to be known as Mel...She's Welsh and is up here on holiday trying to discover a taste for our whisky. Mel, this is Jock. He's a taxi-driving friend of mine."

"How very nice to meet you, Jock. But aren't you taxi drivers usually on the *other* side of the pub door? It must be very difficult for your customers to get hold of you," she smiled artificially.

"Jock's having a night off tonight, Mel. Now, here...you must join us upstairs. We're just having a few drinks after work. You two take a seat and I'll bring the drinks up."

He ushered both towards the stairs as Macmillan bowed his head slightly and spoke; a sibilant whisper in Rees's ear. "Well, this takes the bloody biscuit. I should have known I couldn't trust you."

"Well, if you answered your phone from time to time, it might not have been necessary," she hissed.

They approached the table and Macmillan did the introductions. "Hector, this is a friend of Willie's. Name's Mel. She's a nurse. He's asked her to join us."

McLeod half-rose and shook Rees's hand.

"Any friend of Willie's..."

"What a lovely Scottish name...Hector. It's so romantic," she flirted.

"Aye, it's Scottish but it's also Greek, French but mostly Spanish. Common as muck..."

"Well, I think it's lovely."

Macmillan groaned silently at Rees's coquettish behaviour.

As the evening's banter continued, McRae returned with more drinks and Rees rose to assist by taking them from the tray.

"Jesus, she's trim. Very pretty," whispered McLeod in Macmillan's ear, nodding in Rees's direction.

McLeod thought quickly in an attempt to maintain distance between Rees and the task at hand.

"I saw her first."

"But I'm better looking. It's no contest."

"Someone as gorgeous as that probably has several suitors."

"Suitors?...Were you brought up in a Victorian household?"

"Well, boyfriends...admirers."

"Only one way to find out, eh?"

Over the subsequent two hour period during which there was a lot of laughter, McRae and McLeod drank copiously while Rees and Macmillan were slightly more circumspect.

Climbing the five stairs to the pub gallery where the group was seated, publican John Waterson approached the table and started collecting empty glasses. "Oh, Willie, I forgot...a fellah came in earlier and asked me to pass this note to you next time you were in." He fished in his pocket and handed an envelope to McRae.

"Thank you, mine host," responded McRae. He continued talking while opening the envelope disinterestedly. Waterson left the table clutching several empty glasses. McRae read the note and nudged McLeod lightly in his ribs, proffering the note. "Wonderful penmanship...sadly a skill no longer taught the younger generation! Here."

McLeod unfolded the note and read it. Its content was brief. 'YOU ARE NOT SAFE'!

It was signed, '*Alba*'.

McRae asked Rees and Macmillan if he might seek their indulgence so as to have a quiet word with McLeod outside, their consent subsequently permitting each of them to whisper furiously at the other regarding their behaviour. Had McRae and McLeod overheard their initial exchange they would have heard McMillan growl, "A *nurse*? You told him you were a bloody *nurse*?"

*

McRae and McLeod stood on a sloped Hope Street outside the pub and lit their cigarettes. Sporadic large rain drops fell on the pavement as they smoked, hinting at a downpour. They stepped back against the wall of the pub to shelter themselves.

McLeod spoke first, his face only inches from McRae's. "Whoever the hell this *Alba* is, he's only saying what I've been telling you!"

"Ach, I'm flattered, Hector. All these people running about trying to damage my belongings, reading my mail, looking to frighten me off...it just means I'm worrying them. Maybe we've got them on the run!"

"Aye, or else they have more dastardly plans for you, Willie. We need to offer you more protection. I've said it before but you just shrug it off! You canny keep throwing double sixes! Remember, last year they killed Hilda Murrell, a sweet old lady who just wanted to grow roses behind her cottage in Shropshire but who got too troublesome over the case she was making about the management of nuclear waste...just like someone else I know!"

McRae spoke conspiratorially. "Well, maybe if I get out of town for a while, Hector. I've decided I'm going up north to my wee place in Dornie tomorrow. It's the Easter holiday weekend and I need time to think and to write. I mentioned that I've a file on alleged paedophiles at the highest reaches of government. 'The Untouchables' they're called, apparently! Worryingly, it's alleged that some of them are in the intelligence services. It's extremely concerning – not just because these pederasts prey on young, innocent children...and that turns my *stomach* as well as firing my wrath...but importantly, it means that if their sexual deviance is known to those in power, they can be blackmailed and controlled by those in Government or in the security services to whatever ends they require of them. I need to work out in my own mind how best to deal with this and to establish to my satisfaction that I'll not be slinging mud where none is merited."

"Christ, Willie, that's dynamite. No wonder we're getting notes saying you're unsafe."

"Aye, Hector. But in my estimation, if I can make it stand up in the court of public opinion, it'll bring the government down!"

"More power to your elbow, Willie!"

"Well, there's more. We now have information via Miss Brown that there's a report out...this McCrone Report commissioned by the Heath Government that states that Scotland's been robbed of its oil and they've deceived the Scottish public over the amounts of oil and gas that lie under the North Sea. It's been labelled Top Secret so getting access to it won't be easy. I've all the Dounreay files about dumping nuclear waste to make sense of and

there are a number of concerns being raised regarding the decon-
tamination of Gruinard Island, where the MOD tested their
wartime anthrax bombs."

McLeod interjected enthusiastically. "And remember, you
have some evidence that drugs traffickers are using remote corners
of the west coast to bring their contraband ashore and that our
Royal Navy are doing hee-haw to stop them due to under-
resourcing and government cut-backs..."

McRae pursed his lips. "Aye, so. And God alone knows how
they get away with that. There's government men everywhere
and behind each of them is a spook of one kind or another. The
whole of that part of Scotland is swarming with Soviet, American
and British spies. There's even rumours that the wee post office
at Arrochar stocks daily editions of *Pravda* and the *New York
Times*!"

McLeod drew heavily on his cigarette and added to McRae's
listings. "Aye, and you've also got the submarine bases at Faslane,
Coulport and Rosyth. There's the NATO munitions store at Glen
Douglas and the armament depot at Beith. There's the Z-Berth
at Loch Ewe and over at Applecross is where they monitor their
submarines' acoustic signatures. All of us would be better off if
these places were all consigned to the dustbin of history but we
have to face facts, Scotland has more secret agents drinking in
pubs all over the west coast than Bratislava had at the height of
the Cold War...and all of that suggests that this 'Alba' whoever
they are knows something about you that we don't. You *have* to
be careful, Willie."

"Well, I've a lot to ponder but we have information that's
dynamite, Hector. This could be a huge break for nationalism. It
could make our dream reality. Independence for Scotland...
because the Scottish public will be outraged at the behaviour of
the Westminster Establishment if I play my cards right." He took a
long drag on his cigarette and coughed heartily before recovering.
"But tonight I intend to relax with you and our new friends."

"And speaking of spooks and spies, we're comfortable that
our two new friends in there are who they say they are? That
they're not inflitrationists?"

"Och, Hector. You see plots in every conversation; suspicion in every coincidence. You mark my words, young Melissa in there is no *agent provocatrice*. She's little other than a very fetching young lady." He dismissed McLeod's concerns with a wave of his hand and changed the subject. "Tomorrow I need to pop into work in the morning for a meeting and few other things but I'll leave at lunchtime and drive to my cottage in Dornie. I'll be safe there."

"Then let me come with you, Willie. I'll watch your back."

"Ach, away and don't be daft, Hector. I'm a big boy and I need the time on my own to work through all of these issues. Besides, on the strength of this evening's performance, it looks like you might prefer to spend some time with the fragrant Melissa in there and if you came up north it'd just turn into a drinking session."

McLeod ignored the comment about Rees, "Aye, like you won't let a drop pass your lips all weekend."

McRae smiled, dropped the stub of his Gold Flake cigarette to the pavement and ground it underfoot. "Look, let's go back in. I've an Islay Mist calling my name! But before we do, let me give you the broad picture of what I have on paedophilac practices at the very heart of our government and within the intelligence services." He opened his palm and used his fingers to count off the political heavyweights named in his files.

*

Macmillan and Rees had by now resorted to speaking to each other through clenched teeth but were wreathed in artificial smiles as Mcleod returned, McRae stopping at the bar to order another round.

"Everything okay?' asked Macmillan.

"Absolutely," responded McLeod, still preoccupied by McRae's words outside. "Willie's just getting in another round,"

"Jesus, Hector, I must be approaching my limit," said Macmillan. "I'll soon start talking complete keech!"

Unused to Glaswegian terminology for faeces, Rees nevertheless interpreted it accurately, bit her lip and her rejoinder remained unsaid. Instead she offered, "I'll need to be getting back to the Central Hotel as well. My head's swimming."

"You're a bit too late with your protests, grinned McLeod. Willie's already got the tray loaded up. Anyway, the Central Hotel's just down the hill. Three minutes away. I'll walk you down after this and make sure you're home safely if you like. It's still early." He consulted his watch. "It's just gone eight-thirty."

"How gallant of you", simpered Rees, oblivious to the unspoken protest of Macmillan.

A further forty minutes were spent in pub banter following which moves were made to head for homes. As the rain ebbed, all four stood outside chatting while McRae waited for a taxi. Upon its arrival, McLeod and Rees waved farewell and began the short journey down Hope Street to her hotel. Macmillan considered intervening in whatever plans Rees and McLeod had in mind but thought better of it on the basis that neither would appreciate his interference and he would look jealous or childish. At *least,* he told himself *that'll be how it'd play out the next time me and Rees have a confrontation.*

* * *

McRae stepped unsteadily from the taxi and paid his fare leaving a tip more extravagant than would have been the case four whiskies earlier. Lifting his hefty briefcase, he climbed the nine stairs from the pavement to the entrance door of his Balvicar Drive apartment, opened it and slowly walked up the internal staircase to his top floor apartment, mumbling drunkenly to himself all the while.

After entering and steadying himself at the door of his bedroom, he left his briefcase in the hallway and went through to his kitchen where he poured himself a further whisky, another Islay Mist, this measure perhaps four times that served earlier in the Pot Still...this measure devoured in a single gulp.

To bed, laboriously. No attempt was made to remove other than his jacket and tie. Before sleeping, he felt for his jacket pocket lying on the chair next to his bed and found his pack of Gold Leaf cigarettes from which he withdrew a single one. He lit it from a bedside lighter and slumped back on his pillow singing softly and sleepily. *"Campbeltown Loch, I wish you were whisky; Campbeltown Loch, och aye...Campbeltown Loch.....I wish you were whisky........I would drink you dry."* He dragged on his cigarette and his head lolled back in sleep. His cigarette arm lolled to the side of the bed.

*

Only a few minutes had passed when McRae was awakened by infant flames that licked at his dangled wrist. His bed linen had caught alight. Suddenly sobered, he yelped in pain and in shock. "Jesus!"

He struggled to rise from the bed, his limbs refusing to obey his instructions quite as commanded. With as much alacrity as could be mustered, he extinguished the small flames that had begun to take hold on his shirt before much skin damage had been caused. The blankets, however, were another matter and flames began to mature on the bedding. Still befuddled with drink, McRae tore at the bedcover and pulled at the sheets now ablaze and hauled them through to the adjacent bathroom where he dumped them hurriedly into his bath, newly installed only a month earlier.

McRae's bathroom furniture was white; fashionable according to the salesman but made of acrylic plastic, a tough, highly malleable material with excellent resistance to wear and tear. These properties make it ideal for many applications including McRae's bath. Unfortunately, acrylic is flammable and as it burns, releases carbon dioxide, carbon monoxide and formaldehyde, all of which made its presence known in the McRae bathroom.

Coughing fitfully while turning on the water taps to douse the flames, McRae was horrified to notice that the acrylic inset bath was now set ablaze and thick acrid smoke bellowed towards the ceiling. Confused and alarmed, he staggered through to his lounge where he picked up his phone and dialled 999.

* * *

McLeod and Rees had decided to have a coffee in the Central Hotel's lobby rather than another drink. Each flirted with the other until McLeod placed his cup in its saucer.

"D'you mind if I make a call on one of the lobby phones, Mel? I just want to make sure that Willie got home safely. He had a bellyful of whisky tonight."

"He did that...no...please, make your call."

McLeod entered one of the cluster of pay phone booths in the reception area and was surprised when an unrecognised voice answered. "Mr. McRae's phone!"

McLeod gathered himself. "Who's this?"

Strathclyde Fire Service, sir. Who's calling?"

"My name's McLeod. I'm a friend of Willie's. Is everything okay?"

"There's been a fire in his apartment, sir. He's okay and the apartment's not damaged too bad but if you're in the neighbour-hood, I think he could be doing with an arm round his shoulder tonight. He's had a few drinks by the look of him."

"I'll be there in ten minutes."

McLeod walked briskly back to Rees and explained the situation.

"I need to go, Mel. I need to make sure he's okay."

Rees stood. "And I'll come too. I'm a nurse, remember. I might be of some use."

McLeod considered the offer only briefly. "Makes sense. Let's go."

Rees signalled to a passing waiter. "Medical emergency. Must go. Room 215. I'll sign for the coffees when I get back."

They crossed the road to the taxi rank in Gordon Street finding perhaps ten couples in the queue before them. McLeod headed straight for the couple at the head of the queue who were preparing to board the taxi that had just rolled forward. He thrust a ten pound note into the hand of the young man.

"This is an emergency, my friend. This'll take you both home free. Sorry we have to jump the queue."

*

Arriving at Balvicar Drive, the taxi slowed and bumped its way gingerly over the hoses that crossed the street from the two fire tenders that had parked, engines still running noisily outside number six. McLeod and Rees exited, paid the driver and turned to see McRae seated on the stoop of the neighbouring property. A grey blanket hung around his shoulders and, as ever, a Gold Flake cigarette was lodged between fore and middle finger. He recognised his two friends and waved an acknowledgement beneath the blanket, hardly rippling it so weak was his gesture.

"Jesus, Willie, what happened?"

"How did you know...?"

"I phoned to check you were home safe. Fireman answered."

Rees interrupted. "Are you injured, Willie?"

"A wee bitty burned on my wrist. It's nothing."

"Let me see."

McLeod took over again as Rees began to ease McRae's arm from beneath the blanket."

"Is this these bastards at their dirty work again, Willie?"

McRae shook his head wearily. "No...not at all. Not this time." He raised his right arm and dragged on his cigarette. "I'm a fool to myself, Hector. I smoked in bed. I'm a sixty-one year old man of some accomplishments, a respected solicitor and I can't undertake the simple task of falling asleep without setting the bloody house ablaze."

"If this is your only injury, it's nothing, Willie. Some salve cream and you're as good as new. No other injuries?"

"Only to my dignity, Mel. I'm an eegit!"

McLeod remained preoccupied by the prospect of the involvement of the security services. "Where's your briefcase, Willie?"

McRae tapped a bulk beneath the blanket on his right side. "Safe and sound, Hector. Safe and sound."

After a further ten minutes on the stoop, a fire officer approached the threesome and informed them that it was now safe to re-enter. "There's not too much damage bar the smoke, sir although your plastic bath melted and looks kinda like a modern art exhibit now."

Another half hour was spent seeing McRae settled and abed. He continued to insist that he would head for his cottage in the west Highlands the following day.

"Then I'll come round here tomorrow and make sure everything's tidied up for when you get back, Willie."

They bid him goodnight and left, McLeod accepting Rees's offer to come along and help him tidy up the next day.

* * *

London, England

The living room was comfortable, if dowdy. A television in the corner showed a black and white BBC2 repeat of 'To Kill a Mockingbird' starring Gregory Peck. Beneath the apartment outside, revellers were leaving the Duke's Head pub in Highgate High Street in high spirits and in small knots of twos and threes.

Two glasses of red wine having been consumed, Rosemary Roberts reached into her purse and retrieved a small slip of folded paper on which was written a series of eleven numbers. If they were increased by a factor of one and punched into a telephone keyboard in reverse, they'd connect her to an old friend.

She stood and reached for a jacket that she'd earlier placed over the back of an adjacent chair and put it on. Stepping over to the box television, she increased the volume slightly hoping to persuade any passing felon that the house was occupied, and left. She made her way slowly downstairs and out on to the street where she walked the short distance to an unoccupied phone box. Stepping inside she entered coinage and consulted the row of numbers on the piece of paper she held in her left hand. Cupping the phone under her chin, she added a factor of one to each number and started to dial them reading from right to left. The phone rang three times and a voice answered.

"Hello."

"*Alba*, it's me."

"Any problems?"

"I travelled north as planned. I met with Mr. McRae and provided him with the information. I told him everything."

"Go well?"

"I met with both him and a friend of his. They were both charming and accommodating...but I was forced...well, I *chose* to reveal my identity."

"That wasn't part of the plan."

"I think I'm safe. He seems a man of integrity."

"I'm grateful. You did the right thing."

"This remains entirely between us?"

"You know it will. And I repeat, I'm grateful."

Roberts searched for words to end the conversation, unsure whether to suggest a future meeting. "I'll go now." She placed the telephone on the receiver and returned to her flat and to Gregory Peck.

Chapter Fourteen

FRIDAY 5TH APRIL 1985

Glenmallan, Loch Long, Scotland

Hancock watched from his cottage window as a police car drove leisurely along the loch road at the bottom of his path. *That's the third this morning,* he thought. Pondering further their appearance in a rural part of Scotland not usually blessed by a police presence, he exited his cottage, walked round the side of his abode and stepped carefully round to a small outhouse where he collected his toolbox and a small bucket of galvanised roofing tacks. He retraced his steps and walked down to the main road at the loch-side.

Half an hour passed during which only a dozen cars passed, none of them police vehicles. Shortly thereafter, a mile along the glen, a white car appeared which aroused Hancock's suspicions. As it closed he spotted the livery and rooftop light-bar and satisfied himself that it was a police car. It disappeared behind some pine trees and he stepped forward, upending the bucket, spilling the nails on the road. As the car drew nearer, he stepped out and began to wave at the vehicle indicating it should stop.

It pulled up some twenty yards from him and a uniformed police officer stepped out from the driver's side putting his hat on as he did so, fumbling its placement on his head and appearing momentarily as if a tipsy bus conductor. The passenger's door opened and Carnegie emerged, still in plain clothes. Together they walked towards Hancock.

"Morning sir. Problems?"

"Sorry, officer. I'm fixing the wooden stakes on my fence here and I dropped all these tacks on the road. I was worried that you'd puncture your tyre."

Constable Carruth looked at the road surface. "Aye, they might have caused a bit of damage, right enough. Hold on."

He returned to the vehicle and turned on the car's blue flashing roof lights, reversed to the side then drove forward to the right, blocking the road.

"Live here, sir?" asked Carnegie, still standing with Hancock, awaiting Carruth's return.

"For the past twenty years."

"Seen anything suspicious recently?"

Like what, officer?"

"People or cars you didn't recognise..."

Hancock stroked his chin and attempted to look thoughtful. "Nah...everyone knows everyone else round here."

Moving to the boot of the car, Carruth took out a portable 'Police Stop' sign and walked past Hancock and Carnegie some forty yards before setting it up in the middle of the road. He returned to Hancock.

"Right sir, let me help you gather these up and we'll be out of your hair." Both men stooped and began collecting the sharp, stubby tacks. Carnegie shook his head at such a menial task and made no attempt to assist.

Hancock offered conversation whilst on all fours. "You're the fourth police car I've seen this morning, officer. Has there been an accident?"

"Not that I'm aware of sir, we're just doing some spot checks on the roads around the loch. Just checking cars."

"Not an axe murderer on the loose?" he teased.

Jim Carruth smiled. "Just routine, sir."

"I'm more used to seeing you check cars down in Helensburgh or Dunoon where there's more traffic, that's all."

"Well, you pay your taxes same as them, sir."

They picked up the remainder of the tacks. Carruth threw a final handful into Hancock's bucket.

"There you go, sir."

"*Gracias, merci beaucoup, danke schön, grazie mille*...All different languages but there's only one translation. Thank you, very much."

Carruth looked at him strangely and nodded. "*Je vous en prie, mon ami!* You are welcome, my friend."

Carnegie looked at them both as if they'd each grown a second head. He addressed Hancock.

"Remember to let us know if you see anything out of the ordinary, sir?"

"That I will, officer.

Carruth collected the road sign, placed it in the boot of the police car and waving amiably, drove past Hancock's equally affable farewell. Carnegie ignored both gestures.

Hancock watched the car as it drove onwards towards Arrochar along the loch-side.

Now why would they be out here checking vehicles? Four police cars? I'd better be careful. He walked back up his path, returned the tools and tacks to his outhouse and re-entered his house.

* * *

Glasgow, Scotland.

Macmillan's phone rang just as he'd risen, thrown two paracetamol in his mouth and was washing them down with a glass of milk. Anticipating his caller, he lifted the phone. "Hope you're not phoning from a stranger's boudoir at this early hour in the morning!"

"Fuck off, McMillan. What I do in my down time is my own business!"

McMillan exploded. "*Down time?* In this kind of job there's no such thing! You're doing it again. It's Belfast all over again.

Getting involved where you've explicitly....*explicitly* been told to perform only a support role. I turn up in fulfilment of my duties only to find you simpering away at my main target and making eyes all night at his fucking right-hand man!"

"I wasn't *simpering*!"

"Well, you shouldn't even have *been* there. You may have compromised the entire project!"

"Or I might have stumbled across crucial information that might have taken you months to find out!"

"Well, it better be worth it because I'm this far"...unseen by Rees he positioned his left thumb and forefinger an inch apart..."*this* far from reporting your delinquency and asking for someone else who'll do as they're bloody well *asked*!"

"Calm down for God's sake, Jock," said Rees attempting a measure of conciliation. "I need to meet you this morning. I've arranged to meet Hector over at Willie McRae's house at two o'clock tomorrow afternoon. Willie set it ablaze last night, suffered minor injuries and Hector and I attended to support him."

"*What*...and you didn't think to contact me immediately? I've to wait until I read it in the papers or something?"

"We were all pissed last night. Everything's sorted but I need you and your taxi to take us both to Willie's for two. How about we meet outside the Central Hotel at one-thirty. I'll explain on the way."

Macmillan's interest was now intrigued. His temper ebbed. "No. Not there, there's a rank in Gordon Street and if it seems that I'm jumping the queue there might be a complaint made by peeved taxi drivers. I'll pick you up in Jamaica Street. Outside the side station entrance."

* * *

McRae, as was the case most mornings, appeared seemingly unaffected by the surfeit of alcohol he'd consumed only hours earlier. He'd arrived at his office precisely at the time he'd stated, made his calls, kept his nine-thirty appointment and had enjoyed three cups of strong coffee. Any innocent observer would have presumed that strong drink hadn't featured in his consumptions in some days. His secretary, Ann Mahon had served him in that capacity since he'd established the firm of Levy & McRae in 1949 and had only seen him under the influence at Christmas parties and other office occasions where drunkenness was permissible.

McRae read the morning copy of the Glasgow Herald at his desk whilst sipping at his fourth coffee of the day. "Dear me," he said to no one in particular, "another car bomb in Newry kills two." He shook his head in dismay and scanned further down the front page. "Huh, our beloved Secretary of State for Employment, Mr. Tom King celebrates a downward trend in unemployment while in Scotland, seventy-five youngsters chase every job vacancy. Dear God, four hundred and fifty men to be laid off at Yarrows shipyard? Independence can't come soon enough." He folded the newspaper without opening it and called out to his secretary.

"Ann, have you the file on Mr Graham? I'd like to make some notes and I want to write to a Mister William Hill with whom he's in dispute."

His secretary came through with a buff folder. McRae withdrew a letter and scribbled notes in its margins before picking up a dictation device and composing a further flowery confection in support of his client.

"Right, Ann. You can type that up. I'll sign it before I leave this afternoon. Have we ink and paper in that photocopier? I've got a few things I want to copy before I leave."

"Away to your wee but and ben in Dornie this weekend, Willie?" McRae's business partner, lawyer Ronnie Welsh had his head round the door.

"Aye, I am that, Ronnie. It'll be wonderful smelling the heather and the pine, watching the sea foam and listening to the streams burble. I've a briefcase full of reading and a load of work to do for the Party. It'll be a memorable couple of days work and with any luck we might even be able to describe it as transformational...that's the word, *transformational*."

"And is this a celebratory weekend? Will Islay Mist make an appearance?"

"Well, as well you know, Ronnie, that particular tincture is never that far from my elbow. But no, this weekend is a working weekend. The Islay Mist serves merely to assist my powers of reasoning in that I'm prone to be *un*reasonable if denied my potation." He laughed as he continued to sort the papers he sought to photocopy.

"Well, I'll hold the fort for you, Willie. But I've a client coming in about now so I'll see you on Tuesday after the holiday weekend."

"Tuesday it is, Ronnie. Have a good one!"

McRae gathered a sheaf of papers and stood for some twenty minutes passing them through the photocopier while organising them into four separate bundles which he then placed within large A3 envelopes. His secretary, Ann knew better than to interfere with political business but hovered nearby lest her assistance might be of use. McRae didn't even acknowledge her so focused was he on his task. *Better safe than sorry. Just in case the originals go missing one night. You never know with this mob!*

Roused from his thoughts, he raised his voice above the hum and throb of the photocopier and called Ann to his side. "Can you get me my cousin, Cathy McRae's number? I want to give her a call before I head up to Dornie."

"Would you like me to get her on the phone?"

McRae shook his head. "That would be impolite. I'll call her personally."

Moments later, having reassembled his original documents, he returned to his desk and called his cousin in Dornie using what little Scots Gaelic he had.

"*Madainn mhath Morag. Ciamar a tha thu?* Good morning, Cathy. How are you? It's Willie here. How's your arthritis?"

"Willie! *Tha gu math, tapadh leibh.* I'm well thank you...and my arthritis will be the end of me. I can hardly walk to the road end now."

"Well, you're the one who's refused to administer my medicine all your days."

"Your medicine comes at forty per cent proof, Willie McRae. It's the devil's potion."

"I can't argue with you Cathy...but here, would you ever do me a wee favour?"

"Anything, Willie. Are you coming up to Dornie?"

"I am, Cathy. I'm leaving this afternoon and wondered if you'd be good enough to put the fire on for me so I don't come into a cold house. I'd hope to leave this afternoon and I'm in no rush so I'd expect to arrive in the early evening. It'll be light until the back of eight tonight."

"Well, you drive careful in that big Volvo of yours and I'll get the fire lit for you. Mind and look in tomorrow sometime for a cup of tea."

"I'll do exactly that, Cathy. See you then. *Beannachd leat.* 'Bye."

* * *

Glenmallan, Loch Long, Scotland

Blinking the sweat from his eyes and grunting at his exertions, Hancock lay underneath his van and wrestled the final self-tapping screw into the lower edge of the sill that formed the base of the driver's door. He laid the screwdriver on the ground and shook the sill to ensure its solidity. Satisfied, he unscrewed the entire piece and reached behind himself to feel for his .308 Winchester sniper's rifle. His fingers found the scope, allowing him to manoeuvre the rifle and drag it to his side where he raised it and placed it in the space created within the hollowed-out car sill of the Ford Fiesta van. Placing the lower half of the sill in place, he screwed it back in place and tugged at it one more time to ensure that it would pass any rudimentary inspection undertaken by police should he come across them on his route north. Finally, he took some road dust and applied it to the brightly polished screw heads, dulling them.

He looked at his watch. *Half eleven? Time flies. I'd better get going.*

* * *

Glasgow, Scotland.

He called it 'tidying up his desk' but McRae merely shuffled paper around so that some small surface of his desk was visible midst the disorder. He checked his four pieces of luggage; a briefcase containing some work matters in case he found time to deal with them, the bulging briefcase containing his confidential files, a small black attaché case containing a change of clothing and toiletries and a cream and tan shopping bag containing the Scots Magazine and other reading matter. He checked his suit pocket... *money, wallet, hanky, keys*...and ventured through to his front office.

"That's me off, Ann. I'm just going to dump this stuff in the car and visit Agnew's for some cigarettes and whisky to tide me over. I'll be back on Tuesday. You have a nice weekend, now. Stay away from young men in those discos. It's not the Joe Loss Orchestra these days!"

His secretary, a widow-woman of mature years, looked at him over her horn-rimmed spectacles and smiled at his gentle bonhomie.

"Chance would be a fine thing!"

*

McRae walked along to his maroon-coloured Volvo parked in West Nile Street and unlocked it, placing all but his bulging briefcase on its rear seat. Carrying his leather satchel, he locked the door and walked the short distance to Agnew's off-licence where he bought Benson and Hedges cigarettes in the absence of his favourite brand and two bottles of Glenmorangie. Eschewing the need for a carrier-bag, he walked back to his car to find it being inspected by Constable Donald Morrison, the local beat police officer. They knew one another well.

"Willie, I *thought* this was your car." He noticed McRae struggling with his briefcase and whisky bottles as he tried to retrieve the car keys from his trouser pocket. "Here, let me help you with that." He took the bottles. "I'll no' breathalyse you Willie seeing as how the bottles are still sealed!"

They both laughed as Morrison held the bottles while McRae organised his entry to the car.

"I've got them this time, Donald". McRae patted his brief-case. "I've got the buggers this time...The Government...I've got them."

"Have you now, Willie?" said Morrison, completely oblivious to McRae's meaning. "That's good!"

McRae slowly leaned his heavy frame into the driver's seat taking the whisky bottles from Morrison and placing them in the passenger's seat. He wound down the window as he closed the door. "I'm off for a wee break up in my wee *clachan* in Wester Ross."

"Heading north?" asked Morrison. "Here, just do a U-turn in West Nile Street. It'll save you going round the one-way system. I'll hold up the traffic."

McRae's Volvo was facing into oncoming traffic but Constable Morrison stopped both flows and allowed McRae to manoeuvre his Volvo in one motion up the hill towards the roads that would take him north and out of the city. McRae offered a smiling thumbs-up in recognition of the favour.

As Morrison stood in the middle of the road, arms extended to halt traffic, he noticed two suited men running and splitting, entering two cars; one a silver coloured Triumph Acclaim and one a Austin Riley coloured black and with distinctive white-walled tyres. Almost before the doors were shut, both cars performed a U-turn as had McRae and accelerated away, wheels spinning, each running a red light. *Eegits!* Then more reflectively, anyone *would assume that these people were trying to keep up with Willie.* Morrison lowered his hands and permitted the free flow of traffic. He walked to the pavement and pulled his left hand across his bristled jaw in contemplation. *That was two guys I noticed earlier watching Willie coming down the street to his car.* He dismissed the notion. *Ach, probably nothing!*

* * *

The entrance door of McRae's flat at street level was ajar allowing Macmillan and Rees to enter and make their way up the staircase at the top of which McLeod was busy trying to haul the remnants of the plastic bath into the hallway. Assisting him in this were his pals Tommy Docherty and Tam O'Neill.

Rees shouted a greeting as they approached the top of the stairs bringing McLeod to the stair-head banister.

"Oh, hi, Mel." He noticed Macmillan behind her. "Hi, Jock. Didn't know you were coming along."

Macmillan waved a smiled greeting, patting his chest intimating a pretend breathlessness. "Mel thought a taxi might come in handy to get rid of some of the things damaged by the fire."

"Good idea, Jock." He beckoned O'Neill and Docherty to join him. "Guys, this is Mel and Jock. Two friends of mine and Willie's"

A flurry of *pleasedtaemeetchas* followed and after some direction from Mcleod, they began to remove some of the smaller items to Macmillan's taxi as a prelude to a visit to Polmadie Refuse Works a mile distant. Rees took to cleaning soot-covered surfaces before advising McLeod that a painter would be required to be hired to return the bathroom to its original condition. A further hour saw the place liveable as long as a quick wash at the kitchen sink could substitute for a bath. Macmillan returned from a second trip to nearby Polmadie Refuse Works and climbed the stairs. McLeod spoke to the foursome.

"Many thanks to everyone. Willie would be the first to suggest that we need a drink after this. Unfortunately I've arranged to visit my mother this afternoon and I won't get back until late tomorrow." He picked up his jacket. "We'll catch up later. I've a train to catch. Thanks again, everyone."

As the group began their exit, he turned to Rees and took her arm, easing her apart from the other three, "Hey, listen...I was sorry our coffee ended so abruptly last night. I enjoyed your company and was wondering if you had any free time before you headed back to Wales."

Rees smiled widely. "I was going to suggest that we meet up for a few drinks but you have your mother to..."

"Well...she's getting on a bit. I like to keep in touch but she's in a care home up in Stirling. If the boys thought I'd be free tomorrow night, I'd be press-ganged into throwing drink at my face in their company in the Auld Smiddy."

Rees fingered his jacket collar affectionately. "Perhaps if you're back tomorrow evening we could have a few drinks and you could join me back in the hotel for that coffee we had to abandon last night."

"If you'd prefer, I have an international reputation as a skilled and inventive chef!"

"Really?"

McLeod grinned. "Nah, but I'd be delighted if you wanted to join me in my home for dinner. I could only promise that it probably won't be burned entirely beyond recognition."

"That would be lovely. Where do you live?"

McLeod fished in his pocket. "Here's one I made earlier." He handed her a business card advertising his accountancy services which he provided from his home office.

"Thirty-seven Courthill Avenue. Where's that?"

"I work from home. Round the corner from the Auld Smiddy."

"I'll ask Jock if he'll drive me over if he's working."

McLeod demurred. "Hmmm, not sure about that. He might be my rival for your affections."

"Jock? I'm sure he wouldn't give me the time of day!"

"Well, that's not what he was saying in the Pot Still the other night and I don't want him to spirit you off *en route* to my house."

Rees took a moment to attempt an understanding of McLeod's comment. "Eh...well I'll get there one way or another. Tomorrow night? Eight o'clock?"

"Can't wait!"

*

As the group stood on the pavement talking, McRae's Volvo eased round the corner and parked in a usefully free bay opposite his house. McRae levered himself from the driver's seat and hailed them.

"Hello there boys, *Alba gu bràth!* Thanks for your help with the house."

"Forget something, Willie? asked O'Neill.

"A wee detour. Just collecting some files I forgot, boys. I'll be away north to my cottage in jig-time."

McLeod and Rees approached.

"How's the arm, Willie?" asked Rees.

"Ah, dearest Melissa. My arm is just fine. I've been driving without impairment all morning."

"Need any help?"

"I'm fine, Hector. You two go on about your business and we'll meet for a glass when I get back down."

Some banter with the group followed and McRae went upstairs carrying only the leather briefcase which wasn't to be left unattended in the car under any circumstances. The rest of his baggage he left in the boot of the car.

*

Returning to the taxi, Macmillan, with Rees in the rear seat, drove off and waved farewell as they passed the other three standing on the pavement outside number six.

Macmillan's earlier frustration with Rees had eased. "I had a look round Willie's house. Nothing untoward. Tidier than I'd have anticipated for a bachelor."

"Well, *you're* a bachelor. Do *you* live in a tip?"

Macmillan avoided the subject. "Still, a useful morning. I got to meet Docherty and O'Neill."

"*We* got to meet them...and I'm having dinner with McLeod tomorrow tonight. His place."

Macmillan erupted. "For the love of God, you're meant to be a *support* to me, not fucking take over the assignment. This is Belfast all over again. At the slightest opportunity you shoulder your way into an operational role...you don't listen to guidance and when we strike an agreement, the first thing you do is...."

Macmillan continued in an escalating monologue for a further mile until he found himself in Glasgow's Renfrew Street unsure exactly where he was. Rees allowed him to settle.

"Jock...I understand your frustration with me but let's face facts. McLeod is a key target of ours..."

"Of *mine!*"

"Of *yours*...and he's asked me to visit him in his house tomorrow evening. What responsible officer would reject such an opportunity...whether in a support or operational role? You should be pleased."

"I'm just not sure about the ethics of this."

"Ethics? Because I'm going to be in a potentially amorous situation with a target who also happens to be a good-looking hunk?"

"Exactly. It's a clear conflict of interest."

Rees measured her response, concealing her smile. "Hector *said* you'd be jealous! Didn't want me to ask you to taxi me over to his place. Said in the Pot Still you told him you fancied me the other night..."

Krakatoa couldn't have matched the explosive force of McLeod's response. A flurry of curse-words and invective mingled with loud denunciations and condemnations filled the taxi until Macmillan remembered he'd switched the recording facility to 'on'. Angrily he switched it off and withdrew the tape. "This is going in the fucking *bin!*"

Rees was in no mood to relent. Her mischief continued. "Look, Jock. It's perfectly okay for you to have feelings for a colleague...it's just that it's a clear conflict of interest...same as Hector!"

Macmillan recommenced his angry diatribe as Rees laughed uncontrollably in the rear seat.

"Jock...Jock...I'm teasing."

McLeod quietened, still simmering.

"Nothing will happen between Hector and me," she reassured him before taking a beat. "I'm saving myself for *you!*"

Krakatoa erupted once again; Rees clutching her sides laughing.

* * *

Walking back towards their nearby homes in the Cathcart area, McLeod, Docherty and O'Neill discussed the events of the previous evening and their role in the clear-up. O'Neill wasn't happy.

"So who're these new friends of Willie's? We don't fuckin' know them...they've just arrived on the scene and now they're in the inner circle? Ever since they arrived we've all been interviewed by Special Branch. Bit suspicious, eh?"

"Ach, don't be so paranoid, Tam. It's hardly surprising that we were interviewed because of the killing of those cops. They're chasing down everyone who's ever had a connection with the independence movement. Jock's a good guy. He was on the march with us. He was flung in jail with me and he's been a brilliant help from day one. He's one of us!"

O'Neill's gruff demeanour continued. "Well, I wouldn'y trust him to look after my pint while I went for a piss," before easing back on his curmudgeon pedal. "And who's the bit of stuff?"

McLeod allowed a grin to spread across his face knowing O'Neill's penchant for expressing his views in a challenging manner. "Bit of stuff?"

"Aye. I mean who the fuck *is* she? She turns up out of nowhere? I thought we were meant to be careful about who we consort with."

Docherty chimed in, laughing lasciviously. "Is that what you're trying to do, Hector, 'consort' with her?"

McLeod continued the banter. "Just you guys leave her alone. She's a young lady up from Wales on holiday. I'm just acting as a kind of tour guide. She wants to see the mountains of Scotland."

Docherty continued his teasing. "Aye, I'd bet you'd like to tour *her* twin peaks, eh, Hector." They all laughed although O'Neill remained surly at what he argued was his friend's indiscipline as they closed on the Auld Smiddy and the inevitable suggestion of a quick pint.

* * *

After a sustaining nap in compensation for his sleep deficit the previous night, McRae returned to his vehicle and noticed that his rear, near-side tyre was flat. He inspected it. Initially, annoyed at the delay this would cause, his mood became more anxious when he inspected the tyre and noticed that its wall had been slashed. Cursing quietly, he placed his briefcase on the road, removed the other luggage and pulled the spare tyre from its mountings under the floor of the boot. *Nothing for it! I'll just need to jack it up and change the tyre. Could've done without this! It means I'll be driving in the dark tonight instead of admiring beautiful scenery all the way up to Dornie.*

Removing his suit jacket, he set to.

Chapter Fifteen

SATURDAY 6TH APRIL 1985

Glasgow, Scotland

At eight o'clock in the evening, Rees entered the rear of Macmillan's taxi at the Central Hotel, sat back and crossed her legs.

"This'll be your way of being fashionably late, eh?"

"Treat 'em mean, keep 'em keen."

Macmillan turned in his seat to look at Rees's attire. "Christ, not exactly police mufti. If you paid by the square inch for that outfit, it must only have cost thirty bob!"

Rees laughed again. "Jock...it's a dinner date. I have to look the part!"

"Aye, well, I can confirm, Detective Sergeant Rees that you look the part. And if they're ever looking for plain-clothes officers to take part in an assignment involving high-class ladies of the night, I'll recommend you."

Rees groaned..."Once a Stornoway boy...*always* a Stornoway boy!"

Macmillan shook his head disapprovingly and drove towards Cathcart.

* * *

McLeod's home was well decorated, almost minimalist in decor, clean and tidy. The low tones of The Eagles offered a peaceful easy feeling as they sat in conversation after the meal. As promised, McLeod had managed to avoid burning the main course although the starter was somewhat underdone and the sweet course, purchased in a box from the local supermarket, hadn't fully been defrosted.

"That was lovely," lied Rees as she raised her glass of wine and clinked McLeod's. She looked round the apartment. "You have a lovely place here...and you work from home?"

McLeod rose from the table. "Let me show you round."

They walked together to the hallway where McLeod pointed out the rooms that it fed. A bicycle stood propped up against a wall.

"Two bedrooms?" asked Rees. "Not sub-letting?"

"No need. Business is good. I look after the accounts of a lot of voluntary organisations; Non-Governmental Organisations as some describe them. I prefer to support non-profit distributing entities which try to do some good rather than help the fat cats make even more money."

"How noble!"

"Aye well, don't mock. I try to live by my values."

Rees realised she'd jarred, cursed the fourth glass of *Merlot*, and attempted recovery. "No, I'm sincere. I think it's wonderful that you're not just another accountant chasing the mighty dollar."

McLeod smiled his acceptance and suggested they move back through to the living room where they sat together on his red fabric settee. Tentatively, he placed his wine glass on the nearby coffee table and took Rees's from her grasp, putting it next to his. He turned to face her.

"Enjoy the meal?"

"Your lovely red wine has dimmed my memory. I've had one too many, I suspect."

"Me too."

McLeod leaned into her and kissed her tentatively on the lips. She responded, placing her right hand tenderly on his face and holding the embrace. McLeod positioned his hand softly on her shoulder and continued his caress.

From the hallway, a phone rang startling both. Rees pulled back from McLeod.

"You'd better get it," she suggested.

"It can wait," responded McLeod, grinning.

"Might be your mother or Willie reporting in?"

McLeod pursed his lips and agreed the possibilities. He rose and walked to the hall where he lifted the phone. Rees listened to his end of the call.

"Doctor McRae...as I live and breathe...It's good to hear from you, Fergus." Seconds passed. "No!...Never!" he sputtered. More time elapsed. "This is awful. What's his condition?" A further silence. "Anything, Fergus. Anything. Please keep me informed."

Rees rose from the settee upon hearing the concerned tone in McLeod's voice. He returned to the room, his face ashen. "It's Willie. He's been in an accident. They've taken him to Raigmore Hospital in Inverness but he's in a coma..."

Rees's hand rose involuntarily to cover her mouth in shock. "Dear God...what happened?"

"That was Willie's brother, Fergus. He's a Doctor. He wanted to let me know...from what he says it sounds serious. Said a doctor who was travelling north with an SNP Councillor found him slumped behind the wheel of his Volvo. Apparently, the Councillor recognised Willie. He's still alive...his chest was moving and he was still breathing". He said that the doctor had found that one of Willie's pupils was dilated." He shook his head trying to comprehend. "You're a nurse, Mel. What does that signify?"

Rees's nursing career had briefly preceded her occupation in the police force. She hesitated before replying, hoping her memory hadn't let her down. "It can be a sign of traumatic brain injury, Hector. It could be very serious."

"God...how serious, Mel?"

"Don't know...a coma's a coma, I suppose. Are you going to visit him?"

McLeod shook his head. "Fergus asked me not to. Said he'd rather it was dealt with as a family matter." He sat down. "I think

152

that Fergus is worried that because it's Willie it'll become a bit of a media event..." He lifted his glass of wine and studied it as a thought came to him. "Jesus, I hope he wasn't drunk!"

Rees puffed out her cheeks and blew. "Shit, that would throw the cat among the pigeons!"

"He's had a couple of convictions for driving under the influence already and one's outstanding. They'd throw the book at him."

"They would, Hector. But it sounds like that's a minor consideration at present. He may not pull through!"

"*Jesus. Really?* Fergus says he was found down a pretty steep incline off the A87 on the banks of Loch Loyne. I've been up there before. It's the middle of nowhere." He suddenly realised the seriousness of Rees's prognosis. "You really think he might die?"

"I'm no doctor and they can work miracles these days but if it's a brain injury, it might eventually prove fatal or may lead to considerable impairment." She gathered herself. "Look, I'm happy to stay but I think it'd be better if I headed off."

McLeod nodded, only partially aware of Rees's comment. After a moment, comprehension kicked in. "Yeah, sure... I'll call you a taxi."

Rees hoped her next proposal wouldn't raise suspicions. "At this time of night it might take a while. Why not phone Jock. He told me he'd be looking for hires on the south side after dropping me off earlier. He'd be over here in jig-time and I know he'd be anxious to help."

McLeod grimaced, still only half-aware. "Makes sense."

*

McLeod walked Rees to the pavement and awaited Macmillan's arrival. The conversation was stilted as McLeod remained lost in the shattering news he'd heard only thirty minutes previously. The taxi could be heard before it arrived and it drew up sharply before them, Macmillan exiting wordlessly and placing his arm comfortingly around the shoulders of both.

Rees prepared to depart. "Thanks for a lovely evening, Hector." She kissed Mcleod lightly on his cheek. "You get back inside in case Willie's brother calls again. I'll fill Jock in on the way back to my hotel."

McLeod awakened from his reverie. "You'll call me tomorrow?"

"Of course I will."

Macmillan drove back towards Glasgow but pulled in to a cul-de-sac just off Pollokshaws Road and turned the engine off as Rees reported back on the evening's events. He listened thoughtfully.

"Willie might not make it, Jock. It sounds a serious injury."

Macmillan nodded his understanding. "You'd better get on the phone to London before they read it in the papers. Mo McGinnis in MI5 will want to be advised immediately."

"If he dies, d'you think they'll pull the operation on us?"

Macmillan shook his head. "We have two objectives. Infiltrate the group surrounding Willie and secure information that might threaten the security of the state. If we uncover circumstances that require us to protect ourselves or to act in order to protect the best interests of the state, then we have permission to take action. We've managed to achieve the first objective but if there's a controversy over Willie's accident or if there's an outpouring of nationalism, they'll want us to stay undercover and remain close to Hector and his boys."

Rees nodded her silent agreement. "So, what now?"

Macmillan turned on his engine. "We get some shut-eye. Tomorrow you get back in touch with Hector and keep close to events. He's obviously the man who's trusted by his brother so he'll be first to hear what's going on. Hector doesn't own a car so tell him that this taxi is at his disposal...no charge...whether it's to drive him to the pub or to Inverness. Tell him I'll do anything for the cause and that I've become very fond of Willie."

"And you?"

Macmillan began the process of turning the car to face the main road. "I'm going home, get some sleep, then I'm going to look through my underwear drawer."

"Eh?"

Chapter Sixteen

SUNDAY 7TH APRIL 1985

Glasgow, Scotland

Macmillan awoke from a listless sleep, showered and dressed. A banana and coffee met his breakfast needs. He washed his cup, dried it and placed it in a cupboard along with other crockery before returning to his bedroom and making his bed. He selected a clean shirt and pulled on a pair of chino trousers in an attempt to look presentable. Looking at his only footwear, his scuffed training shoes and casual attire, he cursed quietly and decided on a purchase of something more proper.

His ablution needs having been addressed, he turned to a chest of drawers containing his socks and underwear. Taking both handles of the drawer, he withdrew it and edged it slowly from its mounting. Carefully he took it to the bed where he upturned it, cascading the nether-garments onto the duvet. Sellotaped on the underside of the drawer was a small envelope. He peeled it from the wooden base and opened it. Inside was a Metropolitan Police Warrant Card. He fingered it and read its content. It showed a good photograph of him; easily identifying the bearer. Beneath his likeness was his name, beneath that his rank of Detective Inspector, showing his operational responsibilities as Special Branch. A minute passed as he gave thought to his next move. He held the card casually in front of the mirror taking care to partially cover his name. *Not bad. Only a pedant would want closer inspection.* Making his mind up, he folded the small wallet containing his warrant card and placed it in his front trouser pocket. A glance at the sky from the bedroom window suggested a quiet, dry morning. *Unlikely there'll be anything happening so early. I'll nip up to Byres Road and buy a suit and decent pair of shoes...maybe a tie.*

* * *

Hancock lay prone on a rise overlooking a rough footpath which led up the hill from Loch Eilt near the small village of Glenfinnan in Lochaber District, some miles south of Glen Affric. He peered through the sights of his .308 Winchester. *Fucking hippies!* He placed a bullet in the chamber of his rifle and aimed it at a rock some yards in front of a party of four back-packers who were making their way along the heather-clad track some fifty yards in front of him, heading east to west. Setting the crosshairs on the rock, an easy target from that range, Hancock eased his finger back on the trigger sending the rifle's projectile crashing into the rock face eliciting shocked cries from the four walkers.

Hancock rose before them holding his rifle and shouted. "There's military manoeuvres going on here. Live ammunition! Go back all of you or you'll get hurt. Didn't you see the signs?"

The four back-packers stood motionless and bewildered. One man in the lead answered. "We saw no signs!"

"If you proceed there's a good chance you'll be shot! It's live rounds that are being used today."

The foursome held a short conversation and the lead walker offered a conciliatory wave. "We'll go back. Sorry!" They turned and moved back towards the loch.

Hancock watched them go before lying back on the ground and facing the sky. He placed his hand over his eyes and squeezed. *Now why the fuck did I do that? There was no need, Jimmy boy. You're losing it! Now you've been spotted!*

Moments passed as Hancock thought through his options. Collecting his rifle and checking again on the disappearing four-some, he set off up the hill to an old bothy half a mile from his position. He rebuked himself again. *The worst that could have happened was that they'd take a break at the bothy. They'd never have stumbled across my hide.*

*

Some several minutes later he'd arrived at the bothy, a stone-walled, tin-roofed enclosure designed to give basic, emergency shelter to walkers caught in Scotland's winter snows. He circled the primitive structure and satisfied himself that no one was in the vicinity. Laying his rifle against one of its walls, he walked some twenty paces to a flat boulder just outside an area trodden down over the years by the small number of people who'd made use of the facility. Turning again to ensure that he wasn't being observed, he moved the large rock with some considerable effort revealing, when he did so, a locked metal box. From his pocket he took a key and opened it, removing a sack containing three pounds of Semtex. He shouldered his rucksack to the ground and opened it, placing the explosive inside. With further exertion he replaced the rock over the now empty box and disturbed the earth surrounding it with some heather to remove any evidence of recent footprints. Checking the vicinity once again for any onlookers, he set off back down the hill towards Glenfinnan.

* * *

Rees decided to leave matters until the afternoon before contacting McLeod. When she called the phone was answered before the second ring.

"Hi Hector…"

"Oh, it's you, Mel. I…I thought it might be news of Willie."

"Well, don't sound *too* disappointed," she responded, trying to raise the tone slightly. "How are you coping?"

"I've just been sitting next to the phone. I can't face the guys in the Auld Smiddy until I know what to tell them."

"I've not seen anything yet on the news."

"No...not yet...so maybe no news is good news."

"Let's hope so." She paused. Would you like me to come over...just to give you some company?"

McLeod permitted himself a mild chuckle. "That would be great, if you didn't mind. Might take my mind off things."

"Well, I'm just sitting here in my hotel room watching the news. I'll hop in a taxi and be there shortly."

"See you in a wee while."

*

Rees rang McLeod's doorbell and waited until she heard footsteps. She beamed her best smile at the approaching shadow viewable through the opaque, stained glass door-window. Her smile left her face as soon as she saw Mcleod. He'd obviously been crying. "Hector...wha..."

"He's *dead*, Mel. Willie's *dead*. He was *shot*! A bullet through the head. Fergus just phoned."

Rees stood back in surprise before embracing Mcleod. They stood at the door entry hugging for some time before Mcleod broke the silence. "You'd better come in."

Rees removed her jacket and sat next to Mcleod on the settee noticing an empty whisky glass on the table. She gestured towards it. "Thought you never touched the stuff?"

"Needs must, Mel. I'm pretty shaken up. Fergus says it was suicide."

"Suicide? Never!"

"Says that's what the police are telling him and he sees no reason to doubt them. He reckons that Willie was a depressive and an alcoholic and that he was pretty much bound to end up dead one way or another."

"Well, we *all* end up dead one way or another...but there was no way Willie McRae killed himself, Hector. We were with him before he went north. He was upbeat...he was fine."

McLeod nodded. "Apparently they took him to Raigmore hospital in Inverness where they took the view that his condition was sufficiently serious to require him to be taken to a hospital in Aberdeen. Fergus says that the blood on his head that everyone assumed was from a wound caused by the car crash obscured the entry point of the bullet. It was discovered by a nurse when they were cleaning him up for theatre."

Rees's cheeks reddened. "A man is shot in the head and they miss the wound for the best part of twenty-four hours. Jesus Christ!"

Tears rolled down McLeod's face as he poured himself another whisky. He held the bottle towards Rees, displaying its label. "Islay Mist. Willie's favourite. Just in case he ever came in looking for a wee glass. He won't be needing it now."

Rees held McLeod's free hand. "What do you want to do now, Hector?"

McLeod drained the glass in one gulp. "Fergus is still saying it's a family matter. Says he'll let me know when there's more information."

"Well, we'll be getting that from the television any time now, Hector. Senior SNP politician shot dead...whether by his own hand or by the assassin's bullet, it's front page news."

McLeod's voice cracked. "You don't understand, Mel. This is serious. He was *warned*...Willie was *warned*."

"How do you mean 'warned'?"

"He had his flat broken into several times. Nothing stolen. His house up in Dornie was broken into. Nothing stolen. His office was broken into. Nothing stolen. He was being followed by Special Branch...so was I...Christ we were almost on first name terms with them. And then...twice recently he was given a message saying he wasn't safe! *Twice!*"

"Who warned him?"

"Buggered if I know. Someone calling themselves *Alba*. But he was about to produce evidence that would bring down the Government. He had information...secret information that he said would have brought about Scottish independence..." He hesitated. "I've said too much already."

Rees remained calm. "If what you say is true, you might also be in danger."

"I don't have Willie's secrets, articulacy, influence. I'm a nobody. I'm a threat to no one."

"But if people *have* come after Willie, they'll know you're his closest confidant. They don't know if you have the same information that he had. You need to be very careful now, Hector. Maybe Willie's brother is right when he says it's better to leave this as a family matter. You could be in danger." She thought further. "Look, why not get away from this house until things settle. I'd bet that Jock would put you up. He told me he'd a spare room."

McLeod dismissed her various suggestions with a shake of his head, "Aye, well Fergus or no Fergus, I'm not leaving it like this. I'm going to get to the bottom of what happened. I mean, how could the police have decided it's a suicide when there's not even been a post mortem?"

"It'll just be loose talk, Hector. You're right. It'll take a wee while. Especially if the body's in Grampian Region. The post mortem'll have to take place in Highland region where the death occurred."

McLeod reached for the bottle again and allowed a silence. He paused before pouring another drink. "You seem to know a lot about police procedures!"

Rees stiffened. "No, it's post mortem procedures. At least that's the rules in Wales. It might be different up here."

McLeod held her gaze before looking away and splashed himself another whisky.

"S'pose."

Rees and McLeod talked together for a further hour during which the remnants of the bottle of Islay Mist were disposed of entirely by McLeod who was by now, quite drunk. He slurred his words.

"Look, Mel. I'm comp'ny for no one. You sh'd go. It'd be... It'd be better if I was on my own."

Rees had been looking for an opportunity to report to Macmillan and to London and agreed the proposition on the basis that she'd return in the evening and make sure he was okay.

"I suspect it's just the drink talking, Mel but I want y' to know that I 'ppreciate your friendship. You're lovely and wonderful and...Christ, I'm not too clever at talking to members of the opposite sex. I'm a man's man...'s why I've reached the grand old age of thirty-five as a bachelor. I'm shy with women. Anyway, it would be nice to see you later."

Rees smiled reassuringly. "Well, I think you're lovely too. I'll come over at eight and I'll bring a couple of pizzas. You've had enough drink to float a battleship. Sleep will come soon but you'll be fine by this evening if you lay off the hard stuff now."

" 'S all gone now, Mel. Only had one bottle in the house."

She kissed him on the cheek. "You lie down. I'll see myself out."

* * *

Macmillan folded down his shirt collar, straightened the tie he'd bought and considered his besuited image in the bathroom mirror when his doorbell rang. *Who's this,* he wondered?

The door entry system allowed him to quiz anyone who sought entry using an intercom. He pressed the button on his phone receiver. "Yes?"

"It's Mel. Let me in."

Another breach of protocol, Macmillan told himself. *She was told not to contact me here at the flat. Anyone could be watching!* He bit his tongue and pressed the buzzer allowing her entry, using the time it took her to reach his apartment to compose himself.

Rees entered and stepped back as she observed Macmillan's attire.

"Heavy date?"

Macmillan closed the door and realised the suit, tie and polished shoes he'd been trying out were somewhat in contradiction with the undercover garb he'd been wearing recently. He looked abashed. "You weren't supposed to see me like this just yet." He hesitated. "I'd an idea."

"It'd better be a good one because I've just come from Hector's and after a few serious whiskies he shared a bunch of stuff that kind of throws the cat among the pigeons."

"Like?"

"Like Willie's dead."

Macmillan couldn't hide his incredulity. "*Dead?*"

"He was shot."

"*Shot?*"

"Would you stop repeating what I *say?* scolded Rees. Bullet through the head. They only discovered it when they were preparing him for theatre in Aberdeen. He had his house, cottage and office broken into several times without anything been stolen. He had information he was planning to release that would have brought down the Government. He had other, secret information that would convince the electorate to vote for Scottish Independence....and he'd been warned twice recently by someone calling themselves *Alba* that he wasn't safe!*"

Macmillan took her arm. "C'mon through."

They talked while Macmillan made them coffee and sat mulling over the implications of McLeod's information. "You need to get on to MI5 and let McGinnis know what's what."

"I did that on the way here. McGinnis wants us to remain undercover and close to Hector. You were right." She placed her cup on a coaster, noting as she did so that for a bachelor, Macmillan was more house-trained than she'd given him credit for. "She actually talked about coming up here to see what was what."

"Would that be helpful?"

"Hard to say. In MI5 she has quite a fearsome reputation. Bit handy with a gun, she's seen service on the front line in Northern Ireland and in the civil war in Lebanon. Apparently she did some work in India and Pakistan. You only saw a friendly neighbour from the Isle of Lewis but she's no shrinking violet." She took another sip of her coffee. "So what are you going to do? Going to talk to McGinnis?"

Macmillan shook his head. She'll decide whether she wants to come north. I don't mind. I'm quite clear what she expects of us." He gestured towards the heap of Sunday newspapers that lay in various states of disarray on his coffee table. "I've been trying to make sense of all of these incidents involving the killings of the four police officers and the military policeman...the bomb destined for George Younger. Can't help wondering if Willie and Hector are involved."

"Not in my book. We've both been in Willie's company. A passionate man but not a murderer. Same with Hector. I'm frankly impressed by his approach to life...trying to live it by his values. Again, a committed nationalist but neither a murderer nor a conspiracist."

"I'm inclined to agree. But they must have insights and contacts currently denied us. There's not much information in the papers..." He tugged at his tie. "Hence the get-up."

Rees made a face suggesting she didn't understand.

"New approach." He produced his warrant card. "I think we need to get information directly from fellow officers."

"But that would mean breaking cover."

"Perhaps...but we'd be careful." He took a deep breath. "I can't believe I'm saying this, but I might need you to operate front and centre."

"Jesus...an *operational* role...and me a mere woman. Just so I can carry your briefcase?"

"No. Acting both together and on your own."

"What does this cost me? A session on the director's couch? Money? Flattery?"

"I'd settle for professionalism!"

"Fuck off! Who's been responsible for bringing all of this information to the table, eh?"

Macmillan held his hands up in surrender. "You're right. I was wrong to speak as I did when I drove you over to Hector's. If you get this quality of information from him who am I to care if you shag his brains out?"

"John McMillan! If your old mother up in Stornoway heard the way you speak to young ladies!" Her mischievous streak returned. "So you're not jealous? Hector was quite sure you'd feelings for me. I mean, I'll keep myself pure if there's even the smallest chance that there's a place in your heart for me."

Macmillan had the good grace to smile widely. "Sorry. I was a bit of a tit, wasn't I?"

"Yes, you were...but I forgive you." She squeezed his knee in what she hoped would be seen as a friendly fashion. "For all we argued and fought over that Belfast stuff...you're a good guy. I always respected you and I'm pleased we're working together on this. I think we make a good team. I always liked the way you'd think outside the box. Loved the fact that you took risks and I enjoyed watching you being cheeky to people who are senior to you. I like your *chutzpah*!"

"Aye, well...thanks...I like your...your...your ability to like me," he finished lamely.

They both laughed.

McMillan held out his hand. "Truce?"

"I'm back in Hector's arms tonight...carrying pizzas. No chaperone."

Macmillan offered a watery smile and his open hand. He repeated his question. "Truce?"

"Truce."

* * *

Still drunk, McLeod sat in the rear of a taxi and took a ten pound note from his wallet in payment for the journey from Cathcart to Glasgow's West End. "Keep a pound, driver," he offered, his hand open awaiting change. "Pound tip," he repeated. *Mel was right*, he thought as the driver fished around in a bag for change. *I could be in danger. My pal Jock'll see me all right. I mean he offered to help any way he could. If I could stay a couple of nights in that spare room that he gave that English woman...that would be good...that would be good.*

"Hold it!" he exclaimed, addressing the taxi driver. He lowered himself slightly as he saw Macmillan and Rees walk together from the street entry of his apartment. Macmillan was dressed in a business suit. "Wait a minute, driver!"

Rees positioned herself at the rear door of the vehicle awaiting entry as Macmillan moved to the front. They entered and after a few moments, drove off.

"Follow that cab," said Mcleod, his intoxication not lessening his feeling of being ever so slightly melodramatic.

"Always wanted someone to say that, sir...'follow that car'! Ten-four!"

"Eh?"

"Ten-four! It's what cops say when they're telt tae dae somethin'."

"Just follow the taxi but don't look like you're following it," urged McLeod.

"And how am I supposed tae dae that?" enquired the driver.

"Don't get too close but don't lose them."

"You a polis? A spy?"

"Just follow the taxi. Big tip."

The driver eased back on his questioning and concentrated on fulfilling the task set him by McLeod. The journey lasted but ten minutes and ended when Macmillan pulled into a parking bay and emerged to feed the meter.

"Keep the tenner," growled Mcleod as he left his taxi and watched as Macmillan and Rees crossed Hope Street and entered the Central Hotel, chatting amiably.

I knew Mel had a thing for Jock, he thought. *Well, she's going to get a piece of my mind. Numbers...numbers...my specialty... numbers. What did she say her room number was the other night? Two, one, five. That was it, two, one, five. I'm sure that's right! Okay, here goes nothin'."*

McLeod crossed the road and stood for a moment at the hotel's entrance, gathering himself before opening the double glass doors and walking to the wide, elegant stairway that led to the bedrooms with as much insouciance as he could muster.

*

Ahead of him, Rees opened the door to her hotel room and both she and Macmillan entered. Rees went directly to the small drawer in a dressing table on top of which were scattered various items of make-up. Surreptitiously, she swept up the previous evening's underwear that she'd left untidily next to the mirror and tucked it away in a drawer. Macmillan took a seat on the edge of her bed and disinterestedly inspected his warrant card. Rees removed her own police identification from the small drawer and threw it in the direction of her colleague for his inspection.

"That makes us both semi-legal, I suppose"

"We're going to have to play this cute, Mel. We need to be able to bluff our way into the confidences of cops up here."

"I guess so…"

There was a knock at the door. "Room service!"

Outside, McLeod stood with his index finger covering the peephole, denying identification.

Rees, puzzled, approached the door and eyed the peephole. *Can't see anything,* she thought, opening the door regardless.

McLeod stood in statuesque pose, his pointing finger remaining in mid-air where he'd used it to cover the peephole. A drunken smile and bleary eyes suggested to the world that he wasn't firing on all cylinders. "Thought I'd pop in for a swift one, Mel. Don't mind do you?"

Rees was sufficiently surprised to offer nothing but an open mouth in response and stood aside as McLeod stepped past her waving cheerily at Macmillan.

"And there's my pal, Jock. How are we Jock? A wee afternoon dalliance, eh, Jock?'

Macmillan realised instantly that Hector's presence was as a result of drunken jealousy and responded appropriately.

"Good to see you, Hector. Mel was just saying how much she was looking forward to visiting you this evening."

"Aye, I'll bet she was." He looked at Mel who stood holding the still-opened door. She closed it as she spoke. "Is this you taking my advice, Hector and getting away from your home for a bit?"

"Aye…something like that." Confused at the absence of obvious carnal activity and the calm demeanour of Rees and Macmillan, he sat on the edge of the bed next to Macmillan. Drunkenly he glanced at the card held in Macmillan's hands and screwed his eyes better to register its significance. On the face of the card was the portcullis, crown and lions rampant logo of the

166

Metropolitan Police. It took a moment for him to understand its significance. He took the warrant card from Macmillan who offered no resistance.

"Aw, *Jesus!*...Wee Tam was right! You're a bloody *cop!*" He looked again at the warrant card and threw it on the floor and tried to stand before falling back to a seated position. "And I thought I was a good judge of character. I fell for it. I trusted someone who probably shot my best friend!"

"No, Hector..."

"Aye, deny everything. That's what you're taught, isn't it?" He thought further. "So have I just walked into the lion's den, eh, have I? Am I now the next one that gets bumped off? "

"Hector, if you'd just listen..."

"I'm listening to no police officer." He stooped and with effort, picked up the card from the floor and read it once more. "Oh, you're only a fucking detective *inspector*! A *top* cop. None of your shite here! None of your common or garden polis here, eh?"

A silence endured as McLeod shook his head slowly, forming a question he didn't want to ask. He looked at Mel. "And what about you, Mel? Are you in bed with Jock , so to speak."

Rees folded her arms as she calculated her response. With an audible sigh, she stepped towards the bed and lifted her own warrant card which lay just behind Macmillan on the bed. She handed it to him. "Detective Sergeant Melissa Rees. North Wales Police Authority." She waited for a moment as McLeod grasped the import of her revelation. After a few moments he responded, speaking softly.

"So I'm betrayed, am I? By a guy I thought was a top man. Someone I'd have called a friend. Betrayed by a hussy who *used* me...and I fell for it. Hook, line and sinker. The hale jing-bang!" He laughed derisively and began shaking his head slowly, drunkenly, without speaking before uttering, "Can't believe it. Wee *Tam* sees through you...Wee *Tam*, who can hardly put a verb in a sentence...*he* sees through you and I defend you and befriend you" A thought suggested itself to him. "Here...I'll tell you this, you guys are good at what you do. When it comes to sleekitness, you guys have it covered. As they say, the polis aren'y bastards...they're *clever* bastards!"

Macmillan rose and pulled the single chair from a corner of the room and sat it square in front of McLeod. He sat down and faced him directly. "Okay, Hector. Enough of this. Look at me!" He spoke sternly. "*Look* at me, Hector." McLeod met his gaze. "Let me make a few points. First, yes we're both police officers. At present, I'm Special Branch. Mel's MI5. Presently seconded back to us in Special Branch."

McLeod placed both hands over his eyes in dismay. "Jesus Christ!"

"Pay attention, Hector. Secondly, you're in no danger from us...although it may be that there are other forces at work. Third, Mel really *does* like you. That part's true. She and I have discussed what we worried was a conflict of interest. You weren't deceived by her. Her feelings for you are genuine."

Rees stared at the side of Macmillan's head promising herself she'd slap it at the first opportunity.

"Fourth, you're upset about Willie's death. Well, believe it or not, so are we. I can't share all of our mission objectives with you but believe me when I tell you that something stinks about this. It seems most unlikely that Willie's death was suicide. It looks suspicious to me. We'd like to find out who was responsible and frankly, we'd have a better chance of success if we could count on you to help us."

Rees's eyebrows were somewhere above her hairline as Macmillan addressed McLeod but she held her own counsel as he continued. "So here's what we're going to do. You're safe here. You're with friends...even though you'll find it hard to accept that for now. We're going to stay here until you sober up. We're going to enjoy the best coffee and sandwiches the Central Hotel can provide until you can string some words together. Then, Mel and I are going to answer all of your questions until you are satisfied that we have a genuine interest in pursuing the same goals you do in getting to the bottom of Willie's death."

McLeod listened stony-faced to Macmillan's monologue. He turned to Rees. "Is that right, Mel? Do you really like me?"

"Hector, we've only just met..."

"Knew it..."

"Hector, let me finish. We've only just met but Jock's telling the absolute truth. He gave me a row for developing feelings of affection towards you. I like you. You're a good looking guy, charming, educated and passionate. I'm impressed that you live a life based on your values...and...I like you! The police thing complicates things...but I *like* you!"

McLeod took a moment to process the information with which he'd been provided. "I need to sleep. That okay?" His head lay back on the pillow before either had time to respond and he fell asleep as if a giraffe felled by a tranquilliser.

*

Rees removed McLeod's shoes and made him comfortable as he slept on her bed, his length filling the queen-size. Macmillan, now in shirt-sleeves chewed on a sandwich pensively, still seated on the single chair in the room. Rees sat at the edge of her bed. She placed her elbows on her knees and studied the whorls on the floor carpet.

"So, where do I start?" She raised her head and met Macmillan's gaze. "By asking you what the fuck you think you're doing revealing everything to Hector, by thanking you for giving me a boyfriend I didn't know I had, or for returning me to the uniformed service in *Llandudno* once my superiors find out we're now in cahoots with the guy we're meant to be surveilling?"

"We are where we are, Mel. We've just been compromised completely. I've been giving it some thought. In some ways could work to our advantage if Hector plays ball."

"What's London going to say? McGinnis will go ape-shit!"

"Yeah. Thought about that, too. I'm afraid McGinnis doesn't get to hear. Your reports to her from now on are a concoction that we agree in advance."

"Jesus, the way this is going I'll be lucky to get a uniformed job in *Penrhyndeudraeth* as a traffic warden, *tops!*"

"Thought you liked the way I was cheeky and assertive with senior staff?" smiled Macmillan.

"Yeah, when it's you that's doing it."

"Thought you liked that I take risks?"

"Yeah," acknowledged Rees accepting the point, "when it's *you* taking the risks."

"Well, I figure we get Hector on board and keep this back from London until we're ready to let them in on our discoveries." He laughed. "Anyway, we're probably going to be demoted to the ranks for using our warrant cards while working undercover." He bit into his cheese sandwich and spoke with his mouth full. "Sheep as a lamb, eh?"

*

Rees and Macmillan watched television news for the next couple of hours as reports were broadcast of the death of senior SNP lawyer, Willie McRae. Footage of him speaking at conferences mingled with reminders of the role he'd played in sending the Atomic Energy Authority homewards to think again.

McLeod stirred and groaned as he held his head in his hands, massaging his temples. He pulled himself into a seated position on the bed. "Ahhh...Jesus, I've a head on me! I'll need to wear sunglasses to open the fridge! Was I hit by a bus?"

Rees offered little sympathy. "Yeah, you were knocked down on Islay Mist Street."

McLeod looked round the hotel room through eyes narrowed like letterboxes and began to reconstruct his earlier conversation. "Oh...*you* two!"

Macmillan evinced concern. "Hey, you okay, Hector?"

McLeod nodded. "Bit confused. Bit disappointed...in you two as well as myself...Bit anxious about what happens next...but most of all I'm sad. Sad at the death of my friend, sad about what it means for Scotland..." His eye caught the image of Willie on the corner television. He watched it silently, listening to the commentary. "Makes it all real, eh?"

"Aye, it's real enough, Hector. But your decision is whether you'd prefer to remain impotently on the side-lines shouting down everyone in authority or whether you'd like to help me and Mel investigate what's going on here." He allowed some time for reflection. "What would Willie want? Would he just head for the Pot Still and drown in drink or would he want to get at the facts?" He anticipated an argument against his request. "Now, we do all of this quietly. No one needs to know you're involved. You said earlier, that we're good at what we do. Well, frankly, we *are*...but we need you to help us, Hector. *Willie* needs you to help us. If it's suicide, it's suicide. If it's not, you'll want to know. Can we persuade you to help?"

McLeod thought for a moment. "Right now you couldn't persuade me to run from a burning house." He turned to Rees. "What do *you* say, Mel?" he asked sheepishly.

Rees puffed out her cheeks and exhaled noisily. "Jock's the boss here, Hector. But when you were sleeping I asked myself whether I was looking at the face of a murderer, the face of someone who conspired in the deaths of police officers, someone who was underhand, devious...or did I buy the idea that Hector McLeod was someone who tried to live by his values, who was a passionate Scot, a committed nationalist and essentially a man of peace. And as I asked myself, I remembered that my assessments had been formed when you were completely unaware of the role I was playing. *I* was the one playing a role...not you." She sat on the edge of the bed and placed her hand lightly on his lower leg, the nearest part of his body to her. "I'm not saying I understand your politics. But I *am* saying that you're a genuine guy and I've enjoyed getting to know you. It's for you to decide if you want to throw your lot in with us. But I've a suggestion. Help us! Help us get to the bottom of what's going on and you can pull out without anyone knowing you were involved at any time if you don't think we're being completely honest with you."

"Mel means as honest as we can be, Hector," interjected Macmillan. You're not a cop and we're not potential suspects in conspiracy to murdering police officers."

171

McLeod gave thought to the request made of him. The low tones of the television had moved on to advise watchers of the next day's weather. He leaned on his elbow and moved uncomfortably from the bed, returning his feet to the floor. "Does this hotel do room service? I could murder some chips." He smiled as he asked. "And you're both right on one matter...that's the only thing I could murder!"

Chapter Seventeen

MONDAY 8TH APRIL 1985

Inverness, Scotland

The Procurator Fiscal's office on the outskirts of Inverness was, from time to time, used to a few reporters attending the announcement of a post-mortem. Seumas Tait had had a busy morning and groaned inwardly at what he imagined would be requests for questions and the frustrated reaction he'd generate upon refusing to answer them. Walking into the small room used for announcements to the media, he sat behind a small table and opened a folder within which was a statement he proposed to read. Looking up, he found that the small throng he expected hadn't attended and that he was faced instead by a local reporter from The Inverness Courier, whom he knew and a young stringer for what transpired was the Glasgow papers. He rose and read from his statement.

"Ladies and...eh...Gentlemen, he corrected himself. "The Procurator Fiscal in Scotland has responsibility for the investigation of all sudden, suspicious, accidental, unexplained or unexpected deaths and any death that occurs in circumstances that might give rise to serious public concern. The purpose of my presence here today is to make a statement regarding the death of Mr. William McRae, a solicitor from Glasgow. Mr. McRae died following the termination of life support in Aberdeen Royal infirmary at three-thirty pm on Sunday, seventh of April following a motor vehicle accident on the A87 on the evening of Friday, fifth of April. A post-mortem examination found that a bullet was lodged in Mr. McRae's head and that it was this and not the motoring incident which killed him. The examination was carried out by Doctor Colin Keenan, a pathologist employed by the National Health Service assisted by Mr. John Kennedy an anatomical pathology technician. The pathologist carried out the post-mortem examination having been provided with a clinical summary of the police report and the deceased's medical records. His findings were provided to me and I have concluded that Mr. McRae committed suicide. His relatives have been so advised and have accepted the verdict. None of Mr McRae's organs have been retained and the body has been made over to his relatives for cremation. I can advise that I have considered what effect disclosure of further and detailed information would have on the often confidential and sensitive nature of communication between Procurators Fiscal and Crown Counsel and have taken the view that it is not in the public interest to disclose any further information. Mr. McRae's family is in agreement with my decision." He folded the sheet of A4 paper, replaced it in the folder he'd brought with him and left the room in silence.

* * *

Fort William, Scotland

Jimmy Hancock sat in the snug of the Ben Nevis Bar in Fort William and opened an edition of the West Highland Free Press left abandoned by a previous customer. He scanned the front page disinterestedly while he supped at his pint. Articles about rural life fought for coverage with a host of small ads and the journal was about to be discarded when his eyes fell on a small, side article reporting that a 'lone gunman' had opened fire on a group of hillwalkers. One Johnnie McManus from Wemyss Bay was reported as having been in a party of four which was shot at by a 'crazed gunman' who spoke of signs alerting them to military manoeuvres. However, upon return to the village and having quizzed locals, they'd discovered that no such operations had been scheduled and it was very suspicious according to all concerned. 'He fired at us and the bullet hit a rock just in front of the group. The shrapnel went everywhere. My brother Ali thought we were all going to die', read Hancock.

He shook his head. *I'm a fuckin' amateur. If this is followed up they'll have a decent description of me.* Now uncomfortable in the public house, he finished the remainder of his pint and left, heading towards the quiet forest track just outside of Fort William where he'd parked his van; his home in the meantime.

* * *

Macmillan seated himself in a chair in his lounge and addressed McLeod and Rees who each sat sipping the coffee he'd made for them. He waved a folded copy of a newspaper. "This morning's Glasgow Herald makes interesting reading. There's the briefest obituary and an account of his death that doesn't mention him being shot, 'died following a motoring accident', it says." He leaned forward. "Okay we need to split into three. The two boys from Special Branch, who've been following you, Hector...they might have an interesting view of proceedings. However, I can't interview Detective Sergeants Gall or Carnegie because they arrested me last Saturday on the march and view me as a bad man. Hector can't speak with them as they'll view him as a tartan terrorist so it falls to you, Mel. Your job is to find out what they can tell us and in order to do this you'll need to reveal yourself as Special Branch...but I'm giving us both a battlefield promotion. You and I now work in the Professional Standards Section. We play it cute and we might just get away with it." He turned again to McLeod. "I need to know more about the final movements of Willie. I gather he was in his office before he drove north so his secretary..."

"I know her. Ann Mahon," informed McLeod.

"Well, you'll need to wander in and find out what you can. Anything out of the ordinary, who did he meet or speak with on the morning before he left, what was his mood...anything you can throw into the pot when we gather together again."

"And you?" asked Rees.

"Well, I'm going to drive up to Loch Loyne to visit the scene of the crime if that's what it was. I might try to find out more from local officers and other witnesses if an opportunity presents itself but I'll keep in touch and we'll reconvene when I get back down"

Rees eyed him with some scepticism. "You're going to drive north in an old Glasgow taxi? Don't you think it'll look a bit odd to the Highland crofters up in Glencoe or somewhere?"

Macmillan reflected on her challenge. "Beggars can't be choosers, Mel. Stealing or hiring a car might bring its own problems...but you make a good point." He smiled. "Maybe I'll tie a sheep to the roof and stick a bale of hay in the boot."

Rees returned his grin, unconvinced. Macmillan continued.

"Hector, you go about your business as normal other than a lunchtime visit to Willie's office if you're agreeable to that." He stood, lifting his empty coffee cup and moved towards the kitchen. "Mel, you contact MI5 and tell them we're developing a close relationship with Hector and are hopeful that this will bring us further information on the reaction among nationalists to Willie's death. Keep it light and general." He picked up his empty coffee cup. "More coffee anyone?" He walked to the kitchen, catching Rees's eye as he did so, beckoning her to join him.

She gathered both remaining cups and joined him, making play of washing them under the tap. She raised her jaw silently and gave Macmillan a quizzical look, inviting an explanation as she did so.

Macmillan whispered to her as he used the adjacent cold tap to fill the kettle noisily. "Tell McGinnis we want pistols. Tell her we're not sure of the extent to which Hector's involved with the paramilitary side yet and would prefer to be armed. My preference is the American Glock 17. You make your own decision if you feel it's necessary...but things might get a bit leery round here for a while...and I need it as soon as possible. The local boys'll supply it to you here in the hotel and you can get it over to me when I return from up north."

* * *

Rees returned to her hotel. McLeod accompanied her to the front door and bid her goodbye more formally than was earlier the case telling her he'd try to meet with Ann Mahon in the morning.

"Any news from your contacts about Willie's funeral would also be useful," urged Rees.

Still suffering from his Olympian whisky consumption, McLeod responded quietly. He seemed melancholic. "I'll try to find out what's what but Willie made it clear once to me when in his cups that he didn't want any kind of ceremony, no grave, no marker, just scatter his ashes to the wind; in nearby Polmadie Refuse Works if that was the most convenient way of removing his earthly being from the planet. It'll be in his will, I'd bet. And don't bank on any big nationalist funeral...for more than one reason!"

"Tell me more."

"Later, perhaps," said McLeod as he turned on his heel and made for the train platforms behind the hotel.

Rees walked upstairs and contacted London as requested by Macmillan.

Chapter Eighteen

TUESDAY 9TH APRIL 1985

Glasgow, Scotland

Having packed a small case with a change of clothing, Macmillan began his journey north to the remote, heather clad Highland glen that enclosed Loch Loyne in which McRae had met his end. He pulled into a petrol station near Anniesland Cross as he left Glasgow and took as much petrol on board as the tank would allow. The purchase of a one gallon jerry-can filled with fuel and stored in the small boot of the taxi gave him further comfort. *I'll refuel in Fort William if I can,* he thought. *Fuel can sometimes be difficult to find up in that neck of the woods. This trip'll also give me some time to think.*

* * *

McLeod looked at his watch which told him it was just after ten o'clock in the morning. He stood outside the sandstone property at 166 Buchanan Street and looked at the polished, brass name-plate attached to its wall. 'McRae and Company, Solicitors'. Rain had once again visited Glasgow and had begun to run down his neck, persuading him that he'd be more comfortable if he didn't wait until lunchtime as he'd planned but call in earlier during work hours, taking the risk that everyone would be busy.

He climbed the steps and opened the large door to the offices of McRae's law firm.

McRae's secretary, Ann Mahon attended reception upon receiving an internal phone call telling her that Willie's pal, Hector McLeod had asked for her. Still red-eyed, she collapsed into McLeod's arms upon seeing him.

"Oh, Hector, isn't it terrible? Gone so young...and he had everything to live for. Why he felt he needed to take his own life is a mystery to me."

"Yeah, me too, Ann. When I saw him last he was in good spirits."

Mahon stepped back, uncoupling herself from McLeod's embrace. "That's what surprised me too, Hector. He was really looking forward to going up to his cottage. He was chatting away merrily with his partner, Mr Welsh all morning. He was especially buoyant about some work he was doing with one of his clients who wanted to sue a bookmaker. He phoned ahead to his cousin, Cathy to have the fire in his cottage lit for his arrival and his diary was full at his request for the week he returned. Now, that doesn't seem like someone who was preparing to shoot himself in the head does it?" She shook her head sadly. "But that's what seems to have happened."

McLeod remained stony-faced, agreeing her account duplicitously. "By all accounts, Ann."

He changed tack. "Nothing out of the ordinary on Friday morning then?"

"Not at all." Mahon opened her hand and began to count off on her fingers. "He made phone calls, saw a client, did some dictation and towards lunchtime spent some time photocopying some papers to do with his SNP work. He put them all in envelopes but wouldn't let me help him." She hesitated. "I must confess I was rather cross with him in that regard. I deal with the *most* confidential of matters. Have done all my days working with him but he obviously didn't trust me enough to let me near these particular papers."

"How many envelopes, Ann?"

"Four, I think. Size A3. The large ones. Quite stuffed they were."

"Did he post them?"

"Not that I'm aware of. He packed them into that silly old leather briefcase of his that he carries everywhere. But he might have posted them himself after he left."

McLeod acknowledged this possibility and moved the subject back to Willie's demise.

"No word of a funeral?"

"As you know, he spoke often about just being swept up with the sawdust and disposed of. He wouldn't want a big fuss."

"Well, you'll let me know if anything is organised, eh?"

"Of course, Hector."

"I'd better be off." He hugged her again and made to leave but stopped short as a thought occurred. "One more thing. Willie died on Friday. Five days ago. Have there been any police officers round to take a statement from you or Ronnie Welsh?"

"None, Hector. But that'll be because it was suicide, don't you think?"

"More than likely, Ann." He turned again towards the door.

"Mind you, that nice policeman, our local beat officer, Donald Morrison, he came in yesterday morning, first thing. He'd known Willie for years and was most upset. He said something about helping him on his way last Friday by letting him do a U-turn on West Nile Street. Actually, come to think about it, he seemed a bit out of sorts. Probably because of the events of the weekend," she told herself.

McLeod grimaced a smile at her and left, thanking the receptionist on the way out.

* * *

Rees stood in a cubicle in the Ladies' Clothing section of Glasgow's House of Frazer's premium department store in Buchanan Street. She took a suit jacket from its hanger and tried it on, discarding it almost immediately due to its tightness. A second jacket was a better fit and the skirt, if a bit longer then she'd prefer, also hugged her slim figure well. *That'll do*, she decided, almost changing her mind when she read the price tag on each garment.

Back in her hotel room, she pressed into service a white blouse more usually deployed casually and observed her newly besuited form in the long mirror next to her room door. *S'pose I look more like a police officer now,* she thought. New shoes, also purchased in Frazer's, completed the image. She sat in her room chair for some minutes lost in thought before picking up the phone and calling a number she'd written on a piece of paper the evening before. It connected her to Inspector Shona Young in Stewart Street Police Station. *Let's hope the police sisterhood helps me out here,* she thought as the call was connected.

The call was answered in a forbidding tone. "Inspector Young!"

"Hi there, Inspector Young. D.S. Melissa Rees here, Special Branch. We met a week ago on Saturday when we were dealing with the two men arrested after the protest march."

Young was all business. "I remember. How can I help you?"

"I need to speak with the two arresting officers; Carnegie and Gall, from memory. Don't know where they're located."

"Hold on." Rees could hear a desk drawer opening and paper being shuffled.

"Detective Sergeants Anderson Carnegie and Robert Gall. Special Branch like you. Based in Pitt Street. Do you want me to connect you with them?"

"Eh, no thanks. I'll call them later. Much appreciated. Bye!"

She replaced the phone on its cradle noticing that Young had ended the call at her end before she'd moved her own an inch from her ear. *Sheesh! She must be a laugh after work in the pub!*

*

A taxi dropped Rees at Pitt Street Police Headquarters and she stepped through its portal, smiling at the gruff security officer who directed her to reception where, casually flashing her ID, she asked for both Gall and Carnegie. The receptionist busied herself looking through her Rolodex Index system before making a call to determine their whereabouts.

"They're both out on duty, Ma'am. Both out in the Loch Lomond area. I'm told that Sergeant Carnegie can be contacted at the Colquhoun Arms Hotel in Luss this evening. He's staying there while he's undertaking some investigations up that way."

"You've been very helpful, thanks." As she left the building, she smiled quietly to herself. *This might make it easier.* She entered a nearby phone box and called directory enquiries.

"Can you connect me with the Colquhoun Arms Hotel in Luss, please?"

After a while the ring tone suggested connection and the hotel was announced.

"Hi. I'd like to make a reservation for one tonight please. My name's Rees. Melissa Rees."

* * *

Loch Loyne, Lochaber, Scotland

Mid-afternoon saw Macmillan driving slowly along the A87, allowing a single car to overtake him; a Land Rover, the attire of the driver and the sheep dog in the passenger's seat suggesting its use as a farm vehicle. He came round a bend and saw Loch Loyne for the first time; below him and to the left. On a grey day such as was the case today, it was dark and uninviting if still. Marshland, soggy grassland and reeds punctuated every so often by rocky outcrops swept steeply down to the water some three hundred yards away. *Middle of nowhere was right,* reflected Macmillan remembering McLeod's description. He continued along the road and stopped when he noticed skid marks that slewed off the metalled surface and cut obvious rutted indentations on the grass verge. A small lay-by nearby offered him the ability to park safely and he took advantage of it before exiting and walking to the point he assumed McRae's car to have left the road.

He stood between the muddy grooves at the edge of the road and looked first at the road configuration towards the south; from the direction McRae would have taken. *Hmmm, a gentle bend in the road but it's a good distance away, not too sharp, no adverse camber...wouldn't cause a normal driver any problems. No potholes. From the bend it's a straight road past here down the glen, not too steep a descent, keeping parallel with the lochside.* He considered his assessments and noticed skid marks, less obvious but still apparent on the other side of the road heading uphill and south. He placed his upper teeth over his bottom lip as he balanced probabilities. *Could be months old, could be connected with the accident. Difficult to say.* Taking a camera from his pocket he took several photographs of the contour and condition of the road surface before turning his attention to the steep grassy slope which had carried McRae downwards and to his death.

Returning the camera to his pocket, he looked down the treeless hill, noting the obvious tracks of the stricken car and its terminus below a ridge beneath him. He began a descent following the tyre marks, the soft, yielding earth inhibiting easy progress. Twenty yards downhill, a churn of mud and indented peaty ooze occupied his thoughts. *The car clearly rolled here.* Small particles of broken glass in nearby clumps of grass confirmed his assessment. *Damage to windows and the roof, I'd expect. Hope Willie was wearing a seat belt, although a fat lot of good it'll have done him.* A nearby rock showed scarring and colouring in a similar shade to the maroon hue of McRae's Volvo. He stepped a further few yards downhill and crossed a small burn perhaps two feet wide which led to the area where the car had stopped. More tracks leading from the scene suggested that car had been winched back uphill from the road.

He looked again at the acclivitous incline from the lower perspective of the crash site. *What happened here? Did Willie drive off the road in a fit of depression? Was he forced off the road? Was he drunk? Did he survive the crash, take out a revolver and shoot himself in the head...if so, why? Or was the trigger pulled by someone else?* He sat on a nearby rock and spent some time mulling over these questions before climbing the hill and returning to his car.

* * *

Loch Lomond, Scotland

Rees drove her hired Mercedes towards Luss, quite taken by the beauty of the lochside around Loch Lomond. *Wonder how Hector thinks independence for Scotland could improve upon this*, she thought uncharitably as she passed a sign indicating that the small village of Luss was but one mile ahead. Slowing as much to take in the scenery as in anticipation of her destination, she almost turned right into the village until she realised that the hotel sat immediately before her on the left on the main road north. She parked and entered reception, shrugging off the quizzical look from the French housemaid who found her apparent lack of overnight accoutrements surprising.

Having checked her room and found it to her satisfaction, she decided to walk around the small village and strolled down to the loch. *God, it would be lovely to retire to a place like this...almost as nice as the Brecon Beacons in Powys...* She returned to her room and closed her eyes in sleep.

* * *

Glasgow, Scotland

Are you Constable Morrison?"

Police Constable Donald John Morrison stopped in some surprise at being hailed by his name and folded his arms, drawing himself to his full height. "I am. And who might be asking after me?"

"My name is Hector McLeod. I'm a friend...I *was* a friend of Willie McRae's. His secretary mentioned to me this morning that you might have been the last person to have seen him alive, that's all. I was just up the town having a few beers and remembered she mentioned the beat cop for the city centre. When I saw someone in a police uniform in Hope Street I thought I'd ask, that's all."

"Aye, that's me." He shook his head sadly. "A terrible business."

"Sorry if I'm a wee bit under the weather. I've taken Willie's death pretty badly and I've been drowning my sorrows since the pubs opened."

"Well, that's understandable. Willie was a good man."

"And they're saying he committed suicide?"

"Well, he was as cheery as anything when I saw him on Friday. Seemed to be looking forward to a weekend in his wee place up north."

"Aye, he was that. He was full of beans when I was with him the night before."

Donald Morrison was a pleasant man. An officer who built relationships with his public rather than enforced the letter of the law unquestioningly. He unfolded his arms and gripped McLeod's shoulder in a friendly fashion. "Aye, it was a funny business alright, a funny business." He squeezed McLeod's shoulder once more. "Now, you away up the road. Too much drink isn'y good for anyone, even in such sad times as this."

"Willie wouldn't agree!"

Morrison laughed. "Aye, you're not wrong there... Anyway, I'll be off to save Glasgow from bad men. You take care."

McLeod watched him stroll up Hope Street, waving at shop assistants from outside the shop windows, smiling at passers-by. *Wonder what he meant by 'funny business'?*

* * *

Fort William, Scotland

Macmillan took the opportunity of replenishing his fuel tank in Fort William before driving back along the 'Road to the Isles' to the Lochailort Inn on the A830 between Fort William and Mallaig.

Food and sleep, he decided. *But first, a phone call.*

After registering, he took to his room, lifted the phone and rummaged around in his suit pocket to find the card given him two weeks earlier by his old comrade-in-arms, Nobby Clark. He dialled the London number.

"Chief Inspector Clark, Commissioner's office."

"Is that the Chief Inspector Clark who's been promoted well beyond his abilities?"

A high-pitched giggle he remembered from shared days in Belfast responded.

"Or is it the Chief Inspector Clark who has a wee thing about being sick in plant pots in posh restaurants?" Further peals of laughter from both as memories from the past were recalled. "Good to talk to you, Nobby. Still enjoying your cushy life of servitude?"

"Not too bad, me old son. Good to hear from you."

"Nice to hear a welcoming voice, Nobby. Anyway...you said to call you if I needed some help?"

"Anything I can do that doesn't get me clapped in irons, Jock."

"Well, here's the thing." He paused "Can I ask if you're privy to what I'm doing up in Scotland?"

"Listen me old thing, there's nowt goes on that I don't know about down here. Nothing in and around this office anyhow...and in passing, it seems you're held in some reasonable esteem by the powers that be. No accountin' for taste as I say," he finished.

"Well, that's good to know. I might need that esteem to get me out of problems down the line. Look, I'm dealing with this nationalist stuff up in Scotland and the guy I was meant to be getting close to was shot a few days ago."

"Yeah, I read."

"Well, it might be nothing or it might stink to high heaven. I'm up near Fort William where he was shot and I want to ask a few questions. Don't want to speak with the cop who was first on the scene. I want to meet with his sergeant to get an overview on what's gone on here. Can you get me his name, office base and shift patterns? Also, anything about local office politics would be useful and finally I need the name and rank of the Divisional Commander."

"Yeah, I'll make a few calls and get back to you."

They exchanged contact details and Macmillan replaced the phone. *Now for some food and some sleep.*

*

A small room with a bar attached served as a dining room and Macmillan had just forked a piece of sole when the receptionist came through and informed him of a phone call for him being received. He accompanied her to the lobby of the small hotel.

"Macmillan!"

"Hope I didn't disturb anything."

"Hi Nobby, just prevented me enjoying a mouthful of the finest Scottish seafood...any luck?"

"Decent enough. The cop who was first on the scene is one Kenneth Crawford, known as Kenny Crawford. Young cop. Constable. Unusually, all the local cops where he was shot were on leave that night and Crawford attended. His sergeant is an experienced man, Irish background. Name's Henry Donaghey and apparently doesn't get on too well with his inspector, a guy called Baldry, Robert Steven Baldry. There's real bad blood between them, apparently. Donaghey is based in Inverness and he's working day shift this week so he's wearing a uniform between eight and four in the afternoon through until Sunday. Top cop is a guy called Allan Thomson, he's the Divisional Commander; a Chief Superintendent."

Macmillan scribbled names on the back of a tourist brochure advertising the merits of sea fishing in nearby Loch Shiel.

"Big hugs, Nobby. I owe you a beer when we get together."

"Just stay safe, Jock. Here, 'ow are you gettin' on with her majesty, Detective Sergeant Melissa Rees? You strangled each other yet?"

Macmillan laughed. "There've been a few close calls but we're doing okay at the minute. She's still a bugger for doing her own thing!"

"That's what nearly got us shot in Belfast me old son. You tell her Nobby says to behave herself."

"I'll make sure to tell her. Wouldn't bet on it making the slightest difference, though!"

"Let me know if I can be of any further help, me old cock."

"Will do, Nobby."

Macmillan smiled a thank you to the receptionist and returned to his meal.

Half an hour later he sat back replenished and eyed the empty bar weighing up the wisdom of an early nightcap. He pinched his eyes. *Nah, sleep...I need to sleep...*

* * *

Luss, Loch Lomond, Scotland

Rested, Rees looked at herself in the room mirror and refreshed her lipstick. *I'll do*, she thought and left, walking down carpeted stairs to the bar having long conquered any reticence as a woman being in a public house on her own.

She recognised Carnegie immediately. He was standing alone in the small, low-ceilinged bar contemplating an almost full pint of what looked like lager and reading a pub-supplied newspaper spread open on the counter. The bar was empty other than two young men chatting amicably in a small recessed niche at the far end of the lounge. *Here we go*, thought Rees, *attack is the best form of defence*. The barman was busily cleaning glasses but was on his toes, looking out for customer needs. She walked confidently towards his smiling welcome and ordered a glass of *Sauvignon Blanc*, paying him and telling him to keep the change. "Tips jar!"

Taking a sip, she turned to an engrossed Detective Sergeant Anderson Carnegie and placed her glass beside his newspaper. "Will we sit at a table? It'll be more comfortable."

Surprised, Carnegie coughed back a small volume of lager into his glass and took a moment to digest Rees's proposal.

"Eh, wh...what?."

"Perhaps that table over there..." She lifted her glass and used it to point to a table in the corner of the bar.

Carnegie's face was quizzical. "Eh...do we...do we *know* one another?"

"Perhaps you'd like me to buy you a drink first, eh? If I'm going to fuck you at least I should offer a little foreplay!"

"What the fu..."

"But then again, it should probably be you buying me a drink given the service I'm about to offer you."

"Now listen here hen, I'm a police officer and if you think..."

Rees interrupted. "You are Detective Sergeant Anderson Carnegie, Special Branch. You were most recently involved in sur-veilling one William McRae until you made a complete cod of it and fell foul of your superiors," she said extemporising, hoping her empathic assessment wasn't too far off the mark. "You're now up here out of the way of the *able* cops on a manufactured assign-ment. You're in a bar at five o'clock drinking pints, as you've been doing for too many years." She noticed his wedding ring and placed a bet with herself. "You've long ago pissed off your wife and kids and your best pal is your *compadre* Detective Sergeant Robert Gall. You don't just work together, you socialise together and he *understands* you far more than your wife. Your diet's shite. You have boils on your neck that look like bullet wounds. Look at your paunch...*you've* gone to seed, your *life* has gone to seed and your *career* has gone to seed. And now the only thing that stands between you being hounded ignominiously from the force is... *me!*" She removed her warrant card from her suit pocket and slid it towards him, withdrawing it once she'd decided his glance had sufficed. "Detective Sergeant Melissa Rees, Special Branch, Professional Standards Section. Up from London to pass judge-ment on you." She placed her glass on the counter and held her thumb upwards. "I say, okay?" You're spared. "I say, *not* okay?" She inverted her thumb. "Hope your pension contributions are up to date." She gesticulated again towards the corner table. "So...the table over there?"

Carnegie remained statuesque, holding his pint in his hand, his mouth agape. Rees moved towards the table she'd designated and he followed wordlessly. They sat and Rees, now more confident, clinked the heel of her glass against Carnegie's pint tumbler. "What is it you say up here, *Slàinte mhath?*"

Carnegie's natural aggression returned if not in full measure. He spoke in a restrained whisper. "Who the fuck do you think you are, hen? A wee slip of a girl coming up here and talking to me like *that*! I've shat out bigger turds than you."

"Look, I'm quite happy to go back to my room, not trouble you anymore and submit my report. You have one hour with me to save your career. If you choose to ignore the opportunity to fix things, well, I've shat out bigger turds than you as well...and I'm only a wee slip of a girl'...but I'm a wee slip of a girl in the Professional Standards Section who holds your career in the palm of her hand." She sat back in her seat and slowly twirled the stem of her wine glass, allowing a brief silence. "Look...it's Anderson, isn't it?"

Carnegie nodded. "Andy."

"Look, Andy. This is high level now. You were looking after a politician and civil rights lawyer who was of keen interest to senior people in London. He's now in the morgue with a bullet in his brain. You were surveilling him. I've been told by top brass to find out what happened...and to be clear, I've no interest in reducing you to the ranks or seeing you kicked out of the force. I just need to understand more of what went down during the time you were on his coat-tails."

The next half-hour passed in conversation, Rees inviting Carnegie to recall his time spent surveilling McRae. Fortified by a what transpired was a third beer, Carnegie was by now comfortable sharing information and spoke to Rees about McRae, McLeod and the extent to which he believed them involved in the recent bombings.

"So, no proof but it's your gut instinct?"

"Pretty much. We're almost certain McRae was involved with the Scottish National Liberation Army. We believe he could have been their paymaster. We think he helped their leadership avoid capture when they slipped out of Scotland and fled to Ireland last year after a bombing campaign. He and McLeod were almost certainly behind the Dark Harvest Commando operation where they dug up earth from the island of Gruinard that the British Government had infected with anthrax spores during World War Two before depositing it in Porton Down and leaving some in a box at the top of Blackpool Tower. That stuff was toxic and people could have died."

Rees accepted his assertions without comment. "So he committed suicide? You buy that?"

Carnegie shrugged. "It's what they're saying. The man was a drunk. McLeod isn't far behind him."

He's a troublemaker and some kind of hippy accountant. Lives a couple of miles from McRae. In Cathcart, in Glasgow."

"Have you his phoned tapped?"

"For a while. Didn't reveal anything. All accountancy stuff. We visited his home when he was out..."

"Warrant?"

"Didn't bother. Found nothing. I'll deny it if it appears in your report."

"Doesn't need to."

Both now more relaxed, they conversed in more friendly terms.

"So what have they got you doing up here in Luss?"

"Fell foul of the Dep. He's got me and Gall organising road checks for this Lone Wolf guy that's been leaving his calling card when he bombs innocent officers."

"Why up here?"

"There's forensic evidence connecting him with a fucking beetle that's only found in these parts."

"Any leads?"

"Mostly country folk up here. They spend their time meeting in their village halls discussing how best to get the sheep out of their post office. A few eccentrics. One guy was dressed like he was living a re-run of Bannockburn, right down to the kilt and the dirk in the belt...another, mind you it turned out he had Alzheimer's, he was wandering about Arrochar bollock naked. We'd a third guy who insisted on speaking to us in French, German, Italian and Spanish. Fortunately the cop who was driving me spoke all of the languages enough to talk back to him." He laughed. "Aye he was funny. *'Gracias, merci beaucoup, danke schön, grazie mille"*.

Rees's brow furrowed. "That rings a bell. What did he say again?"

"Ach, it was something like *'Gracias, merci beaucoup, danke, grazie'*. We helped him pick up some tacks he'd dropped on the road and he thanked us in all these foreign languages..."

Rees was lost in her own thoughts, asking rhetorically, "Why does that register with me?"

Carnegie continued, ignoring Rees's puzzlement. "Strange guy. Lives in a wee cottage on the lochside at Glenmallan. Opposite a jetty. We found him fixing his fences...with wee daft tacks...just one of the strange characters that populate the more rural parts of our country."

Rees changed the subject. "So where's your pal, Gall?"

"He's up in Crianlarich. Do you want to speak with him as well?"

"Probably not. You've been very helpful. I'll be reporting that you carried out your duties competently."

"So do I get a copy of your report?"

"Nope! You'll just have to wait on the verdict being leased down from on high. I've no influence there but it'd be perverse if they moved against you based on a sound report."

"I'm grateful, D.S. Rees."

"No problem, D.S. Carnegie." She rose and smiled. "Well, I'm getting some early me-time. A book, a bath, a bite and bed then I'm up and off at the crack." She offered her hand. "Nice meeting you."

* * *

Glenfinnan, Lochaber, Scotland

Carrying three blocks of orange coloured Semtex proved easier than Hancock had at first considered. *I'll just hide it in plain sight,* he thought as he placed it inside a plastic container previously used by Dulux as a receptacle for their red paint, numbered 0689. Other, similar paint bins had been pressed into service as containers for nails, screws, putty and cement powder. *Together this'll pass for the typically untidy back of a van being used by the owner of a small croft.* His rifle had been returned to its hiding place in the sill of the driver's door. Satisfied, he decided that the vehicle was fit to pass any road check he might face in return to his home base on Loch Long.

He turned the ignition key and the white van coughed until its engine settled first into a smooth rhythm before stuttering and surrendering to carburettor difficulties. Eventually, Hancock coaxed it into life. With an unnecessary look in his rear view mirror, he guided the vehicle tentatively from its position under a low-hanging birch tree on to a nearby forestry track and back towards metalled roads that would take him to Loch Long. *Let's hope some of the heat has died down around Glenmallan. This Semtex is bloody useless without the American M112 charge to set it off and presently it's lying beneath my floorboards.*

Chapter Nineteen

WEDNESDAY 10TH APRIL 1985

Inverness, Scotland

Macmillan drove towards Inverness following the same route taken by the ambulance carrying McRae only days earlier. A bright sun accompanied him, beaming down on flat farm-land around Fort William that had been tilled perfectly, now resembling brown corduroy. A service station up ahead advertised fuel so he pulled in, replenished his tank and paid.

"Nearest public phone?"

"Just round the corner of the building, sir."

Macmillan ducked his head inside the protective shell of a newly designed phone booth that resembled an oversized crash helmet pinned to a wall and called the number of the police office in Inverness. Connected with police reception at the bar he introduced himself as Chief Inspector Alfred Smith, Metropolitan Police and asked to put through to Chief Superintendent Thomson. After some moments a voice came on the line identifying themselves as the person supporting the office of the Divisional Commander, inviting a short wait. Shortly, Thomson was speaking.

"Chief Superintendent Allan Thomson. Who am I speaking to?"

Macmillan bit his lip and stopped himself correcting the commander's grammatical choice of finishing his sentence in a preposition, an itch he'd scratch more often than not when dealing with colleagues of a lower rank.

"Chief Inspector Albert Smith, sir. Office of the Commissioner of the Metropolitan Police. Thanks for taking my call. I'm on to ask if the Commissioner might ask a personal favour of you. One of his colleagues, Detective Inspector John MacMillan, Special Branch, is in your patch just now and is keen to interview one of London's finest, one William Arthur Miller. He's up in the Highlands just now doing a bit of fishing and while he's north of the border he'll be the perfect tourist but we have him fingered as a member of an East End gang responsible for the theft of jewelry amounting to some two hundred thousand pounds sterling from a shop in Mayfair. MacMillan just wants to put the frighteners on him slightly and pull him in for an hour's interview in your Inverness office."

"Why are Special Branch interested in a common or garden jewel thief?"

Macmillan thought quickly. "This mob is controlled by an Irish overlord, sir; the money goes over to buy arms for the Republican movement in Belfast."

Unseen by Macmillan, Thomson nodded his acceptance. "And what will he need?"

"If you could alert your bar staff to Macmillan's arrival around two o'clock and have a small office set aside, he'd be out from under your feet in an hour. It'd be appreciated...and Chief Superintendent...there would be no need to record MacMillan's presence in your office, if that's possible. We'd like to keep everything about this very quiet."

"Quite understand. It'll be no problem. I'll let downstairs know to expect him. He can use my Inspector's office on the first floor. He's off today. And mum's the word."

* * *

An hour later Macmillan opened the large wooden door of Inverness Police Headquarters and flashed his warrant card at the desk officer.

"Hi! John Macmillan, Special Branch. I gather I'm expected?"

The uniformed officer, a young woman, consulted a piece of paper. "Ah, yes, sir. I'm to take you up to Inspector Baldry's office. You're expecting to be joined by a Mr. Miller?"

"Yeah, later. A few calls beforehand."

They walked together to the first floor office. A milky fluorescent light reflected off beige linoleum in each of the two corridors it took to reach Baldry's office where a flask of coffee and two cups were set out on a tray in anticipation of his arrival. The smell of corridor disinfectant fought for air superiority over the Nescafé. Macmillan thanked his escort. "Before you go, I wonder if you'd be good enough to invite Sergeant Henry Donaghey to join me?"

"Sergeant Donaghey? I think he's finishing lunch downstairs."

Macmillan smiled. "I'd appreciate his attendance immediately. I don't have much time."

"Certainly, sir."

The office was barren of all personal belongings. Painted off-white as were all walls he'd noticed in his walk upstairs, no calendars, charts or pictures decorated them. Baldry's desk was tidy other than a diary, a phone and a folder which Macmillan promptly placed in a desk drawer before sitting behind the Inspector's desk and pulling the tray containing the coffee towards him. He looked towards the door through which he expected Sergeant Donaghey. *Let's hope he hates this Inspector Baldry as much as Nobby says he does.*

A few minutes later the door opened without having been knocked and a burly, red-faced Sergeant Henry Donaghey entered, his face at once aggressive and curious.

"Sugar?" enquired Macmillan as he poured the second of two cups of coffee.

"And why would I want feckin' sugar?" Donaghey's Irish accent was pronounced, undiminished by decades of living in Scotland.

Donegal or maybe Derry, thought Macmillan utilising an ear for regional Irish accents he'd cultivated during his time in Ulster.

"What's this all about?"

"Macmillan feigned puzzlement. "Hasn't the Chief Constable notified you of this meeting?"

"*What* feckin' meeting?"

Macmillan finished ministering to his coffee. "Hmmm, this is awkward." He took his coffee behind the desk and sat on the chair, pushing it slightly and allowing the castors to swivel it so he was side-on to the now blustering Donaghey who continued his rant. "I've not been informed of any feckin' meeting. I haven't a *clue* who the feck you are and I haven't spoke to the Chief Constable in a feckin' *year*!"

"Well, you should know that I outrank you but I've offered you a coffee to demonstrate that I come in peace. No one other than top brass knows I'm here talking to you and you need to know that this interview will not be recorded, will not be spoken of by you but will be of considerable importance to national security." He took his warrant card from his pocket. "Detective Inspector John Macmillan, Special Branch and Professional Standards." He gestured at a chair. "Have a seat, Sergeant. I have some questions."

Donaghey's face, already red, turned crimson. "If I'm being interviewed on some trumped-up, cock and bull disciplinary shite, I have the right to be accompanied by an officer of my choice."

"Aye, Sergeant. But here's the rub. I'm *not* interviewing you on any cock and bull disciplinary shite. I'm having an off-the-record quiet chat about the recent performance of your inspector, Robert Baldry."

"Baldry?"

"Looks like he's in serious trouble over his handling of the recent death of William McRae up by Loch Loyne. I just need some background information. Some colour. And our chat is not being recorded and will not be used overtly. We know you were off duty last weekend and weren't involved. But by all accounts Baldry's not much of a cop and I need to understand more about him. So, again...sugar?"

Donaghey took a moment to distill the import of Macmillan's offer.

"Black," he said, pulling the cup and saucer towards him as he sat down. He took a sip, replaced the cup on its saucer and jiggled the chair closer to the desk. "Baldry's an eegit!"

"By all accounts," lied Macmillan. "Tell me more about the McRae incident. That's the one that's got them excited down in London."

"It was mishandled from the start, sir."

"Some examples?"

"The incident happened on the Friday evening but McRae wasn't discovered until the Saturday morning when a car carrying two Australian tourists noticed a Volvo lying downhill off the A87 but facing back towards the road. Crowe, their name was. Anyway, the man realised it was a crash and that the man inside was still breathing so he climbed back up the hill and waved down a passing car and by all that's holy, didn't it carry an SNP Councillor who recognised McRae? And in the back was only a feckin' doctor...a woman doctor called Messer." He crossed himself. "There *is* a God!" He tightened his lips and shook his head once as if to reinforce his belief. "So anyway, she went down the hill and the report I read said he was unresponsive but alive. His head was covered in blood and they figured this had been caused by the crash. She said he smelled of alcohol."

"So he was drunk?"

Donaghey laughed. "Aye...some would say...but this is where it gets interesting. Another passenger had asked a passing car to contact us as well as an ambulance but all of our local boys were off duty 'cuz it was the holiday weekend."

"Bit strange, eh, Henry," queried Macmillan. "*All* the local troops off duty at the one time?"

"S'pose so. Never thought of it before."

"Had that happened before in your experience?"

"Never...but we had to send a young cop up. Boy named Kenny Crawford. Inexperienced." He took another sip of his coffee, warming to his story. "That'd be the first of Baldry's blunders. He managed everything during the weekend."

"You don't rate him, eh?"

"Like I said earlier, he's a feckin' eegit...but you were saying that this is between you and me, eh? If it ever got out that I was..."

"Relax, Henry. I keep my word. Anything you say is unattributable."

"Well, Crawford assumes it's an accident scene, not a potential crime scene so everybody's wandering around, there's no tape keeping people back, loads of rubber-neckers, people are interfering with evidence and eventually the ambulance comes and McRae's lifted out of the passenger's door..."

"Why not the driver's door?"

"The car had rolled and ended up underneath an overhang with McRae's door wedged against it. It couldn't be opened."

"I've already had a look at the site. Thirty yards or so down the hill from the road?"

"Exactly that, because the next day the recovery vehicle turned up and it only has a thirty yard tow-line and they said it was fully extended." Another sip of his coffee. "And it was the car's momentum that took it there; the ground was so boggy it could never have reached the overhang unless it was going at speed. So anyway, the ambulance takes him to hospital here in Inverness and the good Doctor Messer sits in the back with McRae all the way. When they get to hospital they decide he has to go to Aberdeen to get better treatment but when they get there, a nurse who's cleaning him up for theatre discovers that there's an entry wound beneath the blood on his head. They X-Ray him and lo and behold, there's a .22 bullet lodged in his feckin' brain."

"And this is now Sunday?"

"Aye, Sunday. The day after. So all of a sudden, Baldry's accident scene is a crime scene. Now the tape comes out and the site's protected...but not until the guy who first found him had returned to look for a missing glove...not until the feckin' car's been removed, everyone's been trampling all over it and all of a sudden they find the gun."

"McRae's gun?"

"Well, who the feck knows? Initially I was told that it was about twenty yards from the car although I hear Kenny's now saying it was in the burn that runs underneath the crash site."

"Yeah, I saw it. A wee two foot wide burn."

"So the bold boy finds the gun and holds it aloft like a trophy, in the process buggering up any fingerprints."

"Has it been fingerprinted now?"

Donaghey shook his head. "No need. It was a suicide according to the Fiscal on Monday."

"The gun was found at distance from the car, his driver's door couldn't open but he shot himself in the head?"

That's what they're sayin' and they found a half finished bottle of whisky in the back of the car. So they figured he was driving under the influence."

"What brand of whisky?"

"I was told it was a half-bottle of Grouse."

McRae only drank Islay Mist or Glenmorangie."

"Well, on this journey he made his way through a half bottle of Grouse."

"Was his briefcase found?"

"Not immediately but it turned up by the Sunday evening once we'd been informed that it might be a murder scene."

"And what did it contain?"

"Just some legal stuff. Cases he was working on and the like."

"No large envelopes? No files containing allegations of serious crime? No political documents?"

Donaghey shook his head. "Legal stuff." He thought further. "D'y'know, there was one thing I found strange."

"Just the one?"

"Most of my concerns were about Baldry's mismanagement of the crime scene. But I was told that when the cops were looking around, they found McRae's wallet, licence, some bills and other personal bits and pieces piled neatly on a rock a forty-five feet away...I mean that's near enough the edge of the penalty box. Now given that McRae couldn't get out of his car, he was unconscious, still had his seat belt on, had crashed his car at speed and had a feckin' bullet buried in his head, how the feck he managed to organise himself to place his belongings neatly on a rock fifteen yards away escapes me."

"Me too," said Macmillan.

"And two bullets had been fired. That was also a bit strange."

"Two?"

"Yeah. Now one could have been fired ten years before or it could have been a test shot. He could have been shooting *at* someone near the car or he could have shot it after he'd just blown his own feckin' head off...but that last one sounds a bit far-fetched, don't ya think, sir!"

Macmillan and Donaghey continued their discussion with Baldry's character being blackened at every turn, his sergeant enthusiastically taking what he saw as a God-given opportunity to repay debts long-simmering. He walked Macmillan to the front door of the police station and shook his hand. "Wait here, sir." He turned into an office and returned a few moments later with two sheets of paper. "Don't know if it's any help but here's a list of the contents taken from McRae's car."

"Much appreciated, sergeant," said Macmillan perusing the list.

"Two things then, sir before you go...Baldry's an eegit and it'll take someone like you to draw his faults to the powers that be and secondly, I won't be named in any report, eh?"

"You have my word, Sergeant. No report. You're in the clear." He drew him closer by the elbow and whispered conspiratorially. "And that's more than we can say about your man, Baldry, eh?" Macmillan offered his hand. "And we'll both keep today's meeting confidential if that's okay with you?"

Donaghey smiled and nodded his complicity.

*

Macmillan moved to put distance between him and the police station and found a call box from which he called Rees. They each exchanged findings, Macmillan informing her that before things began to unravel in terms of their new claimed role in Professional Standards, he was going to drive to Aberdeen to interview the nurse and the doctor who carried out the autopsy.

"Keep McGinnis sweet, Mel. Tell her the square root of bugger-all. Let her know we're still in close contact with Hector and that he's beginning to talk due to the amount of alcohol he's taking since Willie was shot."

"I'm seeing him tonight for dinner...no romance, I'm afraid. I think he views me as damaged goods now."

"Glad to see you're still saving yourself for me."

Rees laughed. "He says he's spoken with Willie's secretary and the local beat cop. Says he's got some interesting stuff. He's really on board here, Jock. I think he's to be trusted. He's determined to avenge Willie's death."

"Okay. If I can manage it I'll deal with my interviews tomorrow morning, drive back down to Glasgow and maybe the three of us can meet up to discuss progress. But...and this is important, Mel, you and I meet first and agree what we're going to share with Hector. He still might be complicit in all of this. I'll pick you up in the taxi on the way to meet Hector after I visit the Mitchell Library in the city centre. I want to see what the papers have been making of all this since the Fiscal's announcement.

"Okay. Drive safe!"

Chapter Twenty

THURSDAY 11TH APRIL 1985

Aberdeen, Scotland

Macmillan drove his taxi into the public car park at Aberdeen Royal Infirmary in the city's Foresterhill district high above its harbour and the sharp grey granite of the dwelling houses below. He adjusted his rear view mirror so he could see his face, buttoned his shirt at his neck and tightened his tie, satisfying himself that he was presentable. Ignoring the main reception, he followed the ward directions to Intensive Care where he leaned on a shelf and tapped on a sliding glass window that separated him from a young administrator bent on writing notes on what appeared to be an appointments schedule. She took no notice of him until he withdrew his warrant card and held it against the glass, smiling a smile he hoped would convey a mixture of malevolence and authority.

"Sorry, can I help you?"

"I'd like to speak with the surgeon who dealt recently with a patient called William McRae. He was pronounced dead here in Sunday 7th April, five days ago."

The young receptionist consulted a red, hard-backed folder and drew her finger down the page. "You want Mr. Campbell. He was the consultant on duty that night."

Macmillan took a small notepad from his inner jacket pocket. "First name?"

"Ronald."

"Would you mind contacting him and asking him to speak with me if he's not in the middle of something? It'd be extremely helpful." His smile, he hoped, would now convey a mixture of gratitude and friendliness although to any dispassionate observer, it might be presumed to be possessed of all the same characteristics as was his earlier smile.

The same red folder was examined again, back pages this time. "He should be about to set off on his ward rounds. I'll see if he's available."

Some ten minutes later, a white coated medic appeared, the *de rigueur* stethoscope around his neck, his hand offered in greeting when he was still some yards away.

Macmillan levered himself off the wall. "Dr. Campbell?"

"*Mister* Campbell, actually. I'm a surgeon. A tradition that goes back to the late seventeen hundreds. Don't want to challenge centuries of convention now, do we? And you are?"

"Detective Inspector John Macmillan. Thank you for seeing me."

"Not sure how much I can help, Inspector. The formal post-mortem was held in Inverness on Monday. Suicide, I gather."

"Just a few questions doctor..."

"Mister."

"Sorry...*Mister* Campbell."

"We should speak in here." Campbell looked into a small room just off reception. "This'll do." They entered and sat at a table that suggested earlier occupants who had an enthusiasm for reading newspapers featuring semi-clad young women on their inside page.

Macmillan took out his notepad.

"It was your theatre nurse who first found the bullet wound?"

"Yes, Nurse Margaret Foster was preparing Mr. McRae for X-Ray prior to theatre. She was cleaning the blood from his scalp and noticed what appeared to be an entry wound. A subsequent

X-ray confirmed that a bullet had penetrated the skull and had destroyed all motor functions. The injury was inoperable and was not survivable."

"Was there an exit wound?"

"There was not. The bullet was lodged in his parietal lobe."

"And at that time, you asked permission from his brother, Doctor Fergus McRae to remove supports. He agreed and the patient expired."

"Exactly that, Inspector. Around three-thirty on Sunday afternoon as I recall."

Macmillan made a few notes, thinking as he did. "Did you check his blood for alcohol?"

"Among other things, yes. There was no trace of alcohol in his blood."

Macmillan allowed his eyebrows to rise and gave himself some thinking time.

"Done much of this kind of work, sir?"

"If you mean dealing with patients who have been shot in the head, no. Usually it's my senior colleague, Mr. Bennison-Neal who deals with all of these injuries. They're pretty rare but he's the man when they do occur. Unfortunately he was unavailable that weekend so I stood in."

"Can I ask if you'd done *any* such procedures before?"

"Well, no actually."

"Did you look for powder burns?"

"Powder bur...eh, no."

"The point I'm getting at Mr. Campbell, is that when a gun is fired in close proximity to the skin as is usually the case in a suicide, there are invariably indications that identify it as such. First, the flammable gasses that emanate from the barrel of a gun will scorch the edges of the entry wound. Soot impregnates the surrounding skin, particles of burned powder are forced under the skin and we can calculate distance of the weapon...the further away, the less soot and the wider the coverage, by extension, the closer the shot, the more concentrated is the soot. The bullet, I'm led to believe was a .22. This is a fairly light projectile and it would be common for it to be able to penetrate bone but not have enough oomph to exit the other side of the skull. In essence, these findings would determine whether we're dealing with a suicide or a murder. Standard procedure!"

"I see. Well, I'm afraid these matters didn't concern me at the time. I was focused upon attempting to save the man's life or at least assess his ability to survive the wound."

"Quite so." Macmillan placed his notebook flat on the table and rubbed its spine thoughtfully before containing his discourse on gunshot wounds."

"In circumstances where a gun is held close to the scalp and fired, hot muzzle gasses cause an area of burning around the point of entry scorching the hair. Was this evident when you inspected the wound?"

"Not that I recall Inspector, although his hair style wasn't uppermost in my mind at the time."

"Of course not, Mr Campbell. And can I ask if you checked his *hands* for powder burns?"

"His hands...eh, no Inspector. As I said..."

"Quite so, Mr Campbell. But if someone fires a gun, especially an older gun, there's leakage from the muzzle and cylinder which produces gunshot residue that covers the hand of the person who shot the firearm. Therefore, in determining a verdict of suicide, it'd be important to establish whether such findings were present."

Campbell sighed. "Frankly, Inspector, these are not my concerns." He stood. "I have ward duties, I'm afraid. Might I suggest that you raise these matters with the pathologist in Inverness who undertook the post-mortem on Monday?"

"Of course, sir. But in your washing and sterilising Mr. McRae for theatre, you'd have removed many of the clues I've pointed to which might have helped the pathologist come to a view on the matter. But I thank you for your time and your candour."

*

As Macmillan walked across the car park to make his journey south he was watched from a fourth floor window by Consultant

Mr. Ronald Campbell who observed him with some disquiet. *Hmm, he made a lot of sense. I should have considered some of these points. He made me feel like a bloody first year medical student!* He continued to watch as Macmillan crossed the car park, took the keys from his pocket, climbed into his cab and drove off. *What? A Detective Inspector quizzes me about a possible murder and then drives off in an old-fashioned London taxi? Something not right here.*

* * *

Glasgow, Scotland

Following a phone call to arrange Rees's collection, Macmillan parked in Kent Street outside the Mitchell Library and took the lift to the fifth floor where he consulted the Glasgow and Inverness papers for information on McRae's death. *Hmm, nothing at all in the Evening Times, a short couple of paragraphs in the Glasgow Herald saying it was a motoring accident, an entry in the obituary column saying the same thing and asking everyone but the immediate family to stay away from the funeral...*He swapped papers. *Here's another brief article in the Inverness Courier saying he died of a road accident?* As he folded the papers to return them to their shelf, he noticed another article in the Glasgow Herald. *Jesus, there's a larger piece here on a road death in Plymouth of all places! The media are strangely silent on the demise and either the suicide or murder of one of Scotland's most senior and certainly most controversial politicians...*

He collected Rees from her hotel and they exchanged information prior to visiting McLeod in his Cathcart apartment. Macmillan drove to Pollokshaws whose wide, tree-lined avenues permitted him to pull into the side of the road and allow other cars to pass with ease. He left his driver's seat and sat on a pull-down seat in the rear of the taxi facing Rees in order to continue the conversation face to face.

Macmillan commenced a summary. "This just might be a series of coincidences or else it smacks of skulduggery by a person or persons unknown."

"Bit early for that assessment, Jock."

"Look at what we have. We know Willie was under surveillance by the security forces...Christ, the two of us are in the front line there for that matter! His home, his office and his place up in the Highlands were all broken into several times but nothing was stolen."

"Hector McLeod was under surveillance as well, according to Carnegie. He had Hector's phone tapped and visited his house without a warrant. Found nothing."

Macmillan nodded and continued. "He was known to be preparing an onslaught on government ambitions to deal with nuclear waste up in Dounreay and he was associated with Scottish paramilitary forces."

"Allegedly!"

"Okay. But he's found in a wrecked car in the middle of nowhere, on a road he knows very well. No adverse weather conditions. Up above, there are skid marks on the road opposite that might have been caused by a car trying to run his Volvo off the road. He's found still in his seatbelt, slumped in the driver's seat with his hands folded in his lap. There's a bullet in his brain. There are no local cops on duty so a young cop and an ambulance are sent to the scene. A day later the gun is found yards from the car, his personal belongings are piled neatly on a rock – although the car is tight against an overhang which prohibits the opening of the driver's door. His briefcase goes missing and when it's found, there are no sensitive documents in it. By a fluke, of the people who find him, one recognises him and one is a medic. One stated that he was smelling of drink and they find a half bottle of Grouse in his car – unbroken despite the fact that the car obviously rolled on its way downhill and Grouse whisky is a drink Willie would never entertain but the surgeon in Aberdeen says there was no alcohol in his blood. So, he's taken first to Inverness and then to Aberdeen where all of the routine procedures that would determine murder or suicide are wiped...need I go on?"

"Hmm, does begin to sound suspicious, eh? Rees looked at her watch. "Look, let's go to Hector's. He's expecting us and it'll be interesting to find out what he has to tell us about Willie's secretary."

"Okay. But we probably have to be pretty open with him. We need him to be honest with us and he'll smell a rat if we try to be too clever..." He started the engine. "Did you get hold of that weapon I asked for?"

Rees fished in her large handbag. "Yeah, the Glock Model 17 plus rounds as requested." She took a breath. "I asked for two... one for me...just in case."

Macmillan shook his head in mild disapproval and headed the taxi towards Cathcart.

* * *

McLeod was standing in the bay window watching the road when Macmillan and Rees turned the corner leading into Courthill Avenue. As they walked up the path leading to his front door, he'd already opened it, anxious to hear of their findings.

Coffee and sandwiches had been prepared and Macmillan placed four on his side plate, simultaneously stirring his coffee as the threesome dealt with the social formalities of greeting one another.

"How'd you get on with Willie's secretary, Hector?"

McLeod lit a cigarette in preference to food. "She was terrible upset as you'd expect. Told me Willie was cheerful all morning, he'd phoned ahead to get his fire lit up in Dornie, he'd a busy week of appointments ahead...appointments he seemed keen to deal with. Any idea that he was depressed or that he planned suicide...well, she dismissed that as impossible."

Rees intervened. "You mentioned you'd met with the local beat cop. Morrison was it?"

"Yeah. I'd had a few drinks but not so much that I couldn't function. I bumped into him. Nice guy. He was pally enough with Willie. Ann, Willie's secretary, told me he'd come into the office to express his condolences. She said, he'd told her that Willie was full of fun as he left, that Morrison helped him do a U-turn to get out of Glasgow...but she said he'd said that there was 'some funny business', I think that's what she said he'd said...'some funny business' as he drove away. But he didn't explain further."

Macmillan rose, saying. "Well, by all accounts, it appears that Willie didn't set off with the ambition of putting a bullet in his own head, eh?" As he did so, he removed his suit jacket revealing his shoulder holster containing the Glock pistol.

"Jesus! Are you guys carrying *guns?*"

Rees sought to reassure him. "It's okay, Hector. It kind of goes with the territory. But there's no likelihood of us using them. When we're on duty like this we have to carry them," she lied before changing the subject. "When we spoke on Tuesday, you mentioned that there wouldn't be a big SNP presence at his funeral and that you'd explain later. Want to fill us in?"

McLeod looked uncomfortable. "I'm still not sure I can trust you guys." He thought further. "First you tell me how you got on. I might do a news swap!"

Macmillan met Rees's gaze. "Well, it appears that everything we've learned might contradict the early announcement by the cops up north that Willie committed suicide." He then went on to summarise everything he'd earlier told Rees, his openness earning looks of surprise from his detective sergeant. "Hector, this is becoming something of a puzzle and we won't resolve matters unless we share everything we know. Now, I've been more honest with you than perhaps is wise but I need you to take a gamble that we're on the level and tell us everything you know. Otherwise, whoever was involved in this will walk away and Scotland will have lost a great man to a fiction."

McLeod massaged his left hand with his right, clearly nervous. "Listen, I've got a lot riding on this. I've only just met you guys and already you've turned out not to be what I thought you were. If I'm honest, I'm sitting here trying to balance the wisdom of working together with you to find Willie's killer..."

"If there was one," interrupted Rees.

McLeod bristled. "When I tell you what I know, you'll both believe there can be no doubt that there was a killer...or more than one, who knows? But the notion that the Establishment are trying put across, that he committed suicide is just hogwash. Bullshit!"

"Well, why not trust us, eh?"

McLeod looked at Macmillan attempting to gauge his next move. "There's already been too much violence, too much killing." He rose and walked to his bay window, considering his next action. "Okay, both of you place your guns in that top drawer there. It's lockable. I don't like the idea that I tell you what I know then you put a bullet in my forehead."

Rees groaned. "Hector..."

Macmillan stood and removed his gun. "Top drawer?"

"Yeah. The key's in the lock. Open it, place both guns inside and give me the key."

Macmillan held his hand out towards Rees and waved his fingers upwards suggesting she give him her gun which she did, shaking her head in protest in the process. He placed both pistols in the drawer and handed McLeod the key.

"I only hope to God that I'm not too far off my present assessment of you two. You've let me down once. I don't imagine I'll survive a second misjudgment now that guns are involved." He took a deep drag of his cigarette. "Okay. You know Willie and I were under surveillance. You know his places were broken into. What you don't know was that Willie had a file...a file naming paedophiles operating at the heart of Government. Senior politicians. It would have brought down the Heath Government and might yet see the end of Thatcher's Government in Willie's view. He was also onto a top secret report commissioned by Prime Minister Edward Heath that demonstrated that the oil under the North Sea would make an independent Scotland not only viable but would make the country *per capita*, one of the three richest countries in the world along with Norway and Switzerland. Heath didn't want it to see the light of day...nor does Thatcher, and Willie had all the details in his briefcase. He'd made four files for distribution. I don't know if he managed to post them before he was killed...but from what you say, they weren't reported as found in his possession after the accident."

"Jesus, this is dynamite," said Macmillan.

Rees topped up the three cups on the table. "What about your comment about the SNP not being represented at his funeral?"

McLeod stubbed his cigarette in an ashtray. "The party suspected that both Willie and I were involved with what they viewed as the less acceptable face of nationalism."

"SNLA?" asked Rees.

"Yeah."

"And were you?"

"I've no comment to make on that," he said defiantly. "His family in West Calder was also embarrassed by these allegations although they loved him. They put out a statement in the papers saying no one out with the family circle had to attend his funeral. I didn't get to pay my last respects."

"That must have been very upsetting, Hector," said Rees gently.

McLeod's eyes moistened as he nodded his agreement.

"And he was *warned*, Mel...he was warned. Someone calling themselves *Alba* twice got a message to him saying he wasn't safe and to take care."

"Who's *Alba*?" enquired Macmillan.

McLeod shrugged his shoulders. "Another party member? A friendly cop? Queen of England? Who knows!"

The ring tone of the hall phone interrupted the guessing game and McLeod left the room to answer it.

"This gets murkier by the minute, Mel."

"Yeah. I suppose I'd better let McGinnis know what we've found out, eh?"

"Not quite yet, Mel. We keep the same line going. We've developed good relations with Hector, he's beginning to open up about the SNLA...but nothing yet. This series of coincidences, all the cops away at the same time, the experienced pathologist off duty, the briefcase found without the files, no prints, no examination of powder burns, an immediate determination of suicide, an early cremation...we're looking at the most astonishing clutter of coincidences, the most inept police work imaginable or dirty work at the crossroads. I'd like to find out more before revealing our hand. I've suffered too many 'just step back from your investigation and leave it to the big boys' to hand this over right now."

McLeod returned to the room ashen-faced and sat down. Both Macmillan and Rees realised that something was amiss and attended to him, sitting down on his armchairs.

"What's up? asked Rees.

"That phone call. I've just been threatened by a man who tells me I'm next now that Willie's gone!"

Macmillan moved immediately into police mode. "Tell me exactly what was said."

McLeod reached back in his memory for the words. "He asked if he was talking to Hector McLeod. I said 'yes'. He asked if I was sad at Willie's death. I asked him who was calling and he said, 'I'm the man who's going to kill you when you least expect it'. I don't know where I got the balls but I replied, 'thanks for calling' and he replied by saying something like 'Gracias, merci beaucoup, danke schön, grazie mille. The pleasure's all mine.' Then he hung up"

Macmillan and Rees looked at one another and as one voice they each said simultaneously, "Hancock!"

"Who's Hancock?" asked Mcleod, puzzled.

"Bit of a long shot but there was a guy we worked with in a previous life..."

"A nut-job," interjected Rees.

"He used to say 'thank you' by using the foreign phrases you've just repeated."

Rees slapped the heel of her hand against her forehead. "That's where I remembered it!" She turned to Macmillan. "When I was interviewing D.I. Carnegie up in Luss, he told me he'd been told to ask around for information about the cop killer in the afforested areas of Argyll and Bute because forensics had pinpointed that area as being one that might be being used by this guy who's been blowing people up! He told me he'd met a curious guy who lived in a cottage and had spilled tacks on the road. He found it unusual that he'd been using small tacks to fix a fence and said that he'd finished the conversation with the expression, Gracias, *merci beaucoup,* etcetera. I couldn't place it at the time but it's just come back to me. Jimmy Hancock!"

"Where was that cottage?" asked Macmillan.

Rees thought. "I think he said it was on the shore front of the loch at Glenmallan. Up the hill opposite a jetty."

As Rees and Macmillan discussed the possibilities revealed by the phone call, McLeod opened the drawer and withdrew both pistols. He slid one in his belt and turned to face the two officers.

Releasing the safety catch, he pulled back on the barrel assembly, arming it. Holding it before him with both hands he aimed it at Macmillan.

"For an accountant, you certainly seem comfortable with that Glock, eh Hector?"

"This isn't my first rodeo, Jock. Car keys. Now!"

"Sure thing Hector. And where might you intend to go? Glenmallan?"

"Not your concern, Jock."

"Look, Hector, you and I both know you wouldn't shoot that thing at us. Anyway, I would most probably disarm you before you pulled the trigger."

"Not from a seated position you wouldn't. And you're right. I don't want to shoot you. Not mortally anyway. But I'm quite capable of putting the one of your legs out of action." He turned his gaze slightly to Rees..."And that applies to both of you...so... keys, please."

Macmillan continued to invite reflection. "This is unwise, Hector. How far do you think you'd get? One phone call to our brother officers and the taxi would be pulled over before you got to the end of the road."

"I'll take my chances. A guy's just threatened my life. He looks like being the guy who shot Willie. I'm going after him. You have protocols to follow. I can just take him out!"

"Well, there's absolutely no proof whatsoever. It's just a hunch and if it is Hancock, he's a mean *hombre!*"

"Keys!"

Macmillan conceded. "They're in my jacket pocket."

McLeod stepped sideways and collected the keys, continuing to train the pistol on Macmillan. He retreated into the hallway and with his left hand pulled the phone connection roughly from the wall. He stood at the door entry of the living room. "You're three floors up here. I'm locking you in. I wish you both well and hope that you'll allow me my moment of revenge." He stepped backwards towards the front door, unlocked it and stepping outside, locked both Macmillan and Rees in his apartment.

Rees rose and walked urgently to the bay window. "We'd better get after him quickly."

Macmillan remained seated. "No need. He's not going far."

"Eh, how d'you..."

"He's left his wallet on the mantelpiece. There's no petrol in the tank. I pretty much ran out when I pulled up outside and he won't think to look for the jerry-can in the boot. My suggestion is that we get out of here and make our way to the Auld Smiddy. If I was Hector, I'd be trying to borrow a few quid from *mi amigos*. So he'll head for the pub or to one of his pals. They all live locally. And I'd bet as an organised man, Hector'll have a spare key for the front door somewhere. Let's search his house."

*

It took but three minutes to discover the spare front door key and four to find themselves on the pavement walking towards the nearby railway station, passing an empty Auld Smiddy en route. Rees was still anxious. "Look, Jock. There's an armed man bent on violence driving around the streets of Glasgow. Whatever you say, I'm going to report this. This is going to end badly."

Macmillan stopped short. "Alright, you win. But I'll phone in. You check out Homelea Road over there while I make the call. There's every likelihood that the taxi's sitting with an empty tank at the side of the road with Hector trying to work out how he's going to get up to Glenmallan."

Rees looked unsure but agreed and Macmillan crossed the road to a phone box, watched all the way by Rees. He gave her the thumbs up and pushed some coin into the phone. Three rings later Nobby Clark spoke on the line. "Office of the Commissioner of Police, Chief Inspector Clark speaking."

"No time for chatting, Nobby. Need another favour."

"Jock! Sure!"

Remember that lunatic Jimmy Hancock? Our friend in Northern Ireland? It looks like he's up to some mischief here in Scotland. Can you pull his file very quietly and find out what the hell Special Branch has got him doing now?"

"Will do, Jock. Give me half an hour."

"Thanks, Nobby. Much appreciated. Can't talk now but I'll fill you in as soon as I can."

Macmillan replaced the phone and repeated his thumbs up gesture to Rees who was still at the corner surveying the street scene. He crossed the road and took her by the arm, guiding her towards a row of houses that led from the main road. "Let's split up. We'll cover more ground that way. We meet back here in fifteen minutes. If he's not found we put our thinking caps back on."

"No need," said Rees. "Look!"

About a hundred yards along the tree-lined avenue, Macmillan's taxi sat parked poorly outside one of the houses.

Walking swiftly, Macmillan moved towards the vehicle, encouraging Rees behind him as he did so. Approaching the rear of the taxi, he stooped into a crouch and peered inside as far as was possible. McLeod sat in the drivers' seat, sobbing quietly. Macmillan pulled at the handle, opening the driver's door and grabbed McLeod's right arm, levering him from the vehicle and on to the pavement.

"Easy, Hector. No need for heroics." He turned him over forcefully and removed the pistol he'd secreted in his waistband before checking inside, looking for the second weapon. Observing it lying on the passenger seat, he called out to Rees now close behind him.

"Mel. Second gun. Passenger's seat."

Putting McLeod's arm in a lock, he bundled him easily into the rear of the vehicle with no resistance.

"Hector, you're an eegit!" He climbed in beside him. "We had a deal. The Three Musketeers, remember?" He eased open the glazed partition between driver and passenger and passed the Glock through the opening to Rees. He lifted McLeod's chin to find eye contact. "Let's start again"

* * *

Instructing Rees to retrieve the small can of petrol he'd purchased outside Fort William and put some in the tank, Macmillan further asked that she take the wheel and drive the taxi to his apartment in Broomhill before bringing McLeod round, coaxing and cajoling him while pointing out the implications of his earlier actions. He counted off the offences on his fingers.

"Stealing lethal weapons belonging to police officers, threatening to shoot them, stealing and driving away a stolen vehicle...if I arrest you for these offences, first offender or not, you're looking at substantial jail time. Alternatively, you screw the bobbin and work with Mel and me to get to the truth of the matter of Willie's death." He held out his hand. "Shake my hand and we work together, all past misdemeanors forgotten." McLeod made no move. "You're upset, Hector. Your best friend has been killed. You're not yourself right now but I need you to step up to the plate. You have insights and contacts not available to me or Mel." He continued to hold his hand out. "Shake my hand, Hector." Slowly, McLeod met his gaze and raised his hand to Macmillan's.

Gradually McLeod's mood improved and apologies were many and heartfelt. The two men fell into conversation but were thrown violently to the side of the cab when Rees performed what felt like an emergency stop and steered the taxi into the kerb.

"Look ahead, Jock."

Macmillan regained his balance and looked through the driver's windshield. Parked outside his flat at a careless angle to the pavement were two police cars, lights still flashing. Beside them a silver Triumph Acclaim, also with a temporary blue light sat, its hazard warning lights alerting other drivers to the partial road blockage. A uniformed police officer stood guard at the common entrance; a 'close' in Glasgow parlance.

Rees engaged the handbrake. "Did you tell the police to meet us at your apartment?"

"Eh, no. Not exactly!"

"Then why three police cars?"

Before Macmillan had had an opportunity to respond, Rees pointed upwards. "Look, Jock. In your bay window. It's Carnegie."

Macmillan leant forward and lowered his head to improve his perspective. He narrowed his eyes. "Well, so that's our friend, Detective Sergeant Anderson Carnegie? He's obviously been brought back from the wilderness." He thought for a moment. "Looks like our cover's blown, Mel. Wouldn't surprise me if there was also a contingent in your hotel room right now. They'll have decided that we've gone off *piste* and are buggering up their investigation."

"What alerted them?"

Macmillan shrugged. "They have my address since I was arrested. Or perhaps DS Carnegie up there in my flat or Sergeant Donaghey in Inverness weren't convinced by our Performance Standards line...Might have been the doctor in Aberdeen smelled a rat and phoned in. Whatever the reason, we're going to face some interview time denying charges of professional incompetency at best for the next few weeks unless we come up with some pretty impressive results."

"Perhaps it was when you phoned to alert them to Hector being on the loose with a gun?"

McLeod looked anxious.

"Eh, that call never took place. Sorry, Mel. I phoned Nobby Clark and asked him for the low-down on Hancock."

Rees shook her head. "Lying and deceiving a colleague. How's Hector meant to trust us when we don't trust each other?" She smiled as she said it, reversed the car slightly and performed a slow U-turn, driving back down the hill towards the Clyde Tunnel.

*

Arriving in Govan on the south bank of the Clyde, Macmillan stepped from the taxi and phoned Clark in London.

"Hi, Jock. Some news but not a lot." He took a piece of paper from his inside pocket and flattened it on the desk with one hand.

"Whatever he's up to in Scotland, he's doing it under the deepest cover. His file has been filleted. He's apparently on an official assignment up north. Has been for two months now but there's nothing else. No details of his duties, no contact numbers. Got this, though!"

He started to read from the paper before him, explaining. "Found a psychological assessment of him written up four months ago. It's lengthy but let me read you some of the more salient text. 'Hancock displays many characteristics which place him very high on the spectrum of psychopathy. He is possessed of high levels of emotional intelligence meaning he can charm when he needs to but also scores poorly on empathy which allows him to carry out actions without the need to feel compassion for their results. He scores highly as a sociopath and is more spontaneous and intense than other people. He is likely to do bizarre, sometimes erratic things that most people wouldn't do. He is unbound by normal social contracts and his behaviour will often seem irrational or extremely risky. He lies easily and scores highly on recklessness and impulsivity. This allows him to make quick decisions but does not suggest that these decisions are likely to be wise ones. He is untroubled by remorse or guilt. He is highly intelligent. Many top criminals are possessed of these characteristics and are routinely assessed by medical professionals as having traits which lead them to believe that the subject is a psychopath. In this instance, however, Mr Hancock is in the service of Her Majesty's Government. Dependent upon the particular assignment he is allocated, he may perform very well indeed. I would not, however recommend him for any task that requires diplomacy, tact or patience.' It's signed here by a Doctor Ian McAlpine who has more letters after his name than he's got in it!"

"Thanks, Nobby. Listen, these pints I owe you are piling up. We'll have quite the shindig when this goes away." He glanced at the taxi where Rees and McLeod appeared to be in easy conversation. "One more thing, pal. Is there any sign down in London of Mel and I being in the bad books?"

"Jock, it always surprises me when you're *not* in the bad books...but it's quiet right now. The Commissioner's not mentioned anything and there's been no telephone traffic suggesting you're

anything less than Superman and Supergirl saving a grateful nation."

"Much appreciated, Nobby. But don't be surprised if the chatter soon starts about us going rogue or something. I think we're on to something but we're not exactly fighting using Queensbury Rules. However, don't try to contact us...especially at my Glasgow apartment. You'll be talking to Strathclyde cops if you do. I'll get back to you when I can." He ended the call. "Take care, brother!"

* * *

Hancock eased his troubled van off the road at Glenmallan and switched his lights off. It was dark now and his cottage showed no signs of having had been visited following his departure a few days earlier. *But then, it wouldn't,* he told himself. As casually as he could make his arrival appear, Hancock walked up the pathway to his front door leaving the Semtex in the rear of the van and taking care to avoid each of the three trip wires he'd placed to alert him to anyone using it if he was in the croft at the time.

Checking each room in turn by torchlight, he satisfied himself that there had been no intruders while he was away. He turned on an electric light so dim it almost failed to match the lux of the small torch. He stooped and fed his Rayburn cooker with a mix of rolled newspapers, small pieces of kindling, larger pieces of wood and some peat. Leaving it to ignite, he returned to the van and brought the contents of the van into his small kitchen where he pulled at a floorboard and withdrew one of two American M112 charges. Placing it on the table beside the Semtex he took the explosive charge and looked at the ingredients before him. He smiled, *Guy Fawkes has got nothin' on fuckin' me!* He stepped over to a cupboard whose door was attached to the frame but by one hinge and removed the Union Flag of the United Kingdom and spread it on the surface of the table.

Chapter Twenty-one

FRIDAY 12TH APRIL 1985

Glasgow, Scotland

Following an uncomfortable night sleeping in the taxi, Rees, Macmillan and McLeod ate an early breakfast in the University Cafe in Glasgow's Byres Road.

"I know it's a risk, Mel but before we head up to Glenmallan, I want to talk to this beat cop, Morrison that Hector spoke with. Sounds like he might have information he wasn't prepared to share with a civvy but might just share with a fellow police officer." He chewed on some toast. "If he was on day shift yesterday, he'll probably still be on day shift today. He'll be based in Stewart Street so if we're quick about it we might be able to catch him coming out of the station. It'll give authenticity to our meeting." He turned to face McLeod who was dipping his toast in egg yolk. "Hector, I need you there to identify him. Mel, you're the getaway driver!"

"Here we go again! Support staff. Shall I make you a cup of coffee and take some notes while you spring into action Detective Inspector?"

"Later, Sergeant," said MacMillan, suddenly impatient.

*

As beat police officers left Stewart Street Police Station in ones and twos to attend their duties, McLeod nudged Macmillan. "On the right. Big chap."

Macmillan exited the taxi and strode the few paces to the front door of the police station where Constable Morrison was finishing a conversation with another officer. Macmillan stood by as the pair separated.

"Constable Morrison, unless I'm mistaken."

Morrison eyed his interlocutor. "You're not mistaken. How can I help you?"

Macmillan produced his warrant card briefly before replacing in in his pocket.

"Jock Macmillan. Detective Inspector, Special Branch. I was just about to catch you inside before you headed off. Got a second?"

"Always happy to help our brothers-in-arms. What can I do for you?"

"You witnessed Willie McRae leaving Glasgow for his holiday home in Dornie?"

Morrison eyed him with a new suspicion. "I did."

"Anything unusual about his departure?"

"Well now, I'd have thought that you boys would be right on top of this!"

"Well, we're not, Constable Morrison. Which is why I'm asking the question. Why do you think we should be on top of this?"

Morrison smiled. "Because it was obvious that your people were keeping a very close eye on Mr. McRae that day."

"Say more."

"I helped him get into his car on West Nile Street; he did a U-turn and was chased up the road by two of your colleagues in unmarked cars."

"And how would you know this?"

"Because I've a good memory for numbers, Inspector. I returned to the office later and checked the registrations of the cars, BGS 425S and PSJ 136X. Both numbers blocked, which is our system's way of revealing them as being used by Special Branch."

"And they followed Mr. McRae?"

"Two officers. Car each. Chased after him like a bat out of hell! One of them ran a red light to keep up with him."

"Did you tell anyone back at the office? File a report?"

"If Special Branch is involved, I don't want to be the one who fingered them."

"Good man!" Macmillan fished in his pocket. "This is an inventory of Mr. McRae's belongings found by Northern Constabulary after his death. I'm told you knew McRae. Does it make sense to you?"

Morrison took the two page list and perused it. "Looks like exactly the kind if things you'd take with you for a weekend away; changes of clothes, medications, magazines, his work stuff...all seems okay. Don't understand why..."

"Anything missing?"

Morrison consulted the list again. "Ah...no cigarettes! I helped him into his Volvo and he had two cartons of cigarettes. Willie was never without his smokes." He looked again. "*Grouse* whisky? Willie never drank Grouse. He drank Islay Mist or Glenmorangie. Never Grouse. And the malt whisky I handed to him in the car has gone missing from this list. Oh, here, I can see why you're in plain clothes and I'm pounding the beat, Inspector."

Macmillan took the inventory and returned it to his pocket. "You've been very helpful Constable. Much appreciated."

They shook hands and Morrison went on his way, looking for a member of the public at whom to smile.

* * *

Macmillan returned to the taxi and joined both in its rear reporting his findings to Rees and McLeod. "So we know now that he was followed by two Special Branch cars, we know he was carrying information that he felt might bring down the government and lead to Scottish Independence and we understand that *that* information was not contained in his briefcase when it eventually turned up."

McLeod began the process of lighting a cigarette, allowing it to dangle from his lips as he spoke. "Well, it seems to me that it's an open and shut case."

Macmillan demurred, "I'd rather have it that to any reasonable person, it would seem that there's an argument suggesting motivation and that there's also circumstantial evidence suggesting the involvement of security services in the acquisition of materials that might be prejudicial to the safety and security of the country."

"Aye, weasel words, Jock. It's well seein' you're a lawyer. It's the safety and security of the British Establishment, you mean."

Rees opened the rear window slightly to permit some of the smoke from McLeod's cigarette to escape. "Yeah, but if you also consider the scene of the accident..."

Macmillan continued his analysis. "Well, we have the possibility...no more...of his car being forced off the road. We know he left Glasgow in good spirits and find it difficult to accept that he'd just run his own car off the road, pull out his pistol and fire it twice, shooting himself once in the head. We know he couldn't open the door of his car, that he was still strapped in when he was found but that his personal papers were stacked in an orderly pile some distance from the vehicle."

"Then there was the gun itself," added Rees.

"Aye. The gun is found, dependent upon which version of Constable Crawford's testimony is ultimately agreed, also far from the vehicle or underneath it. They don't check it for prints because once it was established that he'd been shot, the immediate verdict is suicide. When he's taken to Aberdeen, no check is made on powder burns...either at the wound site on his head or on his hands. He's disinfected in preparation for theatre, pronounced brain dead and life support is switched off. There's currently no evidence that I'm aware of that the bullet actually came from Willie's gun although I'd suspect that there aren't too many assassins going around carrying a pea-shooter with a .22 capacity. The Fiscal reports on the Tuesday morning, only thirty-six hours after his death and eighty-six hours after the crash that he was killed by his own hand, delivers a suicide verdict but the papers only carry a story saying it was a road accident. He determines that there's no need to retain any organs or both parts for future reference and the family are contacted and arrange a cremation effectively destroying all the evidence."

"Then there's the mystery of the blended whisky."

"Good point...Willie's favourite malts are missing as are his cigarettes, the pathologist finds no alcohol in his blood but we're told he was smelling of whisky! There's a half empty bottle of Grouse...unbroken despite the car rolling...which might well have been used to stink him up a bit."

McLeod nodded his approval. "And in the meantime we've a guy with Special Branch credentials whom we know to be an explosives expert, apparently blowing the head off a military defence cop, blowing up four beat cops, sending a letter bomb to the Secretary of State for Scotland and now threatening to kill me!"

Macmillan and Rees exchanged glances. "What's our next move, Jock?"

"Well, we have to take seriously the allegation that some of those named as paedophiles in Willie's dossier are senior members of the Intelligence Services and *may*...I repeat *may*....be disinclined to see us bring this investigation to any sort of proper conclusion."

"They'd ignore all that we've uncovered?" asked McLeod incredulously.

"If it suited their purpose, they'd give it the full ostrich!" He shrugged. "That said, I suppose Mel and I could write this up and send it to McGinnis. She'd clap us in irons for a while so they could rebuke us for not reporting our findings as we unearthed them and for consorting with a suspected SNLA terrorist...

"I never confirmed one way or the other that either Willie or I were involved with any organisation..."

"Aye maybe so, but you'd be arrested and held, accused of all sorts so they could interrogate you about this stuff. And just so you know, Hector, we record everything that's said inside this taxi. I should have mentioned."

"Jesus! I think maybe you should have!"

"You've said nothing incriminating but I'll review the tape just to make sure."

Rees interjected. "So maybe the first option of playing this by the book isn't our best bet?"

"The key to this seems to be Hancock," said Macmillan. "We've absolutely no proof. But we know him to be capable of these acts from our time with him in Belfast. He's an explosives expert. We've had his capacity to kill confirmed by a recent psychological report on him and we finger him because he uses that daft way of saying 'thank you'. It's a long shot but maybe we track him down and see where it takes us, eh?"

"Well, I've got nothing to lose," said McLeod. If I stay at home and sit on my backside, it looks like I'll be his next victim."

"If it *is* him," corrected Rees before adding, "What's your personal take on it, Jock?"

Macmillan laced his fingers and brought his hands together in a tent. "If I'm pushed to an analysis of what's going on here, I have to say it looks a lot like the powers-that-be down in London – or some of them – have decided to deal with the Scottish question by deploying Hancock in a 'Black Ops' assignment. He behaves as if he's a Scottish terrorist and provides the media with a stick to beat Scottish Nationalism over the head."

"How does killing Willie lock with that theory," asked McLeod.

"My initial guess is that Willie stumbled across some very damaging information that would seriously wound the government and whoever facilitated this assignment found it just too tempting to remove Willie as part of the wider benefits of this operation."

"Why don't you two just report these findings to your bosses in London and walk away? Surely you're part of the same security service that employs Hancock to do what he's doing if that supposition is accurate."

"Well, you don't know the full detail of our operation, Hector but I wasn't sent up here to pursue an overtly political goal. I was sent up along with Mel to infiltrate Willie's camp in order to secure information pertinent to the security of the state. We did that but you brought that part of the operation to an end when you discovered our warrant cards. However, if we come across

226

circumstances that require us to act in order to protect the best interests of the state, we are permitted to do so."

Rees dissented. "Well, I'm not quite sure that London had in mind us withholding crucial security information and taking initiatives without consulting them."

"You may be right, Mel. But we're not automatons. We use our initiative. We make decisions when we're on the battlefield. My assessment is that we need to find out more of what's going on. I've no proof right now that there's a security service operation being run in parallel to our own. My 'Black Ops' theory is just that right now, a *theory*. All I know is that following the death of Willie, our nearest target is one Hector McLeod and he's been threatened by someone. Now, if we happen to bump into the man who made that threat, then all well and good. If it also happens to bring a halt to the bombings that have been going on, then many people will have cause to thank us."

"They won't believe a word of what we have to tell them."

Macmillan spoke sternly. "Listen carefully...both of you. We tell them Hector received a phone call from someone celebrating Willie's death and saying that he had information about who shot him. He asked Hector to meet him in Glenmallan. Hector was desperate to go but we smelled a rat and worried that we might lose our main contact to a violent act. We came along to support him quietly..."

"Jesus, you think on your feet, eh," said McLeod.

"Trust me, he's built a career on lies and exaggeration," responded Rees.

"Creativity is always useful in pursuing bad guys. And this particular lie has the benefit of having its roots in the truth but gets us all off the hook quite neatly."

McLeod listened to the exchange avidly. "Well, for sure I'd have cause to thank you both if this matter was brought to a conclusion."

Macmillan brought the discussion to an end. "So, let's all go to Glenmallan, eh?"

* * *

Glenmallan, Loch Long, Scotland

An hour later, the black taxi climbed the road from Gare Loch before descending steeply to Loch Long. At the foot of the hill, Macmillan pulled into a makeshift lay-by and turned off the ignition. An inscription on a nearby stone stated, *'This road was made from the Castle Rosneath to Tenne Clauch in the year 1777 by his Grace John, Duke of Argyll.'*

He turned to face his passengers. "Okay. Absolutely no heroics. Glenmallan is just up the road a bit. Hancock's cottage shouldn't be hard to find. Whether he's there or not is anybody's guess. However, we work on the basis that he's there, he's armed, he's been given some kind of remit...and he's crazy! I'm going in alone to talk with him..."

Rees bridled. "I'm armed and dangerous too, Detective Inspector!"

"You are, but if Hancock is on top form, he's like Popeye on spinach. Your job is to remain with Hector and protect him. If you hear gunshots, I'll be looking for backup. You remain in the taxi and keep an eye on the outside of his cottage."

"So much for working in partnership."

"That's a direct order, Detective Sergeant!"

Exasperated, Rees drew her pistol and pointed it at the back of Macmillan's head as he began to manoeuvre the taxi from its stationary position. "*Bang!*" she whispered, catching McLeod's eye as she did so. She blew imaginary smoke from the muzzle of the gun and shared a smile with him.

Ignorant of the pretended drama behind him, Macmillan followed the road along the shoreline until he saw a jetty jutting into the loch. Carefully he parked twenty yards on the landward side of the road, out of sight of the cottage.

"Don't worry if I'm a while. I'm going to try to talk with Hancock. If he bites, I might be some time. If you hear shots, come a-running! Hector, don't even *think* about leaving this taxi. Mel, perhaps you'd sit in the driver's seat in case we need to leave this neighbourhood quickly, eh?"

Now approaching late morning, the loch was still. A slight breeze caused the few boats moored there to clink and creak as they strained gently at their moorings. Macmillan realised he was still wearing his suit and felt somewhat out of place midst the marine and farm detritus as he surveyed the harbour from the roadside. *Still, a suit might have advantages here,* he reflected.

Slowly he walked forward until the small cottage came into view on the hill, smoke rising from its chimney. *Hmm, thought I could smell peat.* Warily he scanned the two windows facing the road but didn't detect any presence in the darkness behind the half-opened curtains that framed the glass on each side. He eyed the path carefully and noticed almost immediately the three trip wires crossing it. *Christ, with improvised devices like those, it's definitely Hancock,* he thought. *Now, are they here to warn him or to do damage to anyone who approaches?* He considered his options. *Nothing ventured...*

Macmillan walked up the path cautiously avoiding the taut fishing lines designed to accomplish a task he couldn't be sure of and approached the door of the croft. He knocked the door three times hoping it sounded confident and untroubled.

Inside, Hancock had placed his improvised Semtex explosive device below the floorboards along with the rest of his armaments. The boiling kettle he was busily watching so he might enjoy a cup of tea was abandoned as he went into a crouch, an automatic reaction to any hint of danger. He gathered his thoughts. No alarm? How could his alarm system have failed him? He armed himself with his favourite Walther *Polizeipistole Kriminalmode* pistol, placing it in the rear waistband of his trousers, approached the door undoing the latch and opening it.

"Hi Jimmy," said a smiling Jock Macmillan. "You'll need to do better with those trip wires. I could see them from the road!"

Hancock's face, initially expressing curiosity and wariness now conveyed astonishment. "You?"

"Aye...me, Jimmy! Jock Macmillan. Late of Belfast, now in the Office of Constable. A senior one mind you. Up here to say hello." He folded his arms. "I come in peace, Jimmy. Are you not going to invite me in?"

"But how did you..." Urgently he looked behind Macmillan to assess any further danger. Finding none, his gaze returned to meet Macmillan's. "How did you know where to find me? No one knows..." He faltered again as his mind worked busily to determine the circumstances in which he found himself.

"Relax, Jimmy. We're on the same side. Working for the same team." Macmillan decided to attempt to relax Hancock. "If I may?" Slowly he ventured into his jacket pocket and produced his police identification. "Special Branch!"

Hancock had overcome such anxiety as he'd had and was now aggressive in his questioning. "So what the fuck are you doing up *here*?"

Macmillan decided to replay his approach to Sergeant Donaghey in Inverness. He stepped past a confused Hancock without resistance and entered the cottage. Looking round, at the basic comforts of the house, he continued his approach of speaking confidently. "Two sugars if it's coffee, Jimmy. Three if it's tea!"

"Make yourself at home, won't you?" he replied sarcastically.

*

Hancock permitted Macmillan into his kitchen and cleared a second chair used only as a shelf for clothing in order that his unexpected house-guest might find somewhere to sit.

"So you'd better tell me why you're up here, eh Macmillan."

All in good time, Jimmy. I've been sent up here from London to have a chat with you...but first, how are you doing? Haven't seen you since Belfast."

"Belfast was a long time ago...what...six years...seven?" His curiosity remained an itch he had to scratch. "So why have London sent you up here?"

Macmillan satisfied himself that his presumptions about Hancock's role had been proved accurate and decided to probe further without exposing himself. "Your role is top secret, Jimmy. But there are a lot of people in London who are anxious about the fall-out if things unravel and there's some unanticipated public awareness of your activities."

"Fuckin' pussies! That lot don't realise the need to shed some blood to achieve their objectives."

Still making intelligent guesses, Macmillan played to what he saw as Hancock's probable prejudice against politicians. "You know how it works, Jimmy. It's not your fellow professionals who are getting antsy about your work, it's the politicians...and they're the top boyos on this one. Senior politicians."

Macmillan's empathic understanding proved to be accurate. "Politicians! I've put my life on the line for these bastards so many times and what do we find? At the slightest pressure they want to back off. So you've been sent north to tell me to calm down, eh?"

"Not exactly. I've a measure of discretion. They're jumpy and want to know where this goes next." He pushed further. "So where do you intend to take this?"

Hancock laughed. "If you knew the carnage my next wee caper will cause..."

"Well, that's kind of the reason I'm here, Jimmy."

Hancock's mood darkened. "I'm telling you nothing. Even when we were in Belfast you were a bosses' man. Always the smart guy. But you couldn't pull the trigger could you? Always had to wait for someone like me to do the dirty work. You'd be the one sitting trying to rationalise everything while I was out hunting the bastards trying to damage the state that employs us."

Macmillan concurred. "You certainly were no slouch when it came to shooting people, Jimmy. And you've not lost your touch, have you?"

"Don't patronise me, Macmillan. You still think I'm a fool, don't you? You always did. Well, *I'm* running this project up here and I'm just doing what I was asked to do, like the good soldier I am. And if a few men die, it's just the way things go."

"And your assessment is that this needs to continue?"

Hancock snapped. "I told you I wasn't going to answer any operational questions." He rose and pulled the Walther PPK from his belt, pointing it at Macmillan. "Are you carrying?"

Macmillan sighed, having anticipated Hancock's reaction to his presence. "Of course I am. You wouldn't expect an operational officer to be knocking about the streets carrying a water pistol, would you?"

"Still a Glock?"

"Still a Glock 17."

"Then just you hand it over here until I'm sure what's going on."

The Walther PPK pointed at his head persuaded Macmillan that anything other than compliance was futile and he passed over his Glock.

"No second pistol or a knife?"

"Only my bare hands. But you'll remember my proficiency with them, eh?"

Hancock bristled. "I was drunk that night."

"Aye, maybe so...but that's all in the past, Jimmy. I'm here to conclude the operation you've been given. Too many people have been killed for London's taste. Mission accomplished, soldier."

Hancock cocked his pistol threateningly. "*I* say when its 'mission accomplished'. And I've one more task to complete before I hang my boots up. Biggest yet."

Hancock stepped backwards and stooped. Whilst maintaining his gaze and his gun directly on Macmillan, he levered a floorboard with his fingertips and removed it. Deepening his crouch, he felt for and removed the sack containing his improvised explosive device. "Just realised you might save me some time. My car's buggered and you have one on the road outside. Perfect. You can help me finish the job by taking me to Glasgow."

"And what mischief have you in mind there?"

Hancock laughed. "There's a nationalist pub called the Auld Smiddy in Glasgow. Frequented by all sorts but there's a nationalist contingent meets there most nights. They'll hear from me!"

"Can I assume that's an explosive device there, Jimmy?" Macmillan nodded at the brown sack at Hancock's feet.

"And a big one at that! They'll hear this blast north *and* south of the border!" He gestured towards the door of his cottage. "No more chat. You're going to drive me to Glasgow."

"Well, okay...but I've a couple of surprises for you."

"And what are they?"

"I'm accompanied on this assignment by your old comrade-in-arms Melissa Rees...now Detective Sergeant Melissa Rees, Special Branch."

"Christ, not *that* bundle of trouble!"

"My sentiments exactly. But London wanted people who knew you." He took a pause before continuing. We're also accompanied by a new recruit...a long-haired undercover cop but wet behind the ears...name's Ciaran Conor. New and harmless."

"Jesus, you people travel team-handed, eh?"

"...and there's one other thing!"

"Which is?"

"We've been traveling around Glasgow in an old London taxi. Helps reduce suspicion...and costs," he added unnecessarily.

"Fuck's sake," said Hancock exuding frustration with every syllable. "I need bullets and weapons, there's a problem. Top cop here needs transport they give him a fuckin' London taxi."

"Go figure bureaucrats and politicians, Jimmy. You and I know that the kind of work we do is best left to professionals like you and me..."

"Aye, maybe professionals like *me*!" He replaced the floorboard and stamped it down. "Is Rees or that other cop carrying? And don't try to trick me. I haven't decided whether it'd just be better to shoot the three of you and bury you in a glen where you wouldn't be found ever again! If I find they're tooled up they get shot. Simple as that. Now let me ask you again!"

Rees has a Glock. Conor has nothing."

"They're dead if you're lying." He looked round the small kitchen, collected a wallet which he pocketed and a sharp hunting knife which he placed in a sheath strapped to his right ankle. "Before we leave, I just want to tidy up a wee bit. Don't want to leave any incriminating evidence and anyway, cleanliness is next to Godliness, eh?" Without removing his gaze from Macmillan, he stepped over to the other side of the room, a distance that took him two strides and turned a valve atop a large blue metal container whose red lettering described it as holding one hundred and three pounds of butane gas. It hissed as it left its confines. Moving to a work surface abutting the small sink, he placed the folded lid of a cardboard pizza box into an electric toaster, turned it to high heat and switched it on at the wall socket. Hancock lifted the sack containing the explosive device and gestured to Macmillan by waving his gun at him that he should leave the house. "We should probably move, eh?"

* * *

McLeod and Rees sat edgily in the taxi awaiting Macmillan's return. The radio played quietly in the background. As the music gave way to an hourly news report, McLeod urged Rees to turn up the volume. "They're talking about Willie!"

The newsreader introduced the item making reference to the Scottish Lord Advocate, Baron Fraser of Carmyllie. "The Lord Advocate, Scotland's most senior legal authority, made the following statement today in light of emerging rumours that SNP politician Willie McRae had been murdered."

Fraser's reassuring voice evidently sought to comfort. "The irresistible inference to be drawn from all the facts and circumstances surrounding this tragic death is that Mr. McRae took his own life. The investigation provided us with solid evidence indicating firm suicidal intentions following a number of personal incidents which troubled Mr. McRae deeply. His death was neither suspicious nor unexplained."

"Why didn't you permit a Fatal Accident Enquiry, Lord Advocate?"

"Well, I must say that if an inquiry had been instructed, law officers might well have been criticised for using an inquiry only to cause embarrassment to the SNP. All that an inquiry would have revealed would have been deeply unhappy personal details of a very unhappy member of that Party. I trust I have reassured you there is no mystery about his death. It was a sad and unhappy end for Mr McRae. It is now time to respect the wishes of his family and leave his memory in peace."

The newsreader continued, "However, the views of Lord Fraser have been contradicted by his immediate predecessor, fellow Conservative, Sir Nicholas Fairbairn, the then Solicitor General for Scotland who stated that the death of Mr. McRae merited further investigation."

McLeod started, "Wh...what?"

"What's up?"

"That guy...Sir Nicholas Fairbairn....The file....He's one of the people Willie was going to name as a paedophile!"

Rees's brow furrowed. "Then why would he invite further speculation?"

"Double bluff? The confidence of a member of the Establishment who believes himself beyond retribution? Who knows with these types!"

* * *

Macmillan and Hancock walked down the path, Macmillan considering options all the way. Hancock walked closely behind him, holding his pistol against his kidney. From the front they looked like two friends out for an afternoon stroll.

Approaching the taxi, Macmillan took the lead. He hailed his two colleagues and opened the rear door. "Ahoy there, shipmates. Look who I've brought with me. It's our old pal...Jimmy Hancock." He half turned to Hancock. You remember Mel, here don't you?" He leaned into the space inside the rear of the taxi and caught McLeod's eye. "And this young man is Ciaran Conor, Jimmy. A young cop who's trying to learn the difficulties of working under-cover while being dressed as if he's just returned from listening to the Grateful Dead at Woodstock." His eye contact with McLeod lingered in an attempt to ensure that he didn't reveal himself as the person Hancock had earlier threatened to kill.

Hancock moved quickly with graceful energy. He brought the gun up to the open window. "Rees! Niceties later. Macmillan here tells me you're carrying, so pass your weapon over right now and I don't fire this one." He turned his attention to McLeod who sat stricken at the change of circumstances. "You...you just sit there and be quiet."

Macmillan caught McLeod's attention and gestured agreement.

Behind them an explosion rent the sky with such force that all four could feel the heat wave as it hit a nano-second before the blast had Macmillan and Hancock stumble against the vehicle. Orange flames licked immediately at the roof of the croft.

Hancock stepped back to permit Macmillan room to manoeuvre. "Right, into the taxi, Macmillan. We're going on a wee mystery tour."

Both men entered and Hancock sat in the rear seat facing them and the front of the cab, his PPK pointing directly at Macmillan's midriff.

"So, Jimmy. Your mission is as yet incomplete?"

"Listen you..."He bit his tongue and spoke instead to Rees. "Drive to Glasgow. Drive without bringing attention to the taxi or there'll be gunfire. I'll guide you as we approach the city." He returned his comments to Macmillan. "You were always the smart one...always sitting back and doing all the thinking. No balls! Christ, Rees there had bigger balls than you! Well, now it's different. I've a job to finish and you're not going to talk me out of it no matter what they've sent you up here from London to tell me."

"I have to tell you Jimmy, this could be career ending. London doesn't take kindly to disobeying orders."

Hancock scoffed. "What orders? I *have* my orders...and I've carried them out. Today I finish things." He allowed himself a laugh. "Then it's off to Corfu for a few month's rest and recuperation, a few letters to friends telling them I've got the job of a lifetime in Argentina looking after a new wine label but instead, I disappear and I'm back to London with a new name and new responsibilities. Don't you worry, Macmillan. I'm being looked after." He held up his sack. "But before I get the sun on my back, I need to finish things. This wee bag of goodies will blow an entire pub of nationalists to kingdom come."

Macmillan noticed the corner of the Union Flag protruding from the neck of the sack.

"Ah, I see it now. You spend your time in Scotland taking covert action on behalf of the state which persuades people that the SNLA or some such is responsible for terrorist acts then finish by blowing up nationalists with a bomb wrapped in the Union Jack thereby pitting nationalists against unionists, creating the prospect of civil war in Scotland and providing a rationale for military forces to patrol the streets here...just like Northern Ireland."

"Sounds like you've just worked out my mission, eh, Macmillan." He cocked the Walther PPK he'd taken from Rees. "But if you'd *really* been sent up here by my people you'd have known that all along." He pointed the pistol directly at Macmillan's forehead. "So, who sent you?"

Macmillan maintained his composure. "Same troops as you, Jimmy. But my orders came directly from the top."

Hancock laughed. "Aye! Well mine didn't. Mine came from senior individuals who *sneer* at people from the top. My mission comes from experienced people who *understand* how to deal with little local difficulties without troubling themselves too much about the politicians and senior civil servants who know the square root of fuck all about anything."

An angry growl emanated from the throat of McLeod capturing Hancock's attention. "Did you kill Willie McRae?"

"I thought I told you to sit quiet in the corner, son! I'm holding all the aces here and I'll happily put a bullet through your head just so I can get some peace and quiet."

McLeod repeated his question but louder, this time in staccato fashion. "Did...you...kill...Willie...McRae?"

Hancock's brow furrowed. "Who the fuck's Willie McRae? One of those cops in Govan?"

Macmillan took over. "So you killed the military policeman, the cops in Govan, sent a bomb to the Secretary of State for Scotland but weren't involved in the death of Willie McRae?"

"You're beginning to worry me, Macmillan. You say we're both working for the same side and know everything about my operation but you seem to be doing all of your calculations in the back of a fuckin' taxi."

Macmillan continued as he pondered Hancock's comments and a new realisation set in. "Ah, and you had to ensure that the bomb destined for the Minister didn't go off, eh? That'd be too big a calamity. Too much scrutiny by the cops and the media. Just give him a scare and feed the media more propaganda about Scottish terrorists? Create a crisis and turn Sauchiehall Street into the Falls Road?"

McLeod interrupted for a third time, now raising his question by several decibels. "Did you kill Willie McRae?"

"I think this is where you and me need to part company, son. Hancock pointed the PPK at McLeod and fired, his aim being thwarted by Macmillan who threw himself across the cab and grasped his right hand. McLeod slumped forward, his left hand covered in the blood that now seeped from his broken right shoulder. All three men in the rear slammed into the driver's partition as Rees braked severely pulling the taxi to the side of the road at the loch side. Macmillan held Hancock's gun hand as he tried to force it in his direction, taking a blow to the side of his head in the process. McLeod was sufficiently conscious to grasp at Hancock's belt which fixed his other two Glocks to his waist but received the sole of his boot in his face, sending him reeling backwards. Returning to the fray, he managed to fix on the handle of Macmillan's Glock and pulled it from Hancock's waistband. Cocking it, he fired but missed, an instant before a second boot to the chin from Hancock knocked him unconscious.

Rees had by now run around the front of the cab and had opened the rear near-side door permitting the wrestling men to twist and roll, falling heavily from its cabin and continuing their fight at the road side, each still focused upon taking control of the gun in Hancock's right hand. Both men had had professional training in hand-to-hand combat and it showed with single-handed crisp blows and chops raining down on one another whilst tethered together at Hancock's gun hand as though in some macabre dance. Hancock caught Macmillan a glancing blow with a head butt. Together they rose, still glued to one another, each attempting to use muscle, ruse and dexterity to overcome the other. Spinning, Macmillan sought to unbalance his opponent. A knee to Hancock's groin brought a cry of pain but no reduction in pressure to submit. In mid-wrestle, Hancock swept his leg behind Macmillan and he thumped painfully to the ground, releasing his grip on Hancock's gun hand.

Hancock breathed heavily as he looked at Macmillan lying helplessly supine at his feet on the grassy kerb. "Bye, Macmillan. Nice knowing you." He pulled the trigger as Macmillan lay back expecting a bullet but nothing happened. Again Hancock pulled at the trigger but to no avail. Seeing an opportunity, Rees threw herself at him but met with his swinging arm and fell to the ground, blood streaming from a head wound caused by the barrel of the PPK. Frustrated, he re-cocked and attempted a third shot but again the PPK stubbornly refused to fire. Exasperated, he threw the gun towards the loch, ran round the cab, jumped into the driver's seat and sped off. As he left, he fired the second Glock through the open passenger's window missing Rees by a whisker.

*

Macmillan rolled on one side and wearily tended to Rees who was bloodied but conscious. "You okay, Mel?"

"Cut up but nothing other than that."

"Let's get that PPK. He threw it over towards the loch. We'll flag down a car and give chase."

Rees shielded her eyes and sought sight of the disappearing taxi. "There he is there, on the loch side. He's still driving towards Glasgow."

Macmillan picked up the misfiring Walther PPK, cocked it a few times and fired it once into the loch. A bullet sped from its chamber and splashed in the dark waters of Loch Long. "I'll need to review my long-held views on whether there's a God," said Macmillan scanning the road for any approaching vehicles.

*

Hancock cursed as he steered the taxi faster than was sensible around the contours of the loch. His knuckles whitened on the steering wheel as he felt the muzzle of Macmillan's surrendered Glock against his neck.

McLeod articulated his question in staccato fashion. "Now, forth time lucky. Did you kill Willie McRae?"

Hancock closed his eyes momentarily as he realised his oversight. "I told you son. Don't know the man. You heard me say what I've done and it didn't include your man McRae. So why don't we let bygones be bygones. You step out of the taxi and I'll be on my way. No one gets hurt. Eh?"

"Pull in!"

"Fuck off sonny boy. I'm a man on a mission and you don't have the balls to shoot someone in cold blood."

"Well, I've got a Glock. You've got a Walther PPK. Seems we're equal...other than the fact that my gun is pointed directly at your cervical vertebrae and my finger is on the trigger whereas your gun is sitting in the footwell. If I was a betting man, I'd lay odds I could shoot faster than you...so pull this taxi off the road." He indicated an aged wooden barn on a promontory at the loch side. "Over there!"

Resignedly, Hancock braked gradually and drove the taxi slowly towards the barn. Calculating his next move, he swung it slowly around and reversed so it faced the road.

"What now?"

McLeod held the gun in his left hand, his right arm useless. "Face the front and don't move." As quickly as his injury allowed, he placed the gun on the rear seat and used his left arm surreptitiously to open the taxi door. He collected his gun and pointed it weakly at Hancock. "Right! Out! If you make a move towards the floor of the taxi, I'll shoot you dead."

Realising McLeod was now on the other side of the taxi to him, Hancock opened his door and stepped out. Glancing at McLeod to ensure he had space and time, he suddenly bolted towards the half-opened door of the boathouse and entered.

Painfully aware of his bloodied and broken arm, McLeod stepped cautiously towards the wooden barn. Dark inside, he nevertheless caught a glimpse of Hancock at the far end of the enclosure appreciating as did McLeod now that there was no exit door at the far end.

Feeling faint, McLeod stepped back and leaned against the side of the barn. Grimacing at the effort, he closed the barn door and with his foot, dragged a large stone to the foot of the door and jabbing it with his heel, wedged it as tightly as possible. *That'll give me a few seconds,* he thought. Head swirling, he staggered the few paces back to the taxi where he took the wheel and reversed the vehicle back a few yards until it rested against the ancient wooden structure, blocking its doors and denying an exit. Blood loss now threatened unconsciousness but he reached below the dashboard and felt for the taping device. His fingers found the recorder and he removed the tape. *Enough in here to hang more than a few people I'd wager.* He pocketed the tape, elbowed himself from the cab and walked to its front. A distance along the loch, he made out the form of Macmillan and Rees running steadily along the road towards him. *They'll be here in just over a minute,* he calculated. *Still time.*

He reached into his pocket and removed a pack of cigarettes, pulling one from among the ranks by his lips. Replacing it, he felt for his lighter and lit his cigarette, dragging the nicotine into his lungs, further exacerbating the dizziness and weakness he felt. He screwed his eyes as smoke stung and felt for the Glock which he removed from his waistband. Macmillan and Rees were closing but were still some distance from the promontory. Inside the barn he could hear Hancock actively seeking a way out as metal clanged against wood.

Casually, he took another drag on his cigarette before stepping back and pointing his pistol at the nether regions of the taxi. *'Bout there I'd imagine.* He fired twice and waited. Moments later the ruptured fuel tank emitted a flow of petrol which made its way down a slight incline and entered the barn beneath the door.

Macmillan and Rees had reached the road end and turned onto the short track leading to the taxi. *I'll say this, they're fit!* Inhaling his cigarette once more, he flicked it to the ground. A second passed before there was a *crump* and the fuel ignited. Almost instantly a flame two feet wide progressed towards the barn door setting it alight. Realising that the taxi was next, McLeod retreated and took shelter behind a large birch tree some ten yards from the vehicle. Macmillan and Rees had now reached the taxi but stopped short as they, too, appreciated the imminent conflagration. As McLeod slumped to the ground unconscious, the taxi exploded and hastened the incineration of the barn. Shielding his face from the heat with his arm, Macmillan ran towards McLeod and urged the attention of Rees. "Deal with him. You're the nurse, remember?"

Handing the PPK to Rees, he re-cocked his preferred Glock and ran to the far end of the barn which was by now fast alight. *Poor bastard,* he thought as flames leapt skywards destroying the roof and bringing it cascading in on the floor of the building. *Doesn't stand a chance.*

Chapter Twenty-three

SUNDAY 13TH APRIL 1985

Glasgow, Scotland

McLeod lay back on his hospital pillow. "Scotland needs its troublemakers, remember?"

Macmillan and Rees sat at his bedside, Rees with a dressing on her head where stitches had had to be applied to the wound caused by Hancock's vicious blow.

Macmillan responded. "Aye, so you say. And it doesn't need to look far beyond you to find one."

Rees's thoughts were more inclined to the medical. "You lost a lot of blood and your right arm's in a bit of a mess. It's been plated and fixed with screws. That bullet smashed it up pretty bad." She smiled. "You'll need to drink your Pale Ale with your left hand for a while...but you'll live."

"We're going to make our report, Hector. We're not leading this investigation but we do know we'll be asked to provide a statement and we'll be able to report most things accurately although we want to make the point that the petrol was ignited accidentally. That is if you don't want to spend some time explaining yourself to some of our colleagues."

"Oh, it was definitely accidental, Jock," said McLeod disingenuously. "I was dizzy from loss of blood. Thought a wee smoke would sustain me while you two arrived."

"And the two bullets in the petrol tank?"

"I couldn't be sure if Hancock was armed. When he ran from the taxi I felt threatened and fired twice using my left arm. Not surprisingly, I missed as he ran into the barn. The shots punctured the fuel tank."

"And how did the taxi end up against the door of the barn?"

"I was trying to get away. Hancock had reversed it and I tried to drive away to meet you guys at the road end but I didn't have the strength to move the cab and it rolled back down the slope and stopped against the door. When I realised that everything was about to blow, I ran for cover behind a tree. Then you two arrived."

Macmillan held his gaze. "I suspect we can corroborate much of what you say, Hector. They'll quiz you but your story'll hold up. They'll be much more concerned that the information you have doesn't fall into the wrong hands. At least they'll be concerned that you can't prove any assertions you have."

"I want to see Scotland independent, Jock. All of this has just made me more determined. It's just difficult to comprehend the lengths the British Establishment will go to maintain the status quo, blethering on about her Britannic Majesty and patriotism while they traduce Scotland."

"And we're no further forward on how Willie died," reflected Macmillan, ignoring McLeod's diatribe.

"I'm sure in my own mind, Jock. It may not have been Hancock but it sure as hell wasn't suicide."

"Well, it'll all go in our report. Shame you didn't manage to rescue the taped recordings of Hancock before the taxi caught fire, eh?"

"Aye, shame, that!"

"The impact you could have made by releasing a transcript to your followers or the media would have made a substantial impact and might easily have influenced attitudes in Scotland towards independence."

"Aye, you may well be right. Pity the tapes were lost in the fire."

"Because if they still existed and the security forces figured there was even the smallest possibility that you held them, your life wouldn't be worth living. If they took the interest in Willie that they did, can you imagine the attention *you'd* get so they might retrieve the tape?" He allowed a moment to pass between them. From his shirt pocket he took the tape McLeod had removed from the taxi. "Found this in your pocket while you were under anaesthetic."

"Shit!"

"But here's what we're going to do, Hector. Outside right now, your three pals, Tam, Tommy and Sandy are waiting to see you." He nodded at Rees. "Mel here is going to report that she noted that one of them, let's say Tam, was carrying a sizeable tape recorder. I'm going to report that I found this tape in your pocket only later this afternoon. In consequence, no one could be sure that you didn't make a copy tape and subsequently lodged it with a lawyer or someone with instructions to make it public if anything happened to you. That would be sufficient an insurance policy to keep the security forces at arm's length."

"Very noble of you!"

"It *is* actually. But we owe you. You were material in putting an end to a rogue agent murdering public servants and stopping him taking out a public house full of innocent civilians. If that hadn't been the case, we might just have reported everything differently. You'd be called to account for the death of Jimmy Hancock and might even be charged under the Official Secrets Act for stealing top secret tapes belonging to MI5 and Special Branch..."

"But when we get right down to it, we're no nearer finding out what happened to Willie. Who shot him and why?"

"Well, we don't know that right now, Hector. We don't know that. But trust me, a lot of people are going to take an interest in answering the questions you pose. There are too many loose ends and if the cops don't solve this, it'll nag at the body politic like a rag nail."

Macmillan rose, prompting Rees to do likewise. "You've visitors outside. We should go." He offered his left hand to McLeod who shook it. "Your call, Hector. I wish you well in your political ambitions but be cautious about what you share about Hancock.

If we learned anything about the Establishment it's that it's determined, resilient and tenacious. Keep it at bay."

"Thanks for the caution...but I'm pretty resourceful, you know."

"Yeah. But you don't bring a knife to a gun fight. You're completely outgunned here, Hector."

Rees leant over and kissed him on the cheek. "I'll pop back and see you this evening if that's okay."

McLeod smiled. "That'd be grand."

Macmillan ushered her towards the door of the small ward, turning to bid farewell to McLeod as he did so.

"Stay safe!"

Chapter Twenty-four

FRIDAY 20TH NOVEMBER 1985

Budapest, Hungary

Epilogue

The British Embassy in Budapest was bathed in sunshine as Jock Macmillan looked from its second floor window onto Harmincad Street. Two blocks down, a green-grey and languid Danube flowed leisurely towards the Black Sea. Luncheon was uppermost in Macmillan's thoughts when his secretary, Ms. Yates knocked and presented her head round the door.

"Jock, we've just had a call from the airport. The British Ambassador to Poland is in town and has asked to see you. She'll be here any minute. Támas Kovaks has already collected her." She looked over her shoulder lest she was being observed and entered, speaking in a low voice. "Apparently Sir Edward isn't best pleased at the Ambassador wanting to see you rather than him and has made a point of deciding to greet the delegation at Reception before bringing them upstairs to you."

Macmillan raised his eyebrows, gathered his suit jacket from behind his chair and put it on. "Poland? Never been there. Can't imagine what they'd want with me."

"I'll bring coffee and biscuits."

RON CULLEY

"I'm starving. How about coffee and sandwiches, Lesley?"
His secretary smiled. "I'll see if I can't get both."

*

Ten minutes later another knock on his door heralded the arrival
of the austere and haughty Ambassador to Hungary, Sir Edward
Montague-Burke accompanied by a woman.

"Jock, our Ambassador to Poland is passing through and has
asked to meet with you."

Had Montague-Burke proceeded to find further words to
indicate his disapproval of the meeting, he would have been
interrupted before reaching the end of his sentence.

"*Madainn mhath* Jock. *Ciamar a tha thu?* Good morning,
Jock. How are you?"

A smile spread over Macmillan's face. "Well...*Tha gu math,
tapadh leibh*, Ms. McGinnis. I'm well, thank you."

Montague-Burke was nonplussed at the language. This was
Magyar of which he wasn't aware...but they were clearly friends.
He decided to retreat and unearth more of this mystery later. He
bid them goodbye and left.

Mo McGinnis shook his hand warmly. "So, Jock. Deputy Head of
Mission, eh? You'll be British Ambassador to Washington before
long!"

"Don't know about that, Ms. McGinnis. I'm still finding my
feet here."

"Please, it's Mo, and they gave you the most difficult
Ambassador to serve under. He's just one big ego – but he's good
at his job. You'll learn from him."

"I hope so."

"And it's such an interesting time to be out here."

Macmillan steered her over to two comfortable chairs where a
coffee table set for tea, sandwiches and biscuits awaited. "That's
for sure! We had an election in the summer where The Hungarian
Socialist Workers' Party was the only party to contest it. They
won two hundred and eighty-eight of the three hundred and

248

eighty seven seats. And ninety-eight of the remaining ninety-nine seats went to independents selected by the party! That's what passes for democracy here."

McGinnis smiled. "You must arrange to meet the one person not elected under the regime."

"I would but the seat only went unfilled because the candidate was drunk and withdrew his nomination just before the poll. Mind you, change is in the air. Because East Germans are only allowed to travel to other Communist countries, we're seeing a lot of them coming through Budapest and escaping to West Germany through Austria. The border has become more porous. And the Hungarian Prime Minister Miklós Németh has called for the introduction of the market economy as the only way to avoid a social catastrophe. I suspect they're afraid that continued economic decline will lead to social upheaval. We might see the end of Communism here yet!"

Mo McGinnis sat back in her chair and regarded him thoughtfully. "You know, you're a natural, Jock. You've got it all. I suspect you'd still rather be rolling around in the mud shooting at anyone who threatened the state but you've a real talent for people and those who matter in this murky business of ours have you pegged as someone who'll go far...in diplomacy I mean. But right now, someone with your gifts for the street coupled with your intellect and clear abilities on the interpersonal side mark you as someone who'll be a great asset to Montague-Burke. He may be preoccupied by himself but he's not fool enough not to recognise your talents and make sure they're employed to the best of their abilities."

"Well, I *think* I'm grateful to you for seeing me brought into MI6," he grinned. I always said I wanted to see the world. Vietnam was great but this new posting is much more than just dealing with the security side. I'm enjoying it. And I'm not unaware of the fact that it gets me out of the way of any controversy in Scotland." He changed the subject. "And what about you? *Ambassador* McGinnis is it then?"

"Yes. Poor Poland...where I'm dealing with much of the stuff you're dealing with here. Still, like you, I'm an active agent of the intelligence services, though."

Macmillan signalled his understanding and changed the topic, affecting only casual interest. "Any news of Melissa Rees?"

McGinnis bit into a sandwich. "She's returned to nursing. Back up in Glasgow and I think she's seeing that young man Hector McLeod. She's left the business!"

Macmillan nodded his awareness of Rees's decision. "And Hector was treated well following the death of Hancock?"

"He was. We interrogated him for a while and he knows quite a lot because he was privy to the conversation in the taxi but we have the tape so he's no evidence to back up any assertion he might make."

"Well, in our report we stated that we saw his friends outside with a tape recorder so he might have made a copy."

McGinnis' eyes narrowed. "Indeed, although I found your evidence there rather more convenient than compelling. Still, it'll be enough to make sure that some of the lower-brows in our organisation behave themselves."

Macmillan leaned back in his chair and smiled knowingly. "You know, Mo, it was almost as if different elements of the security forces were pitted against one another. Very strange, eh?"

McGinnis nodded. "It did *seem* like that, didn't it?"

A silence held for a moment. "Willie McRae didn't kill himself did he?"

McGinnis shrugged. "The verdict was suicide, plain and simple."

Macmillan invited a deeper level of dialogue. "This is you and me talking, Mo." He waved his arm as if encompassing the room. "No bugs. No recording devices,"

A further silence hung in the air. "You know, Jock. Even in the best of organisations, even those where following orders is an absolute requirement, there are times when it's important to assess for yourself the right thing to do. MI5 has different divisions. Special Branch has many different obligations and directives. People seek different ends and sometimes it becomes evident that two or more elements within a given organisation are attempting to achieve goals which are simply contradictory."

Macmillan concurred. "That's true!"

"And there's something else. You and I are both from the beautiful island of Lewis. We're both Scots. Both British, but both Scots. I'm afraid I've never been able to deal comfortably with the stiff upper-lipped, entitled attitude of some of the privileged elite down in London who treat the nations and regions of the United Kingdom as irritant nonentities. They work on the basis that military adventures and new royal heirs to the throne will remain a favoured way of keeping the minds of the proletariat occupied while they go about the often nefarious business of ruling the country. I quite enjoy taking them down a peg or two now and again."

"We were talking about who killed Willie McRae, Mo."

"Indeed, I'm just trying to provide some context."

Macmillan smiled despite himself. "Now you're even *talking* like an Ambassador."

"Well, the full answer is that I don't know. What I do know is that he was in possession of documents alleging the most serious criminal behaviour in respect of senior politicians and members of our own security services; molesting young children. Now, there are those within MI5 who would take the view that we can't allow moral or ethical matters such as this to enter our considerations when we are tasked with ensuring the safety and security of the British State."

"Do you agree that position?"

McGinnis ignored his question and continued, more abrasively. "There are others who take the view that raping small children is not a forgivable offence and that those who committed those crimes should be brought to account, *whatever* the implications for the state."

"So you would have approved of Willie presenting his evidence?" He thought further. "Did you send me up to Glasgow to surveil Willie or to protect him?"

"The file notes show that I responded to the Minister's request to have McRae investigated. He was viewed as a threat to national security. When he was made privy to the McCrone Report, he was even more of a concern to Ministers."

"And my selection as the case officer responsible?"

"I checked you out thoroughly. A Lewis man but most importantly, someone who'd make his own assessment and who had a track record of speaking truth to power. I was confident that if you found out what *I* already knew, you'd do the right thing."

"But Willie still died. Shot by someone. Shot by security forces?"

McGinnis remained tight-lipped.

"Couldn't you have lifted a finger to help him?"

"I thought I had."

"Sounds like you played the British civil servant to perfection, Mo. Your career's still in the ascendancy, eh? You're in with the bricks. An entirely dependable servant of the British state. An Ambassador now, no less."

Perhaps...but I like to think that I'm *also* someone who makes their own assessment and who does the right thing!"

"And what might that have entailed if you don't mind me asking?"

McGinnis took a breath. Only a very few people know this Jock, but I trust you as a fellow islander?"

"You can, Mo."

"Sometimes, I'm also known as *Alba*!" She stood. "*Saor Alba!* Free Scotland!"

AUTHOR'S NOTES
AND CONTESTED FACTS

1. Where a person implicated in the events surrounding the death of Willie McRae is still alive, the author has used a fictional character using actual names either where the person is deceased or where their role in this historical fiction as presented is tangential or minor.
2. In 1984, there were no traffic lights outside the British Embassy in *Ly Thuong Kiet* Street Hanoi. The new Embassy is presently accommodated within a small number of offices above an apartment store in Hanoi.
3. Prince Philip didn't visit Fairfield Shipyards in 1984.
4. A common spelling of McRae's surname, particularly in the print media, is MacRae. However, his birth certificate shows his name as William McRae, his legal business was named 'Levy & McRae' and his death certificate presents his surname as McRae.
5. McRae reputedly became a member of the Indian Congress party while captaining a destroyer in the Royal Indian Navy. However, his brother, Dr. Fergus McRae disputes this.
6. The Mine Countermeasures Vessel, HMS Middleton was launched on the River Clyde in April 1983 at Yarrow Shipbuilders, Scotstoun not in the Fairfields yard, Govan in 1984.
7. The McCrone Report was a Top Secret UK Government dossier on the economic viability of an independent Scotland based upon its oil reserves. It was written in 1974 by Professor Gavin McCrone, a leading civil service economist, at the request of Edward Heath's Conservative government and forecast that oil would make an independent Scotland "as

rich as Switzerland", giving the country a large tax surplus, on such a scale as to be "embarrassing". He also assessed that this surplus revenue would make the Scottish pound the hardest currency in Europe "with the exception of the Norwegian kronor". These findings were subsequently corroborated by a team of top Whitehall civil servants. The Top Secret Report was suppressed by successive governments and only came to light in 2005 when the SNP obtained the report under the Freedom of Information Act 2000. It was not in the possession of Willie McRae at any point and is only included in this narrative by the author for dramatic purposes. However, the element of this book explaining the McCrone report is accurate in all aspects.

8. The black tinder fungus beetle is only found in Glen Affric.
9. Tory MP Geoffrey Dickens formally handed his infamous paedophile dossier to then Home Secretary Leon Brittan – only for it to be lost or destroyed by Brittan, the police or Home Office officials. Brittan, who acknowledged receipt of the file in a letter, had intimated that the police had been informed. However, the Observer Newspaper revealed on 5 July 2014 that the Dickens' dossier was just one of over a hundred potentially relevant files dealing with paedophilia that had been found to be missing by officials when they did their initial search. The chairman of the Home Affairs Select Committee Keith Vaz told parliament that files had been lost "on an industrial scale". Senior politicians who have been named include the Liberal MP Sir Cyril Smith, the Conservative MP Sir Nicholas Fairbairn, the Soviet spy and Establishment figure, Anthony Blunt, Labour MP, barrister Greville Janner QC, Baron Janner of Braunston and the Foreign Office barrister Colin Peters, who was jailed in 1989 for being part of a network which abused over a hundred boys. Ultimately, Scotland Yard detectives investigated evidence relating to twenty-two political figures suspected of involvement in Westminster paedophile rings, including three serving MPs and three members of the House of Lords. The list of those alleged to have been involved in child sex abuse

included fourteen Conservative politicians, five Labour politicians and three from other parties.

10. Sir Peter Hayman was a long time Deputy Director of MI6. The National Archives at Kew holds a file entitled 'Sir Peter Hayman: allegations against former public official of unnatural sexual proclivities; security aspects'. One document within the file relates to the briefing given to then-Prime Minister Margaret Thatcher concerning Hayman's sexual fantasies relating to children. Sir Michael Havers, the Attorney General, reported to parliament that Hayman had been a member of the Paedophile Information Exchange.

11. In July 2014, Barry Strevens, a former bodyguard to Margaret Thatcher, claimed he warned her that her Parliamentary Private Secretary, Sir Peter Morrison M.P. allegedly held sex parties with under-age boys. Strevens said that despite passing on the allegations to Thatcher, she later promoted Morrison to the position of deputy chairman of the Conservative party.

12. In August 2015, London's Metropolitan Police, Hampshire, Jersey, Kent, Wiltshire, Gloucestershire and Thames Valley police Forces investigated allegations of child sexual abuse by ex-Prime Minister Edward Heath.

13. Four years after McRae's death, The Glasgow Herald reported that the Westminster paedophile ring resembled the Mafia in its organisation and strength and included 'well-placed and influential professional people linked to Westminster and Whitehall'. Two journalists; the former news editor of the Surrey Comet, Hilton Tims, and the former editor of the Bury Messenger, Don Hale, both stated in November 2014 that during the 1980s, they had been served with D-notices, (a legal warning not to publish material that might damage national security).

14. Operation Fairbank, an investigation into the involvement *inter alia* of Members of Parliament in a child abuse scandal in Elm Guest House in London arose from claims of sexual abuse and grooming children at parties held there during the late 1970s and 1980s. The enquiry was led by the Metropolitan Police Service and started in late 2012.

15. As a result of allegations arising from Operation Fairbank, a full criminal investigation, Operation Fernbridge, was launched in February 2013.

16. In November 2014, another operation, Operation Midland, was set up to examine claims of a possible murder, later extended to cover allegations of three murders.

17. Operation Hedgerow, which recorded 650 offences against 150 boys in Elm Guest House, resulted in Colin Peters, a Foreign Office barrister, being jailed for being part of a network of paedophiles who abused over a hundred children.

18. A spin-off inquiry, Operation Cayacos, an investigation into historical claims of child abuse by a paedophile ring linked to Operation Fairbank, is being conducted by the Metropolitan Police.

19. On 11 November 2014, the Wanless Inquiry Report published their findings into the disappearance of the Home Office files on MPs involved in paedophilia, saying that they had 'found nothing to support a concern that files had been deliberately or systematically removed or destroyed to cover up organised child abuse'.

20. It was announced on 16 March 2015 that the Independent Police Complaints Commission was investigating claims that the Metropolitan Police had suppressed evidence of child sexual abuse and prevented the investigation of some allegations between 1970 and 2005, because of the alleged involvement of police officers and MPs.

21. Three years before the death of Willie McRae, Operation Countryman, an investigation into police corruption within the Metropolitan Police, saw just under one hundred officer suspects facing allegations. Not a single officer was dismissed following the £3 million investigation. A subsequent incoming Police Commissioner appointed to clean up the force, Sir Robert Mark famously stated that 'a good police force is one which catches more criminals than it employs'. The Government of the day placed a *seventy year* top secret ban on publication of the details surrounding police corruption in the seventies and early eighties.

22. The Special Demonstration Squad or Special Operations Squad was established by Special Branch supported by MI5, and operated from 1968 – 2008. It was an undercover unit set up to infiltrate entirely legal British protest groups.

23. The deployment of undercover Special Branch police officers and MI5 operatives to infiltrate entirely legal organisations in the mid-eighties is now uncontested. Several MI5 officers have testified to their deployment and leaked documents have confirmed the lengths Prime Minister Margaret Thatcher was prepared to go to defeat 'the enemy within'. One former MI5 officer, David Shayler viewed miners' leader Arthur Scargill's 40-volume MI5 file and confirmed that at least one senior individual within the NUM national office was providing the security services with detailed information about the NUM picketing tactics and details of Scargill's private life. Many more officers were implanted secretly in other organisations in this way.

24. Following widespread allegations of the inappropriate use of undercover police officers in forces across the UK since 1968, a Government inquiry was established in March 2015 to consider any miscarriage of justice which may have occurred as a result of an undercover police operation. The inquiry will consider whether and to what purpose undercover police operations have targeted political and social justice campaigners. At the time of writing, the inquiry has not reported.

25. As undercover officers were withdrawn from a placement, they were often provided with a two-step cover story, usually a month long holiday on mainland Europe from where they'd write to friends intimating the job offer of a lifetime, citing responsibilities in South America where it was presumed they'd never be followed. They would then return to active duty some distance from their old undercover base.

26. In 1949, McRae co-established the law firm Levy & McRae which still exists today in Glasgow's St Vincent Street. In June 1959, upon the retirement of his partner he set up in business as McRae and Company and operated from offices at 166 Buchanan Street, Glasgow.

27. Rather than spending the evening before his death drinking in the Pot Still, McRae was actually attending a ceilidh with his godson, Howard Singerman. The fire occurred upon his return home that night.

28. According to a statement taken from Constable Morrison, the vehicles chasing McRae from Glasgow weren't identified but he noticed the feature of the white-walled tyres. Other reports indicated that two of their registration numbers, BGS 425S and PSJ 136X, were checked and found to be 'blocked'; police terminology indicating that a car was registered to Special Branch. During a *Scottish Eye* television programme on the death of Willie McRae, one of their reporters, Callum Macrae (no relation) reported "We have established from the highest official sources that these cars were operated by Special Branch." A third vehicle, a brown Chrysler registration XSJ 432T was recorded following McRae around two days before his death. This vehicle, too, was on official records as belonging to Strathclyde Police Special Branch. (*Enemies of the State*. Gary Carnegie, Simon and Schuster, 1993).

29. In respect of the actual car crash, Constable Morrison stated in a subsequent police statement that 'I strongly suspected that MacRae's car was sandwiched between the two cars that followed him from West Nile St. Glasgow. This paragraph was deleted from my statement.'

30. There were reports of a rifleman accosting a group of hillwalkers some miles from the scene of McRae's crash a few hours before his death. It was reported that he shot at them and ordered them to leave the area shouting, "I am a soldier." There has been no solid evidence presented which confirms this sighting although the West Highland Free Press reported a 'lone gunman' firing a rifle on a party of hillwalkers just hours before McRae's death. However, they carried this story one year after the event, not a few days afterwards as the author relates in this book.

31. No proof exists that McRae was involved formally with the Scottish National Liberation Army, Dark Harvest Commandos, the Oystercatchers or any other paramilitary or subversive

organisation but rumours were rife that he was. In consequence, in later years, many senior figures in the SNP allegedly
maintained a political and personal distance from him.

32. There was no Sergeant Donaghey nor was there an Inspector
Baldry involved in the investigation of the death of McRae.
These characters were used by the author as a device to tell
the story of the death as tidily as possible. Several police officers, members of the travelling public, car mechanics and
medics were involved in the car crash and its immediate after-
math. This measure allowed the author to tell the story in a
more compact fashion. The facts as presented are accurate
although the actual location of McRae's gun when found
continues to be contested as are the theories pertaining to his
collected belongings.

33. No alcohol was found in the bloodstream of McRae according
to research undertaken by investigative journalists Andrew
Carnegie Scott and Iain MacLeay who published their findings
in a book entitled, 'Britain's Secret War' (Mainstream, 1990).
The authorities claim that there was, but have consistently
refused to make the results of the post-mortem available for
inspection since the event took place to date.

34. The initial autopsy in Aberdeen had had to be undertaken
without having access to the gun which fired the bullet as it
hadn't at that time been discovered. In consequence, it could
not be proved that the mortal wound was caused by McRae's
gun, rendering any verdict of suicide problematic. The body
had also been washed and treated, obliterating substantial
pieces of key evidence. There can be no suggestion of sub-
standard medical care practiced by Aberdeen medics but evidence which could have given definitive proof of suicide or
murder was eliminated.

35. The statement given in Chapter Fifteen by the Procurator
Fiscal in Inverness is an invention that attempts to reflect the
paucity of information provided by the authorities. Despite
numerous requests, the authorities have refused to divulge the
contents of the post-mortem or to allow a current review of
the case. Subsequent routine statements from the Crown

Office assert merely, "The local procurator fiscal investigated the matter fully at the time and Crown Counsel remains satisfied with the investigation into the death of William McRae." Thomas Aitchison, the Inverness Procurator Fiscal and person responsible for the overall investigation into sudden and unexpected deaths in the area, announced that the case had been "fully investigated" and that there had been 'no suspicious circumstances'. However, when Aitchison revealed there were no suspicious circumstances in the case, many considered it a rushed decision. McRae was pronounced dead on the Sunday, a post-mortem was undertaken on the Monday and the Fiscal announced 'death by suicide' on the Tuesday. Efficient...or precipitative? (Death by gunshot at that date had not occurred in the Highlands for over twenty years)

36. Despite the statement on McRae's death by gunshot being made by the Procurator Fiscal of Inverness on Tuesday 9th April, during the following week none of the main Scottish newspapers; the Daily Record, The Glasgow Herald, The Scotsman, the Evening Times, the Sunday Post, the Sunday Mail and Sunday Express corrected their initial story that he was killed in a road accident.

37. A ballistics report released under a Freedom of Information request by leading activist Mark MacNicol of the Justice for Willie McRae Campaign contains a date stamp of 10th April 1985 which was but one day after the Procurator Fiscal's announcement of a verdict of 'death by suicide'. On April 9th, the Fiscal also announced that McRae's death had been "fully investigated" and that there had been "no suspicious circumstances". However, as the authorities had not completed a ballistics report on the gun found at the scene, it would have been impossible for the authorities to rule out another gun being involved.

38. Constable Donald Morrison, now retired, is on formal record as regretting the fact that he did not report the car chase from Glasgow when Special Branch officers followed McRae from Glasgow. He also signed an affidavit indicating that he'd

overheard radio traffic saying that officers of Special Branch were following McRae some time before his death.

39. Retired police officer Iain Fraser, who worked as a private investigator after leaving the police, was interviewed and revealed that he had been asked by a mystery client based in Newcastle to spy on McRae just three weeks before he died. Fraser, now deceased, who upon retiral ran a hotel in Cullen, said he was paid £135 by the caller to watch McRae on a Saturday in 1985. He said: "I had no idea who the client was, but in the murky world of private investigation that was not unusual. The cheque came from Newcastle. I can't remember the individual who signed it, I wished I had kept a copy now, but I had no idea at that time this was going to rear its head again." Fraser was based in the same building as McRae's office in Glasgow. "I was surprised to be asked to do the job as there was a possibility that, having met each other, he may have recognised me."

40. Following the removal of McRae's Volvo and after the bullet wound in his head was discovered, rumours abounded that the car had been returned the following day when the police decided they were dealing with a crime scene rather than a motoring accident. It is alleged by Australian Allan Crowe, one of those who first attended the crash scene, that having lost his glove the day before, he returned to the crash site and asked permission of the two police officers guarding the site to look for it. This took place mid-morning on the Sunday. In doing so, Crowe insists that the car had been returned to the site. This is also confirmed by his wife who was with him. However, following intensive re-interviewing of witnesses by retired Detective Inspector John Weir and retired Detective Sergeant John Walker, via the Justice for Willie McRae Campaign, it has become evident that the vehicle simply could not have been driven back to the same spot through the boggy marsh without following the exact route, speed and trajectory as McRae. It could perhaps only have been returned and placed there by use of an air-lift and there have been no witnesses who have testified to that being the case. It may

have been that the police report was falsified and that the car was never moved from the crash site until later on the Sunday – although this is contradicted by others who earlier inspected the vehicle in Inverness. In consequence, given that the suggestion that McRae's car was returned to the crash site is contested, and in order to simplify the story, all mention of that rumour has been omitted within the narrative.

41. Evidence has been led that McRae had a tyre in the rear seat of his car when it was discovered. Unfortunately, the police report doesn't record whether it was punctured or slashed. This notwithstanding, the concomitant delay caused by having to repair the tyre would have resulted in McRae driving north in darkness rather than in the light; circumstances which may have suited potential assassins.

42. Further rumours and contradictions; that McRae inexplicably had a substantial amount of Chinese Yen in his possession. A further allegation, by SNP Councillor Hamish Watt from Grampian Region, that *two* bullets had been found in McRae's head, has been discounted as he cited his source as John McKinnon, the nurse who was present and in charge of Ward 40 when this was discovered. Mr. McKinnon has subsequently not corroborated this. One factual piece of evidence that has not satisfactorily been explained, however, is the absence of a Scottish £100 note which McRae always carried with him in his wallet as it was the first fee he'd received as a solicitor. No such item was listed as having been found in his possession when a list of belongings was released by Northern Constabulary. Also missing was a bottle of Glenmorangie whisky and the cigarettes he purchased to sustain himself in Dornie. Their purchase was corroborated by Roddy Mackay, the manager of Agnew's Off-sales in West Nile Street.

43. The radio statement cited in Chapter 18 by Scottish Lord Advocate, Baron Fraser of Carmyllie in Chapter Eighteen was in fact a written statement provided to fellow Conservative politician and immediate predecessor in office Sir Nicholas Fairbairn MP.

44. The 'Auld Smiddy' Bar in Glasgow's Cathcart, far from being a nationalist pub is frequented by many unpersuaded of the case for Scotland's independence. The author set elements of the story in that bar just to annoy them.

SO, WHO KILLED WILLIE MCRAE?

There can only be three explanations for the tragic death of Willie McRae; he died as a consequence of an accidental shooting, he committed suicide or he was murdered. It is fairly obvious that the shooting is unlikely to have been accidental, even if it remains possible that the initial car crash may well have been – although road conditions and contouring do not suggest any unusual problems for a competent driver, especially one who had driven the route scores of times before. McRae's gun was a very old, small, light calibre piece that he carried in his briefcase allegedly because he was afraid of the security forces. The notion that following his car crash, he'd toy with it in a manner whereby he'd shoot himself accidentally behind the ear appears fanciful.

Did he commit suicide? This is the assessment of the authorities which presented McRae as a depressive alcoholic, melancholic over his drink-driving convictions and psychologically disturbed over homosexual leanings. However, close friends insist that he was most certainly not homosexual, that he was optimistic and on the day of his death had made arrangements to deal with cases the following week, had asked that a fire be lit for him upon arrival at his destination, had seemed cheery to a number of unconnected people before he set off and many scoffed at the idea of suicide merely because 'he wasn't that sort of person'.

Was he murdered? Well, the answer to that is, we don't know! One reason it's difficult to form a legal view on this is that to prove a murder took place, a verdict would have to be brought in 'beyond all reasonable doubt'. Without a smoking gun or an accused, this is not possible as the evidence to date is largely circumstantial. However, if another test was available, one used in other courts such as Employment Courts or in civil proceedings; that of determining 'the balance of probabilities', quite another verdict might be brought in.

There is no question that security forces were surveilling McRae. It is evident that they followed him from Glasgow hours before he met his death. It is now clear that the government and the security services at the highest levels were populated by people who were engaged in paedophilia and that McRae appeared to have evidence that would prove embarrassing if not fatal to the government of the day. There is also evidence that there were attempts to cover up all allegations and the notion that every file making allegations, every statement and every report alleging paedophilia were somehow lost by the very people who stood accused of these crimes beggars belief. McRae's files have never been found.

Were the security forces surveilling McRae? Did the police investigation at the scene leave key questions unanswered? Did the medical appraisals on McRae fall below compliance with standard investigative police procedures? Was the gun and were his personal papers found at distance from the crashed vehicle when he was clearly unable to leave the car? Was the rushed verdict of suicide precipitative? Was the media, at least initially, complicit? Well, the answers to each of these questions is a resounding 'Yes', 'Yes', 'Yes', 'Yes,' 'Yes', and perhaps less resoundingly, 'Probably'.

In consequence and in view of the stout refusal of the authorities to provide answers that would permit any other assessment, many people yet find it difficult not to arrive at a view that at least in the court of *public* opinion, and on the balance of probabilities, Willie McRae was the victim of state-sponsored assassination.

Lightning Source UK Ltd.
Milton Keynes UK
UKHW011333210420
362053UK00002B/389